A REAL COWBOY ALWAYS PROTECTS

A Wyoming Rebels Novel

STEPHANIE ROWE

A REAL COWBOY ALWAYS PROTECTS

Cover Copy

Is it really a second chance at love if a sexy, charming cowboy proposes marriage only to protect you from a CIA assassin?

Haunted by shadows that will never let him go, CIA agent Logan Stockton walked away from his cowboy past ten years ago. But when his sassy, adorable neighbor gets targeted by his enemies, he'll do whatever it takes to protect her... including taking her back to his hometown as his fake fiancée to hide out.

Skylar Jones has lost too much, and all she wants is to bury herself in her work and forget...but there's one man Skylar can't help but notice. Fortunately, her handsome, brooding neighbor is no more interested in dating than she is...which is exactly how she wants it.

But when Skylar stumbles into the middle of a botched attempt on his life, her safety becomes his responsibility.

Sparks fly hot and fast when Logan takes Skylar to Wyoming as his fake fiancée to protect her. But can they stay alive long enough to find love, especially when his matchmaking family has plans for the two workaholics who are afraid to trust again?

Trope alert! Contains:
    Friends to lovers.
    Slow-burn romance.

Fake fiancée.

Lots of feels.

Laughter.

A hot cowboy burned by love.

Matchmaking family members.

READER REVIEWS: WYOMING REBELS BOOKS

"Heartwarming and romantic." ~Marty L (Five-star Amazon Review)

"Swoon worthy!" ~Five-star Amazon Review

"A masterpiece." ~Frances (Five-star Amazon Review)

"A beautiful, moving love story." ~PLP46 (Five-star Amazon Review)

"A wonderful story about love, loyalty and family ties." ~Sheila L. (Five-star Amazon Review)

"You can't help but fall in love with the Stockton men. No matter how hard they try to hide it, they have good hearts and protect with their lives." ~Lynn (Five-star Amazon Review)

"If you need an awww moment this book is for

you...absolutely priceless." ~My2CentsBookReviews (Amazon Review)

"This is the most amazing heartfelt book I've ever read." ~Grandmaw (Amazon Review)

"A contemporary western that will grip your heart." ~TheBlueLady (Amazon Review)

"This story was so raw and emotional and perfect." ~Therese L. (Amazon Review)

"This is a wonderful, sensual, and mesmerizing love story!" ~Susan1 (Five-star Amazon Review)

"The story is a wonderful journey of coming out of the darkness in the light. Finding out you can have good in your life even after all the pain." ~Lynn (Five-star Amazon Review)

"You will fall in love with them. Heartwarming story. Excellent read." ~Vicki S (Five-star Amazon Review)

"What an amazing series...If you love strong loyal men that just happen to wear cowboy hats and love so strong, then this book is for you." ~Kindle Customer (Five-star Amazon Review)

COPYRIGHT

CHAPTER ONE

THE MOMENT the elevator doors finally opened, Skylar Jones bolted inside, then yelped as she almost crashed into Frances and Howard Stevens, her gray-haired neighbors from down the hall. "Oh, yikes. Sorry." She jumped back into the hallway, horrified that she'd almost knocked them down.

Frances didn't look concerned. She just put her hands on her hips and sighed. "Do I need to worry about you ruining your life and turning into a crazy cat lady?"

Skylar smiled, grateful she hadn't terrorized the stylish, lovely couple. "Maybe, but at least I'll be well-caffeinated, so I figure that's a win. I'm on my way to Charlie's store across the street for coffee, so maybe I'll meet my prince charming there."

Frances, a retired lawyer who still hosted many high-society soirees in their condo building's sixth-floor private function room, eyed Skylar's tie-dyed leggings, fleece indoor/outdoor slippers, and oversized sweatshirt. "You look like a basket of dirty laundry. It's midnight on a Saturday night. A woman your age should be out making things happen."

1

Skylar laughed as she stepped back to allow Frances and her husband, Howard, to exit into the hallway. "I'm working. I have a big project due."

"You're always working." Frances stepped out, her black heels sinking into the thick hallway carpet. She was dressed in an elegant cocktail dress, and Howard was spiffy in a bow tie and gorgeous black suit. "What about dating? Romance? Sex?"

Skylar felt her cheeks heat up. "I'm taking a break."

Frances eyed her. "Seems more like a never-ending drought than a break. I can't remember ever seeing you in anything but sweatpants on a weekend evening."

"Sweetheart." Howard slid his fingers gently around his wife's hand and squeezed. "Let Skylar take her time. She's fine."

Skylar's heart warmed at the affection in Howard's voice as he spoke to his wife.

He reminded her so much of her dad, with his smile, his humor, and his wit. Howard looked at Frances the way her dad had looked at her mom. Being around the gray-haired couple always made Skylar feel safe again, like she had before her whole world had blown up over the last few years.

"I love that you care enough to harass me," she said, meaning it.

Frances winked at her as she leaned into Howard. "Don't let that pig of an ex-husband keep you on the shelf for too long, my dear. Sunshine heals all wounds."

Sunshine. She never saw sunshine anymore. She was working too many hours for that. "I've heard that before. I think from you." She stepped into the vacated elevator and pressed the button to keep the doors open. "It's good advice."

"One date," Frances said. "Go on one date, or I'll disinherit you from my will."

Skylar raised her brows. "I'm not in your will."

"Irrelevant. The point remains the same."

Skylar laughed. "I'll keep that in mind."

Howard tucked his arm around his wife's shoulder. "Frances is relentless, Skylar. You might as well give in, because she's not going to back off until you do."

"I'll take that under advisement." The elevator began to beep, so Skylar released the button. "Have a great night."

"Take a shower at least!" Frances called out, just before the doors closed.

Skylar smiled as she leaned against the wall of the elevator, resting her hands on the brass bar by her hips.

It always made her happy to run into Frances and Howard. They had to be close to eighty, and yet they were so full of fire and life. Being around them made her miss the life she'd once had, the one she'd thought she'd had, and the one she'd thrown away.

Skylar eyed her reflection in the elevator doors as it began to tick down toward the ground floor. She looked comfortable. Cozy. Okay, maybe a little bit schlumpy, but she'd showered an hour ago, and her hair was still fluffy from the hair dryer. So, definitely at least two steps up from a basket of dirty laundry.

Granted, it wasn't the outfit to wear if she was trying to seduce a guy, but since dating was off her agenda for at least the next couple decades, it was perfect.

The elevator dinged to stop on the fourth floor, which housed the building's gym. Who worked out at midnight on a Saturday? Someone with as much of a life as she had, apparently. See? She wasn't the only one.

With a surge of impatience, she looked down at her phone to check the time as the doors slid open. Only three minutes until Charlie would lock the doors to the store. He often closed a few minutes early, but she needed some of his dark roast to make it through the next three hours of work.

She needed to get better at prioritizing caffeine. Seriously. It was one of the basic skillsets of being a workaholic.

"Hey, Skylar."

At the sound of the low, rough masculine voice with the western drawl, Skylar's stomach jumped. She sucked in her breath as she looked up.

There he was, stepping into the elevator. Her devastatingly hot, across-the-hall-neighbor, Logan Stockton. Instead of the jeans he usually wore, he was wearing a sweaty short-sleeved shirt and bike shorts that showed off thighs that were literally corded with muscle. All of Logan was corded with muscle, actually. His shoulders, his biceps, his calves.

Heat flushed her cheeks, and she dragged her gaze off his body and focused on his face.

His brown eyes were as intense as ever, loaded with shadows that never seemed to leave him. His dark, curly hair was cropped short, almost a buzz cut, and his light brown skin was as beautiful as ever. He shot her a smile, that same gorgeous smile that had nearly brought her to her knees the first time she'd met him two years ago when she'd moved in.

There was a time she thought she'd never smile again, but he'd gotten her smiling within five minutes of moving into the building. He still did, despite the fact that he was a completely sexy, irritatingly gorgeous, apparently single, male god, none of which were on her list of things she wanted in her life.

As Logan surveyed her with his decadently dark eyes, she recalled her "dirty laundry" outfit. She had a moment of regret that she hadn't decided to get coffee wearing only lingerie and stilettos, but almost immediately decided that looking like a slob was a much smarter plan, given her current dating goals.

But it did sting just a little bit that she'd run into Logan when she looked as unattractive as it was possible for her to look. Except her hair. At least that was clean. Bonus prize right there.

"Hi, Logan. I didn't know you were back." Not that she kept track of him. Well, she did a little bit. He wasn't around much, and when he was, he pretty much kept to his condo and the gym. He didn't entertain. He didn't socialize. He didn't go out.

Like her. Except he looked incredibly sexy in his Saturday night no-dating attire. So, not like her at all.

He nodded. "Got back a few hours ago."

God, she loved his voice. That faint hint of a western drawl always made her get all dreamy. "How did it go? Your trip?" She didn't know where he went or what he did, but whenever he returned from a trip, shadows seemed to cling to him. From the weight in his eyes, it didn't surprise her that he'd been back only for a few hours. It always took time for the darkness to release its grip on him.

Logan studied her for a long moment. "Good," he finally said. "My trip was good."

He was lying. She could see it in the tense set to his jaw, in the way his eyes narrowed ever so slightly. "How bad was it?"

This time, his eyebrows went up, and a faint smile played at the corner of his mouth. A real smile. Not the one he reserved for polite company. "How do you do that?"

"Do what?"

"Know when I'm bullshitting. No one else can tell with me. I'm a great bullshitter."

She grinned and shrugged. "I'm crafty like that, I guess. Was it really bad?" As she finished her question, the elevator door slid open, and she realized they had reached the lobby.

Suddenly, getting a caffeine hit didn't feel so important. Not when she could stand there, inches from Logan, with the full intensity of his gaze fastened on her like she was his only life-preserver in a hurricane.

Because that was exactly how he looked at her. How he always looked at her. He might not say much, but his intensity was so palpable, she could almost feel it against her own skin.

Logan held the door for her. "It was a shit show," he finally said, his western drawl much more evident than usual in his answer.

Was it because he was exhausted and drained? She felt his weariness in his words. She suddenly understood Frances's need to try to fix her life whenever she ran into Skylar, because she had the same instinct with Logan. A need to lighten the load he was carrying so stoically. "I'm sorry to hear that."

He looked at her, and again, gave her a half-smile that was real. "I believe you mean that."

"I do. No one deserves a shit show." She grinned. "Not even you," she teased.

His smile faded. "Don't be so quick to assume."

"What?" She set her hands on her hips. "That's a bunch of crap right there. It doesn't matter what secrets you carry. No one deserves a shit show, so don't go all martyr on yourself."

He laughed then, a faint, quiet laugh. "You're a force of nature. You know that, right?"

Goosebumps prickled down her spine at the warmth in his voice, an affectionate warmth that seemed to wrap around her like an embrace. "My mom always says that about me. But she doesn't usually consider it a compliment."

His smile widened. "With me, it's a compliment."

A satisfied feeling settled inside her. "Okay, then. Then, thanks."

He cocked his head. "How are you doing? You hear anything about that promotion at work?"

She couldn't believe he remembered. She'd mentioned it in passing months ago, when they'd run into each other in the mailroom. "It sounds like it's going to happen after I turn in my current project."

He smiled, a warm smile that seemed to light up his face. Suddenly, the darkness was gone, and he was back in the present, grinning at her in that way that made her feel all giddy. He was handsome when he was brooding, but when he was smiling, he literally lit up the room. "I'm glad to hear that," he said. "You've worked hard for it."

"Thanks." She smiled. "Frances believes I work too hard. She thinks I'm going to turn into a cat lady."

He grinned. "She thinks I'm going to die old and alone with hair growing out of my ears." His affection for Frances was obvious, which surprised Skylar.

Who would have guessed Logan, the mysterious, brooding cowboy, would fall for Frances like she had? "Maybe we should tell her we're dating, and she'll leave both of us alone."

"What?" His eyebrows shot up so fast that she grimaced. "Us date?"

"I didn't mean I actually wanted to date you." He looked sort of shocked, so she stumbled onward, trying to recover. "I was just bonding over Frances. I don't date, so you're safe from me." Crud. She was making it worse. "Unless you have a cat. Then I might date you. Start my cat lady future early."

The corners of his mouth started to curve up, and he looked like he was trying not to laugh at her. "Sorry. I don't have a cat for you to date."

"Darn. Today is just one big disappointment, then." Mercifully, the elevator began to beep at being held open, and she quickly stepped out into the lobby, taking advantage of the excuse to bail before she made things even more uncomfortable. "I'm going to try to get some coffee before the store closes. Want any?"

It looked like it took supreme effort for him to drag his

gaze off her and look across the street. "Charlie's is still open?"

"Maybe. I'm hoping."

"I'm all set." He released the door. "Skylar—" He stopped.

She paused. "What?"

He met her gaze, and she saw emotions etched on his face. The weariness was back. The exhaustion. But there was something more. Something brighter. Something that seemed to reach inside her and call her to him. She took a step toward the elevator. "Logan?"

He took a deep breath and shook his head, as if to clear it. "Nothing. Forget it. Have a great night." Then he released the doors and let them slide shut.

Whew.

Skylar let her breath out as she turned and headed for the front door of their building.

Logan was always intense, but tonight, it had been more than usual. Something bad had happened on his last trip, something that had nothing to do with boardrooms or business deals. He'd been living under darkness, until that last moment, when things had suddenly shifted.

He'd almost laughed at her. She'd heard Logan laugh only a couple times, and it had never reached his eyes. But tonight, it had flickered in his eyes for that one moment when they were talking about dating and cats, which had probably been the silliest exchange they'd ever had. A small moment, but significant, maybe.

She had no idea what Logan did for a living, but it was something that mattered. To him, at least. Had he almost started to talk about it? Her hot, loner neighbor had started to reach out.

She didn't know what he'd been about to say, or why he'd changed his mind, but there'd been a moment of connection that had never been there before.

As Skylar jogged across the street, she saw Charlie walk up to the door of the convenience store. He was wearing his Chicago White Sox ball cap, but his gray hair was still visible peeking out. He told her he'd owned the store for more than fifty years, holding onto his legacy even when all the fancy buildings began to go up around him. The locals loved him, and he loved the locals.

It had taken a while to win over his friendship, but now? He took care of her. "Charlie! Wait! Let me in!"

He looked up, putting the key into the lock as she ran up, then shook his head at her.

She waved at him through the glass. "Please?"

He opened the door and gave her a dramatic sigh. "Can't you ever get here earlier?"

"I try. I lose track of time. Pretty please?"

He laughed then, and held the door open for her. "One of these days I'm not going to let you in," he teased.

She planted a kiss on his wrinkled cheek as she slipped past him into the store. "You're the best."

"I know." He locked the door behind her. "All I have is dark roast. One cup?"

"That's perfect." Skylar grabbed a bag of peanut M&M's, then paused. "No, I'll take two cups." She was going to bring Logan coffee. Maybe he wouldn't invite her in. Or maybe, for the first time ever, he would.

CHAPTER TWO

THE ELEVATOR still smelled like Skylar.

Logan grinned as he leaned back against the wall, letting the faint scent of Skylar's shampoo drift through him.

Damn, he was glad he'd gotten bored of waiting for the up elevator and decided to jump on the one going down. The minute those doors had slid open and he'd seen Skylar lounging against the wall, looking at her phone, all the chaos inside him had settled. Just like that.

She'd looked so adorable in her massive sweatshirt and fuzzy slippers. Her leggings had given him a good view of her calves and lower thighs, and he'd liked what he'd seen. She had just enough curves to make a man feel like the universe had given him a gift.

Logan inhaled again. The floral scent of her shampoo reminded him of the wildflowers back home, stretching out endlessly for miles on the plains of Wyoming.

He'd left all that behind a long time ago for a career that let him make a difference.

He had no interest in going back to his old life, to the past that had left him with more scars than he could heal.

But whenever he saw Skylar, she reminded him of the good things about his past, about Rogue Valley, Wyoming, where he'd learned to ride horses, muck stalls, and appreciate freedom.

He knew he couldn't allow things to become personal with Skylar, but tonight, he'd come close to crossing that line. She had that effect on him, like some magical fairy darting around him sprinkling glitter on his soul.

His job required him to stay solo, to minimize all personal relationships, to keep people at a distance.

But Skylar tempted him.

Hell, she was more than a temptation. She was the sparkle that he used to bring himself back when the shit got too real for him.

The universe always put her in his path when he needed her, and tonight was no exception.

His workout hadn't cleared his mind.

But seeing Skylar, with her hands on her hips, giving him shit? Talking about dating his cat? The darkness had left for that moment, and she'd given him the gift of her smile.

Dating Skylar. The thought had sunk hard and fast into his gut as soon as she'd mentioned it, in her light-hearted, teasing way. It had felt right, the first thing that had felt that right in a long, long time.

It would be so easy to let himself fall under her spell, to pretend he was someone other than he was. She made him want to be the guy who could do that, who could make that choice.

He'd almost invited her up for coffee, but when he'd seen her smiling at him, those gorgeous blue eyes and glorious blond hair, he'd stopped himself. She was too nice, too genuine, too alive.

He couldn't risk Skylar by bringing her into his world, his secret world that not even his own brothers knew about.

Because if he did, she might die. Or, he might die, and leave her alone.

And there was no way in hell he was going to let anything happen to the one bright spot in his life.

To keep her alive and whole, Logan had to keep her at a distance, and that was that.

No matter how much he wanted it to be otherwise.

Skylar's heart was pounding as she hurried back into her building, a coffee cup in each hand. Was she really going to knock on Logan's door?

Maybe.

Maybe not.

She wanted to.

But he was a stranger. A neighbor. Maybe he didn't feel any of that intensity that she felt when she was around him.

Or maybe he did. He'd almost laughed at the idea of her dating his cat. That glint in his eyes had knocked all the resistance out of her.

She was doing it. If mailroom encounters became totally awkward forever after, then fine. Life was too freaking short, as evidenced by the fact that her dad was buried, and her mom was fading away.

Not her. *Not her*.

Skylar noticed suddenly that the elevator door was closing. She could see someone was already inside, so she picked up her pace.

"Hold the elevator," she called out, but the doors continued to slide shut. "Hey!" She waved her arm between the doors, sloshing coffee as the doors slid back open.

There were two men on the elevator. Men about Logan's age, but wearing all black, as if they were geared up for some night-climbing up the side of her building. They were lean. Fit. Capable.

One of them glared at her, and she saw coffee was dripping off his tight, black jacket. "Yikes. Sorry. I have some napkins. Let me get them for you."

He held up his hand. "Don't worry about it."

"No, seriously, I have napkins—"

"Stop." His tight, clipped command shut her up immediately. His face was hard, his eyes a vibrant green. But what really caught her attention was the star-shaped scar on his right cheek. It was at least two inches in diameter, a strident marking on his skin. It was a scar that meant business.

"Yeah, sure, okay." She retreated to the far side of the elevator, and started whistling under her breath, trying to diffuse the mounting tension.

Neither man looked at her. Instead, they stood side by side, arms held loosely by their hips. They were both wearing black baseball hats, and their heads were angled down, so it was difficult to see their faces. She couldn't even see the scar on the one man's face from that angle.

The hairs on the back of her neck began to prickle, and her heart began to pound. There was something not right about them. Dangerous.

By the time the elevator reached her floor, she practically leapt out, desperate to get away from them.

But they walked out after her.

And they followed her as she hurried down the hall.

She was almost running, but they were walking with easy, controlled strides, looking around as they walked.

She'd never seen them before in the building. Did they live there?

They followed her as she turned the corner to her hallway.

She knew everyone on her hallway. They definitely didn't live there.

Her pulse was thundering as she walked faster. Any doubt about whether she was going to offer Logan coffee was gone now. There was no way she was going into her own condo, where the two men could slip in after her before she could close the door.

Skylar hurried to Logan's door. She was just raising her hand to knock when the two men stopped behind her. She paused, looking over her shoulder. "Are you here to see Logan?"

They both had their heads down, but the one with the scar on his face raised his head slightly to look at her. "You know him?"

"Sort of." What the hell was going on? She was so unnerved she could barely think straight. She stepped back. "If you're here to see him, you go on. I can talk to him later."

Did these men have something to do with Logan's work? Because if they did, suddenly, she wasn't sure she wanted to hand coffee off to him and hunker down on his couch to share stories about being stuck in life.

The man with the scar gestured toward Logan's door. "After you."

"No, I think I'm good." She backed up to her door and leaned against it. Not unlocking it, but ready to retreat as soon as the coast was clear.

The two men looked at each other, then the one with the scar suddenly pulled out a gun and aimed it at her. "Knock on his door."

Holy shit. Skylar froze in sudden terror, unable to drag her gaze off the gun pointed at her face.

"Knock on his door," the man repeated.

Tears started to burn in her eyes. Knock on his door? The

men would kill Logan. And her. She'd seen movies. This never ended well for the innocent bystander.

"Now. If you warn him, you die." He raised his gun and pressed it against her forehead. She could feel the cold metal against her skin. *Holy triple shit.*

"Well, who wants to die, right?" Her hands shaking, she edged toward Logan's door.

The men moved up beside the door on either side of her, so that Logan wouldn't be able to see them. Scarface had his gun pointed at her head, and the other man was watching the door.

Dear God. They were definitely here to kill Logan. *What the hell?* The man had almost laughed at her cat joke. Treasures like that were few and far between. She wanted him alive.

Scarface nodded at her and gestured to the door.

Skylar's mouth was so dry she could barely swallow. She tucked one coffee against her chest, using her forearm to hold it, and then used her free hand to knock on the door. Her hand was shaking so badly she barely managed to get her knuckles to hit the pristine white door.

"Logan?" she called out in a slightly strangled voice as she straightened out the coffee cups. "It's Skylar. Charlie was out of the brownie you wanted, so I just have the coffee you asked me to get."

It wasn't the most brilliant code she'd ever come up with, but in the movies, it always worked to alert the person inside, mostly because the person inside was usually well-versed in spy happenings.

She could only hope that if Logan had people standing at his door with guns, that he qualified as sufficiently well-versed to save her life and his.

Logan didn't answer.

What if he was in bed? Or the shower?

The shower. He probably looked fantastic in the shower.

If she were going to die, thinking of Logan in the shower was a great last thought.

Scarface flicked the gun at her, indicating for her to knock again.

She tucked the cup under her arm again, and knocked a second time. This time more loudly. "Logan," she yelled. "It's Skylar. Come get your damned coffee that you asked me to get, because I'm tired and I don't want to be your servant anymore just because you're hot."

She grinned at Scarface. "That should do it."

CHAPTER THREE

LOGAN HAD JUST BEEN REACHING for the door to let Skylar in when she knocked a second time and yelled at him.

He froze.

He'd thought she was doing a cute flirt the first time she'd knocked, and he'd nearly pulled a quad rushing to get his sweats on over his still-wet-from-the-shower legs.

But now, all his senses went on high alert. He didn't know Skylar that well, but he could hear the edge in her voice, and it made no sense for her to yell at him for making her his servant.

"I'll be right there," he called out. "I just got out of the shower." He stole silently across the room and grabbed his gun from the holster he'd slung over his kitchen chair.

"You and that freaking shower," she yelled. "You're always in there. It's like you're taunting me. You know how I love it when you're in the shower."

Shit. There was definitely something wrong.

He eased to the door and peered through the peephole. He could see Skylar standing there holding two cups of coffee. She looked like she was alone, but as he watched, her gaze flicked to the right side of his door, and then to the left.

He swore. There were people on either side of his door. People who were scaring her.

Fuck. How the hell had anyone found him? Not that it mattered right now. First, he needed to get her out of there safely, and keep them both alive.

He briefly contemplated shooting through the wall, but it was too damn risky. He could hit Skylar.

"Don't worry," he called through the door, even as his mind spun, trying to figure out how to handle it. "I saved some hot water for you. I know you like to lie down and take your bubble baths. You have that coffee ready for me?"

He watched her eyes widen, and then her gaze flicked to the right and left again. She nodded. "I have it ready."

Logan swore. She was a fucking civilian. There was no way she was trained for this. He'd have to assume that she had no idea he'd just told her to throw her coffee at the people flanking his door and then drop to the floor.

He leaned back against the wall, quickly assessing his plan. How he was going to manage it. How he was going to keep them both alive.

He'd have to take the chance that they wanted him dead more than they wanted her dead, so they'd shoot at him before taking her out.

He had to get this right.

That was Skylar out there. His fucking sunshine. Standing there about to be in the middle of a gunfight.

$\sim$

Bubble baths? Why was Logan talking about bubble baths?

Skylar's heart was racing so quickly she could barely concentrate. Scarface still had his gun pointed at her head.

She had no idea how people in movies were able to think clearly when they were in a hostage situation. It was completely debilitating to be so terrified.

The other guy had his gun pointed at the door, exactly where Logan's head would be when he opened it. Unless Logan was crouching. Or lying down.

She paused. Logan had said *lying down*. Understanding flashed through her as she heard Logan slide the deadbolt on the door. He wanted her on the ground. Hot damn! He'd understood her message and was giving her spy lingo back.

She was so on this.

"You have the coffee ready?" Logan asked through the door.

The coffee. Right. *The coffee.* Skylar pushed her thumbs against the lids, lifting them up just enough so they were loose. "I have the coffee ready. I'm looking forward to *lying down* in that bubble bath, if you'll join me." Nice, right? She'd spy-lingo-ed him back that she was ready to throw burning hot coffee in their faces and then dive out of the way.

"Of course I'll join you. I'd never miss it." He turned the doorknob. The instant she saw the door start to open, she flung the coffee at the two men and dropped to the floor.

She covered her head, yelping as the sharp explosion of gunfire shattered the silence of the hallway. Screw spy lingo! This was actual gunfire!

Skylar scrambled across the hallway, trying to get to her door. She was just reaching for the knob, when the guy without the facial scar fell against her door, a bullet hole in the middle of his forehead, blood already blossoming from his head.

Holy crap. She yelped and scrambled backward, only to have an arm wrap around her waist. She screamed and tried to pry it off her, pounding on the rock-hard forearm.

"It's me." Logan's voice was low in her ear. "Come on."

Logan. She stopped fighting immediately as he dragged her back across the hall and into his condo. He slammed the door shut, threw the deadbolt, and then pointed down the hall. His face was focused, his body tense. And he had a gun in his hand. Who was he?

"Get in the office, lock the door, and hide under the desk," he commanded. "Don't open for any reason until I tell you to."

"Okay." Running and hiding sounded like a good plan to her. Skylar didn't waste a second. She sprinted for the door he'd indicated and pulled it open. There were no windows or other doors, which meant no one could come flying through them shooting at her.

It also meant that if Scarface came through the only door, then she had no way to escape. If she went into the office, she would be trapped. Prey.

"Nope." She didn't like being prey or defenseless. "Is there another way out? A back door?" She glanced over at Logan when he didn't respond.

He was behind the island in his kitchen, his gun trained on his front door, as he pulled a phone out of his pocket and dialed. His muscles were taut, his stance ready.

He looked fierce and focused. Relentless. Intent.

He looked like a man who had done this a thousand times.

She sucked in her breath, stunned by the sight of him. He was danger and adrenaline, a solid wall against any threat coming for them. How had he hidden this level of violence from her? How had he been living across the hall from her for so long, and she'd never known what simmered inside him?

Right now, she was glad to have it. But when there weren't men with guns outside the door? Logan Stockton was way outside her comfort zone. Nothing that she could live with.

20

No more coffee dates. No more flirting in the mailroom. No more fantasies about his biceps.

He didn't take his gaze off the front door. "Go into the office, Skylar. *Now*." His voice was pure Western drawl, as if he were too jacked to hold onto the more refined tone he'd taught himself to use.

"But—"

"Now, Skylar. Or you won't be alive to have that bubble bath with me."

Her cheeks heated up. "Heaven forbid I miss out on that." She ducked back into the office, shut the door, and locked it.

The desk was a sterile, black modern monstrosity, but it came all the way to the floor, so she ran around it, crawled beneath it, and then pulled her knees up to her chest.

And waited.

CHAPTER FOUR

IT FELT like an eternity until Skylar finally heard a knock at the office door. The sound startled her, and she jumped, banging her head against the underside of the desk.

She was cramped, shaking, exhausted, and terrified of moving. All her bravado was long gone, replaced with a terror that any second, the door would fly open and she'd be shot right through the desk.

As fun as that sounded, it was definitely a downgrade from her original Saturday night plan of pulling an all-nighter working.

Periodically, she'd heard voices outside the door, which had nearly undone her. She'd waited for the sound of a bullet hitting the door. She'd waited for death.

Instead, she'd finally gotten a knock at the door. Who knew death was so polite?

"Skylar. It's me." Logan's familiar voice brushed over her. "Let me in."

Hah. She wasn't going to fall for that.

She pressed her forehead to her knees and said nothing.

How did she know it was safe? For all she knew, Scarface had his gun at Logan's head, the way he'd had it at hers.

They should have made a code. More bubble bath. Something like that.

But they had no code, so yeah, as far as the world was concerned, Skylar was going to pretend there was no one to kill in this windowless, sterile office.

There was another tap on the door. "It's Logan," he said gently. "It's safe. Let me in."

She shook her head and didn't move. No chance.

"Skylar. Open the door."

God, he was irritatingly persistent. "There's no one in here," she finally said. "Go away."

"I'll withhold bubble baths for a year if you don't open the door."

A tiny smile pulled at her mouth. Bubble baths. Was that their code? Was it their code that Scarface was there, or Logan's code that everything was safe? Dammit. The next time she ran for her life in the middle of a gunfight, she was going to have better plans. "You're evil to even suggest that."

"I'm not evil." He sounded tired. "I need to see you. I need to make sure you're all right."

It was the weariness in his voice that finally got her to move. He sounded human, not like some gun-toting human assault weapon. She crawled out from under the desk, her legs cramping in protest.

She had to lean on the desk to get herself to her feet. Her legs felt weak and shaky, and her hands were still trembling. "Logan?"

"Yeah?"

"You're sure it's safe?"

"I'm sure. It's over." His tone was even, not tense or on edge.

She believed him that it was over. "Okay." She pried

herself off the desk and walked across the office. The carpet was soft and thick under her feet, which she hadn't noticed during her frantic run before. She reached for the door to unlock it, and her hands started shaking again. She tucked them under her armpits. "I can't open it."

"Why not?"

"Because I'm terrified that when I open it, there's going to be a gun pointing at my head."

"Shit." There was a light bump against the door, as if he'd let his forehead drop against it. "I know you're scared, and I'm sorry about that. But I need you to open it anyway. You trust me, right?"

She closed her eyes. "I don't even know you. You're the hot guy across the hall who's been giving me smoldering looks for the last two years. That's not trust."

He paused. "I smolder?"

"It's possible I imagined it to give myself some semblance of a personal life. Either way, it doesn't amount to deep, enduring trust." Her hands were trembling again, and her legs felt like they couldn't support her. She was at the end of her ability to cope.

She wanted to be able to trust him. She wanted desperately to open that door and let him keep her safe. But... hello...gunfight?

"Skylar."

"I'll call the police. Do you have a landline in here?" She'd dropped her phone during the gunfight. She was definitely going to have to work on her resilience in the presence of gunfire.

"The police are already here."

She leaned against the door. "Logan," she whispered.

"Yeah?"

"I can't do this."

"You can, actually." His voice was gentle, wrapping around

her like a solid wall of protection and understanding. "Skylar, what does your gut say?"

She closed her eyes and thought about him. The way he always had that smile for her whenever she saw him, the smile that barely reached his shadowed eyes. She thought about how he always held the door for her in the mailroom. How he stepped back to let her exit and enter the elevator first, his hand always hovering by her lower back. Never actually touching her, but hovering, as if to let her know he was there to keep her safe.

Always close. Always there. But never crossing that line and making it personal.

She thought of his eyes, the way he watched her, his gaze tracking her as if he wanted to say something more, but never did. He was a man who laughed rarely, but when he did, the sound of his voice lit up the space around him.

His laughter, those few times she'd heard it, had poured light into the darkest, most afraid, most lonely parts of her soul.

"Skylar?"

She believed in him. For better or worse, whether it was smart or not, she did. "I suppose there is a small, hopelessly romantic, and desperately foolish part of me that trusts you."

"I'll take that." She could almost feel his smile through the door. "You think you can let me in, then?"

She still couldn't make herself open the door. "I don't want to date your cat anymore."

"I still don't have one, so that works."

Damn him for still thinking her cat joke was funny. She was a sucker for a hot guy who thought she was funny. "Fine, but if I get shot, I will be super pissed and will never bring you coffee again."

"You're not going to get shot. I swear it."

"Okay, then." She had to let him in now, or she never

would. She'd die in his office, a dusty and crusty agoraphobic who wasn't even lucky enough to have cats. She took a deep breath and made herself reach for the door. Her hand was shaking so much she could barely grasp the knob, but she managed to twist it and pull it open.

Instinctively, she jumped to the side, out of the way, but Logan was right there in the doorway, taking up the space, using his body to shield her. If anyone tried to get to her, they would literally have to take him down first.

Logan. Alive. Safe. No more gunfire.

He smiled at her, that same half smile that barely reached his eyes, the one that always made her feel like she was the only person in the world he'd ever bothered to notice. "Hey," he said gently.

"Hi." Tears started to fill her eyes at the sight of him. "Don't ever get in a gunfight around me again."

"Never. I swear."

At that moment, she saw someone move behind him. Fear shot through her and she stumbled back, holding out her hands in protest. "Logan. Behind you—"

"It's okay." Logan moved in front of whoever it was, back into her line of vision. "They're safe."

"Safe?" She shot a look at Logan. "You're sure?"

"Absolutely." Logan's steady conviction broke through her sudden fear, wrapping around her like a warm blanket. "It's okay. I work with them. They're good guys."

She managed to stop her frantic flight backwards, but she was trembling again. She couldn't remember ever being so scared in her life. The two men behind Logan were wearing jeans like Logan was, but they looked more serious. Stoic. Hard. Relentless.

"Hang on a sec, guys." Logan gestured for the others to stay back. "I'm going to come in, okay, Skylar? Just me. I want to check and see if you're all right."

She shook her head, unable to take her gaze off the other men. Dammit. She hated being so terrified, but she couldn't stop panicking.

Logan pressed his lips together, then pulled his gun out of a holster on his hip. "I'll shoot them if they come in here, okay?"

She saw both of the men look at each other. "Where will you shoot them?"

Logan raised his brows. "What do you mean?"

"In the head? In the shoulder? Foot?"

"Do you have a request? I take requests."

She studied them. "Middle of the forehead? I feel like that would be a good equalizer."

"Forehead it is." He glanced over his shoulder. "Did you hear that, gentlemen? Middle of the forehead if either of you scare her."

The taller one nodded. "Got it."

The shorter one, who was studying her just a little too intensely, raised his brows. "You're a pain in the ass, Stockton."

"Agreed." Logan studied her, his gaze concerned. "Good? Can I come in?"

Skylar finally nodded, and Logan immediately crossed the threshold into the office. The minute he came into the room, she felt her tension ease. Her foundation seemed to right itself, shoring up beneath her feet the closer he got to her.

Logan walked over to her, his hands going to her shoulders as he searched her face. "How are you?"

Tears filled her eyes again when she felt his hands settle on her shoulders. She'd been holding herself so tightly, but having Logan holding her suddenly made her shields crumble. "I'm fantastic," she managed to say as she started to cry.

"Skylar." He reached for her at the same moment she reached for him.

CHAPTER FIVE

THE MOMENT SKYLAR felt the strength of Logan's body against hers, the tears came for real. He felt safe. Solid. Protective. His chest was hard, and his arms were chiseled, but the way he held her was pure tenderness and reassurance. She tried to focus on the feel of his body, but she couldn't stop shaking. "I just need a minute," she whispered.

"I'm so sorry." He wrapped her up against his chest as the sobs took over. "Shit, I'm sorry, Skylar."

"It's fine." She pressed her face into his chest, fighting for control, but it was almost impossible to find. "I'm just crying because I'm happy."

He paused. "Happy?"

"Yes. Being in the middle of a gunfight has been on my bucket list for ages. Tears of joy." Her words were strangled by sobs and heavy gasps as she fought for control, but the soft chuckle in his chest told her he'd understood what she'd said.

"Ah... Makes sense." He kissed the top of her head, his arms solid and warm around her. "Accomplishing a big life goal can be emotional."

"Totally." Humor had always been her coping mechanism

with life, and she was so grateful Logan was going along with it. If he gave her some sort of pity party, she'd be completely lost to the terror and shock still trying to grip her so badly.

But he didn't. He seemed to understand she needed to go into denial and deflection mode, which she was deeply grateful for. She turned her head to the side, resting her cheek against his chest while she eyed the men still standing in the doorway. "They're watching us."

"They're voyeurs. It's normal for them. Therapy isn't helping. They're beyond hope."

The grins fell off their faces, which made her almost want to smile. She closed her eyes, pressed her face to Logan's chest, and set her hands on his hips.

She focused on the hardness of his muscles beneath her touch. On the significant height difference between them. On the scent of fresh soap that still clung to his body. She used him to ground herself in the present. "You know," she said, gripping the soft fabric of his shirt. "If you wanted to feel me up, you could have just asked. No need to traumatize me."

"I'm a gentleman. I'd never proposition my neighbor. It creates lifelong awkwardness in the mailroom."

"True. Shooting an armed assailant in the head when I bring you coffee is so much more subtle." The image of the man hitting her door with the bullet hole in his forehead flashed through her mind, and she let out her breath. "I need to go home now."

"You can't." One of the men in the doorway responded, making Logan stiffen.

Logan's response was subtle, but since she was holding onto his sides, she could feel it. His secret. And she was in on it. She liked that.

What she didn't like was someone telling her what she

could and couldn't do. So, she turned her head to look at the man who'd spoken. "Who *are* you?"

"Logan's boss. Director Hamilton. Judd Hamilton." He was the shorter one, with the more serious face. He looked older than Logan, probably in his sixties.

The taller one, who was about Logan's age inclined his head toward her. "Agent Moss."

Director? Agent? Skylar looked back and forth between the three men, trying to wrap her mind around it. "Are you guys CIA? FBI? A secret terrorist organization designed to bring down the very foundation of all that is well and good on this earth?"

Agent Moss grinned. "Some people would consider those not mutually exclusive." He pulled out his wallet and held up his badge. "Agent Moss. CIA."

"CIA." Were they kidding? They weren't, obviously, but it was almost more than she could process. What on earth had she walked into?

"Yep." Agent Moss was attractive, fit, and had a compelling edge. Not as striking as Logan, but no one was.

Since she'd met Logan, every man had fallen short when measured up against him. It was annoying, but a fact of life she'd learned to deal with. "Why can't I go home?"

Director Hamilton gestured at the couch. "May we enter without risk of being shot?"

Logan's arms were still draped around her shoulders, and Skylar was still gripping his shirt, so she felt accommodating enough to nod. "Yes, but keep your hands where I can see them."

A grin quirked the corner of Agent Moss's mouth as he walked in. "Wouldn't think of doing anything less."

Skylar watched them both as they made their way into Logan's office, taking seats on the manly, impersonal leather couch. The office was like the couch. No personality. No warmth. No livability. It was as if Logan were trying to kill all shreds of humanity with his décor.

Which was weird, because every time she'd met Logan, he was almost overwhelming with the raw force of his energy, even as he fought to keep it locked down.

The only thing in the office that had any kind of personality was a photograph on a table in the corner. It was the only thing of interest she'd been able to see when she'd been stuffed under the desk, waiting to die, so she'd pretty much memorized it by now.

It was a picture of nine young men, one of which was clearly a gangly teenage Logan. They were all wearing cowboy hats, jeans, and solemn expressions. Not a smile to be seen in the whole group, but they were standing so close their shoulders were touching.

They all looked like Logan, especially the one standing beside him in the picture. A boy who could have been his twin if they were the same height. Logan and the one standing next to him were clearly mixed race, and the others weren't, but their similar facial structure made it clear that they were closely related. Nine brothers who were united against the world.

She'd never had siblings, and had always longed for them, especially after her dad had died, leaving her mom as the only family she had left. The photograph of Logan and his siblings brought back all those longings for a family she could count on, a family that would swallow her up in their eccentric craziness, always being there for her, no matter what.

With all the boys wearing cowboy hats and boots, Skylar knew where Logan's western drawl came from now, but that picture and his accent were the only remnants of his past that still clung to him. The only signs of connection that she'd ever seen in her solitary neighbor.

"Have a seat." Director Hamilton gestured at one of the armchairs that flanked the couch.

Skylar chose the one facing the door, so she would have time to dive under the desk if someone came in after her. And because it put all the men between her and the door, which she felt was a good plan, seeing as how they all had guns, and she had only her charm and wit.

Logan brushed his hand over her shoulder, then took the chair opposite her. She didn't like him being that far from her, but at least he was between her and the door. She took a deep breath, then folded her arms over her chest. "Okay, so why can't I go home?"

It was Logan who answered. "One of the men from tonight got away. But he knows where you live, and he knows you saw his face."

She sucked in her breath. It had to be Scarface, because she'd seen the other one die. "You think he's going to come back and *kill* me?"

Director Hamilton nodded. "Men like that don't leave witnesses."

Skylar's heart started to pound. "Do I have to go into witness protection or something?" She stood up. "I won't leave my mom. She's in Vermont, and she's all alone and—"

"No." Director Hamilton cut her off. "It won't take that long. We know who he is."

Agent Moss nodded. "It'll be a few weeks at most."

"A few weeks? You expect me to not go home for a few *weeks*?"

Director Hamilton and Agent Moss both looked over at Logan.

So she looked over at Logan. "What?"

He glanced at the picture in the corner, the one with all the cowboys, then looked back at her. "It's my fault you got caught up in this situation. I take full responsibility for getting you on their radar, so I'm taking full responsibility for keeping you safe."

Her heart started to pound. "What does that mean?"

"I'm taking you off the grid."

"To *where?*"

He glanced at his colleagues, then back at her. "It was Director Hamilton's idea." He didn't look happy about it, but his jaw was set with fierce resolution. "It makes sense for a lot of reasons too complicated to go into."

Skylar stood up and set her hands on her hips. She didn't like people making decisions for her, let alone major decisions that affected her life. "*What* makes sense?"

"I'm taking you to Rogue Valley, Wyoming. My hometown. And we leave tonight."

She stared at him. "You want me to walk away from my life? I have a career. I'm in the middle of a big project at work. I have a bamboo plant that needs water. I don't even know you. I'm not throwing my life in a suitcase and traipsing off to Wyoming with you. Put a guard on my door. It's really not that complicated. I see movies. I know how this works."

Logan leaned forward, his forearms resting on his knees. "Skylar."

"What?"

"I want to make sure you stay alive." His voice was low. Rough. Weighted with the same burdens she'd seen in him every time they'd met.

"I appreciate that." She swallowed. "That's one of my top ten goals for the day, actually."

Logan rose to his feet and walked over to her. The closer he got, the more intimidating he became. He was tall. Muscular. And apparently, trained to kill, which was always a great thing to have in one's across-the-hall neighbor.

Or not.

He stopped in front of her, his dark gaze searching hers.

"The last thing I want is to go home to stay. But it's the best way to keep you safe, so I'm going. And you're coming with me."

"I'm not going —" Her protest died at the haunted look in his eyes.

He wasn't exaggerating when he'd said he didn't want to go back there. But for her, he was willing to go. She glanced over at Director Hamilton and Agent Moss. With their serious faces, they were impossible to read.

Scarface might try to kill her, and she couldn't handle that by herself, despite her skill with hurling hot coffee and diving to the floor. Did she want her life in the hands of someone she didn't know and didn't trust?

No. She didn't. Logan was the only one she'd feel safe around again, for at least a while.

She wasn't stupid. The bullets had been real. Scarface had looked her right in the eyes and knew she'd seen him. Her architect skills weren't going to keep her safe, and there was no way she was going to let her mom get a call that her favorite, and only, daughter had been shot because she'd been too stubborn to leave town.

She was trapped. She folded her arms over her chest and glared at Logan. "When I decided to bring you coffee, this was not the maybe-I'll-get-to-know-Logan plan I'd envisioned."

"I get that." He inclined his head in acknowledgement. "Flexibility is an important part of life, however. A good skill-set."

"Not getting me sucked into some sort of CIA blown mission is also an important part of life."

Guilt flickered through his eyes. "I know. I'm sorry."

He totally meant his apology. Not just a little bit. He was all-in on the regret train. His pain wrapped around her, making it difficult to breathe. But she knew it was that pain that would drive him to make absolutely certain that she was safe.

At the end of the day, she wanted to be safe, too.

With a sigh, she let out her breath. "Okay. I'll go with you."

Logan's brows shot up. "Tonight."

"You guys have no appreciation for wasting time." She set her hands on her hips. "Yes. I will go to Rogue Valley tonight."

Relief flooded Logan's face. "Great."

Director Hamilton stood up. "I'll have a plane ready within the hour."

"An *hour*?" All she had was one hour to pack up her life, send all her work files to her boss with some plausible explanation for going off the grid that wouldn't get her fired, and then she'd be on a plane with Logan. Alone. Leaving her entire life behind for a week. Or two.

Or as long as it took for the CIA to track down a man who was, most likely, a trained assassin who was an expert on disappearing.

And killing people. He was also an expert on killing people. People like her.

One simple caffeine addiction, and her life was in shambles. If she'd just stayed in her little condo, tomorrow morning she would have been getting up, taking a shower in her own bathroom, and heading to her computer like the workaholic she'd never dreamed of being.

She was never drinking coffee again.

Then she looked over at Logan. If she hadn't gone for coffee, would he be dead? If she hadn't gone for coffee, she'd be getting up tomorrow and doing the exact same thing she'd been doing for years, slowly sucking her soul dry.

Logan seemed to sense her looking at him, and he glanced

over. When he saw her watching him, he gave her a smile. That smile. That smile that she'd only seen him give her.

Her heart turned over.

Maybe coffee was all right.

After all, it wasn't like she'd actually died.

Yet.

CHAPTER SIX

LOGAN LEANED ON HIS FOREARMS, watching Skylar sleep on the plane.

He'd always thought she looked innocent, too innocent for his life, both past and present. But in sleep? She transcended innocence. The only word he could think of to describe her was angelic.

His angel.

Her lips were slightly parted, and her chest moved slightly with each breath. Her backpack was clutched on her lap, and the desperation with which she held onto it in her sleep told him exactly how strung out she was.

How scared.

Guilt sank deep in his gut for dragging her into this.

Her eyes flickered open, and she saw him watching her. He waited for the smile she always gave him, but this time, it didn't come. A different emotion flickered through her eyes. Fear? *Shit*. "Skylar—"

Before he could finish, her eyes closed again as she wedged herself deeper in her seat, hugging her backpack to her chest as if the bag could protect her from the world. From him.

Shit.

He'd been born into a monster's den, but he'd joined the agency to protect. To do good. To take what he'd been born into and use it for good.

It hadn't worked out exactly the way he'd wanted it, but he had made a difference. He'd done things that the world would never know about, things that had saved lives. Things that would have haunted him, if he weren't doing them for the right reasons.

He was relentless and tireless in his work, never slowing down long enough to think about anything. Except when he was around Skylar, because when he was with her, his mind felt quiet.

When he was around Skylar, he wasn't afraid of the things in his head, because she cleared all the shit out. But now...the woman who had been his sunshine now looked at him like he was the monster he'd tried to escape.

He'd broken into her life and poured violence into it.

He had to fix it. He had to fix what he'd done. He had to clear the path for her.

And he had to do it by plunking them both into the middle of the world that had shaped who he was, the past he'd fought so hard to escape, the life that had made violence a part of his very soul.

He swore and leaned back in his seat, running his hands over his head.

His past was coming back for him. He'd decided not to call ahead to warn his family he was coming. His phone was supposed to be secure, but someone had found out where he lived, and that information had been leaked somewhere.

From inside the CIA?

He wasn't taking a chance.

Not with Skylar's life.

Hell.

He was going home. For more than a day. For more than a couple days.

Something he'd never planned to do again.

He had truly believed that there was nothing that could ever get him to go home again.

Logan looked over at Skylar, and knew he'd been wrong.

Skylar finally opened her eyes, abandoning her attempts to sleep. The private plane had lush leather seats, and plenty of space to stretch out in luxury, so she'd been optimistic about her chances to regroup.

She'd been determined to nap, because she was exhausted, drained, and strung out, but sleep had been impossible. Images of guns and assassins had kept flashing through her mind. Plus, she'd been too aware of Logan watching her, all hunched over with a haunted, intense expression on his face.

She studied him. "Why do you keep staring at me?"

His dark brown eyes had no smile in them. "We need to talk."

So much for her hope that he was going to tell her that everything was a dream, and they were actually flying to Hawaii for a romantic vacation of love, lust, and pineapples. She sighed and wrapped her arms more tightly around her backpack. "Is this where you teach me how to shoot a gun and kill a man with my bare hands?"

Again, not even the faintest hint of a smile, which was too bad. A smile from him would definitely help the tension suffocating her. "No," he said. "It wouldn't help you against him. He's an expert in death."

That wasn't as reassuring as one might think. "So, my only chance to stay alive is you?"

"I'm very good."

His matter-of-fact tone *was* somewhat reassuring, so she considered relaxing slightly. "So, what then?"

"Saturday is the Fourth of July."

"So?"

"So, the holiday is a big deal in Rogue Valley."

Skylar wiggled herself to a more upright position. "At risk of sounding repetitive, so? What does this have to do with Eugene?"

He frowned. "Eugene?"

"The assassin who wants to kill me."

"His name isn't Eugene. It's—"

"Shh!" She held up her hand to silence him. "You appear to be well-versed in having bullets flying past your head, but I'm still a little freaked out and on the edge of a complete panic attack. Eugene is the name for a math nerd who wouldn't even be strong enough to pick up a gun. Calling the guy hunting us Eugene makes him seem less scary, which makes it easier for me to breathe. I like breathing, so can we go with Eugene?

Regret flickered across his face. "It's important to be constantly on the alert."

"But not freaking out, right?"

He pressed his lips together, and then finally nodded. "Freaking out isn't a great plan."

"There you go. Eugene it is, then." She supposed it was all well and good that Logan was being stoic and focused, given that she needed him at the top of his CIA operative game, but it was making her feel increasingly isolated.

She needed a little bit of the Logan she'd gotten to know in the mailroom and the elevator. The one she could draw a smile out of. The one who had pulled her into his arms and held her when she was so scared in his office.

But that wasn't the Logan she was getting right now. This Logan was hardcore special agent, and she didn't really love it. Necessary, maybe. But warm, fuzzy, and comforting? Not so much.

He leaned forward, resting his forearms on his thighs, his hands clasped loosely between his knees. "There will be a Fourth of July parade in Rogue Valley. A town festival. Family stuff. A lot of people and activities. It'll be impossible to stay off the radar completely. It's a small town, and people know me."

She tensed. "So, I'm going to be exposed, Eugene will find me, and then I'm going to take my last breath and die there? I always dreamed I'd die in Vermont, honestly."

His jaw tightened, and his fists clenched. "You're not going to die in Wyoming. I won't let that happen. *I promise.*"

"Well, that's good to know." It really was. Especially since he'd said it like he'd throw his own body in Eugene's path to protect her. He was committed to keeping her alive, and that was great. She took a deep breath, trying to get to a topic that wasn't freaking her out. "Well, if you're not planning to ask me if I've updated my will recently, why are you telling me about Rogue Valley's Fourth of July festivities?"

"We're going to need a cover."

"A cover?" She brightened. "Like a fake identity? I'll be a famous rapper. I could pull that off." She set her backpack on the empty seat next to her and began working a really excellent rap beat, moving her shoulders in a pretty fantastic rhythm. "My name's Skylar and I'm not gonna die there. Cause I got a guy who won't let me die."

The corner of Logan's mouth quirked. "That's pretty impressive for a five-foot-two blond architect from Vermont."

"Right? Never underestimate me. I'm very versatile."

"I wouldn't dare," he agreed quickly, still looking like he was trying not to laugh. "But that wasn't quite what I was thinking."

"I'm crushed." She sighed and flopped back in her seat dramatically. "A famous rapper has been on my bucket list for decades. I suppose you have a cover already planned?"

He nodded. "I need a reason for showing up in Rogue Valley with you. I never go home. I don't have friends. I'm not social. Nothing about this trip will make sense to my family, or anyone in town. People will talk and start asking questions. I can't afford to have anyone dig too deep."

She narrowed her eyes. "What *would* make sense, then?"

He put his hand into his pocket. "There's only one thing that would bring me back home for an extended trip with a woman."

Her heart started to pound at the grim expression on his face. What on earth could make him look so cranky? "I refuse to pretend I'm your personal hairstylist. I can barely blow dry my own hair. No one would believe it. I still think the rapper is the best idea. No one would think twice about a famous rapper that they've never heard of showing up in Rogue Valley for the Fourth of July."

He laughed softly, then pulled his hand out of his pocket. "Not my hairstylist or a rapper." He opened his palm to reveal a white-gold, diamond solitaire ring. "My fiancée."

CHAPTER SEVEN

FIANCÉE? Skylar was so startled that all she could do was stare in shock at the ring. It was sparkly, huge, and beautiful. It reminded her of hopes, dreams, and betrayal that could slice her heart open with one swift swipe.

"Skylar?"

"No." She sat back and folded her arms across her chest. "Nope. I'm good. I'll be your hairdresser. I'm sure I can fake it."

Logan raised one gloriously sexy eyebrow. "I thought women dreamed of getting engaged."

"They might, but there's a couple key things here." She drummed her finger restlessly on the armrest. "First, it's not a real engagement. It's a fake one. Women who dream of diamond rings and getting engaged usually include an actual groom, eternal love, and a dream wedding in their fantasies."

"All right. I suppose that's true." He contemplated her thoughtfully. "What's the second issue?"

"The second issue is that I've been engaged, and it led to such devastating heartbreak that I'll never date again, unless the guy is in prison for life in another country, so there's no chance it could work out."

His brown eyes searched hers. "I'm sorry to hear that," he said gently.

Compassion softened his face, which irritated her. She didn't want sympathy. She wanted to be strong and independent. "I'm fine," she said quickly. "Don't worry about me."

"I always worry about you."

She hesitated. "You do? Why?" He always worried about her? Why? They barely knew each other. That was totally sweet. Unnecessary, of course, but it still felt good.

"Because..." He paused, then shrugged. "It's not important. But if it's a fake engagement, then it's really not a threat to your committed single status, is it?"

She frowned at him. "Well, not literally, but emotionally, it's quite a toll."

"A toll?" He leaned forward, as if he really wanted to know. The distant reserve he'd been holding around him so tightly was gone, replaced with an intense intimacy that made her feel safer. She liked when he looked at her like that.

He made her feel seen, which was both incredible and terrifying at the same time.

"Yes," she said. "A toll."

"How so?"

She sighed at his refusal to let her evade the question. "I don't really want to elaborate."

"Tell me anyway."

She wrinkled her nose at him. "You're a pest."

He smiled, that glorious radiant smile that made her heart flutter every time she saw it. "Some of the folks at work have a more colorful name for me, but I don't deny it. I want to know."

"Damn you for manipulating me with that ridiculously charming smile." She glared at him when his smile widened even further. "Fine. It would be a toll because if I'm wearing that ring, every time I look down and see it, for a split second, my heart will forget that it's fake. And then, I'll be crushed by the horror of having to relive the part of my life I want to forget."

He swore under his breath. "Skylar—"

"Or," she continued, "I'll be blinded by the unbridled ecstasy of believing I fully recovered from that horror show and have a chance for that happily ever after that I no longer believe in, only to be crushed when I realize that it's not true."

Logan got a speculative gleam in his eyes. "All that from a ring?"

"It's not funny." Skylar reached over and smacked his knee impatiently. "Because then, reality will intrude, and I'll remember that the engagement is fake because I'm hiding out from an assassin, and my only chance of survival is my reticent neighbor who claims to be able to keep me alive."

"Ah." He turned the ring over in his fingers. "So, if you put this ring on, it's a triple threat to your emotional well-being: reliving your past, hoping for a future that's not real, and a reminder about Eugene."

"Exactly." She stifled a grin at his use of her name for the assassin. "Since my emotional well-being is already in enough trouble as it is, the answer's obvious." She leaned back in her seat. "Hairdresser it is."

"Nope."

She eyed him. "Yes."

"You don't have to wear the ring." He slid it back into his pocket. "But we're engaged."

To her surprise, she felt a surge of loss as the ring disappeared from sight. Not that she wanted to be engaged to him, or anyone. But Logan was...well...Logan. He was tempting. "How did you come up with a ring so fast anyway?"

He glanced over at her. "I'm not answering anything until you agree we're engaged."

She sighed. "I don't want to be engaged, Logan. It broke me," she whispered.

Logan studied her for a moment, then he unfastened his seatbelt, slid off the seat, and kneeled in front of her. "Skylar."

God, he was close to her. And compelling. Why was he so compelling? She didn't want to get involved with anyone. But Logan did something to her. "What?" She sounded more hostile than she intended and winced.

"I won't break you," he said, his gaze searching hers. "Pretending to be engaged is the best way I know of to protect you. Now that I know that it hits a trigger for you, we can work around it. If I do something that bothers you, tell me. I'll adjust. We can work this out."

She searched his face. "But—"

"I know about triggers, Skylar. More than you could ever know. I have no interest in making you relive a shitty past, trust me." When she didn't answer, he took a breath. "All right. Never mind. I'll think of something else. I won't push you." He put his hands on her knees, squeezed gently, then stood and walked back to his seat.

Skylar watched him as he sat down and bent over, resting his forehead in his palms. His shoulders were tense, his breathing deep and even, as if he were intentionally slowing his breathing so he could focus.

She let out her breath. "This is a shitty situation, huh?"

Logan snorted and lifted his head. "Yeah, you could say that."

Their gazes met, and she saw the weariness in his gaze. The weight he always carried, that would sometimes dissipate when they were talking, like when they had been talking about the ring a few minutes ago.

46

She loved watching that darkness leave him when she teased him. Connecting with him made them both feel better, a gift she was pretty sure he needed as much as she did, especially now.

She bit her lip. Logan was the only person who made her laugh these days. Maybe being fake engaged to him was the universe's gift to help her heal, to finally get past the baggage she couldn't shed on her own.

Giving her a partner to lean on, without requiring her to get romantically involved. If they were only fake engaged so he could protect her, then she was pretty safe allowing herself to lean on him and trust that he'd be there every morning when she woke up, and every night when she went to sleep.

God, that would be wonderful, even if for only a few days.

His eyebrows went up. "You look shifty. What are you plotting?"

She nibbled her lower lip. "If we were to get fake engaged, real rules would apply."

Curiosity flickered in his eyes. "Like what?"

"No messing around with anyone else. I know it's for show, but it matters to me."

He nodded without hesitation. "Agreed."

Her heart fluttered at his immediate acquiescence. How many men would be willing to give up other women for a fake fiancée? Not many. Especially since plenty of men wouldn't even give up other women for a real fiancée.

"What else?" he asked, clearly undaunted by her request.

"Being nice to each other. Treating each other like it's real, at least in public." She wouldn't be humiliated again. Never again. "Always defending one another to others."

He looked surprised by her request, but nodded. "Of course. I'd never consider anything else." He paused. "So, it's a go?"

She took a breath and held out her hand. "Can I see the ring?"

"You bet." He dug it out of his pocket and put it in her hand, his fingers brushing against her skin, making her suck in her breath.

The white gold was cold against her palm, the diamond gorgeous and sparkling. Their engagement would be fake, but to the world, it would be real. If people believed she was his fiancée but hadn't received a ring from him... Her fingers closed over the metal. She deserved more than that.

Silently, she slid the ring onto her finger, her heart hammering as it settled in place. She expected to feel panic and terror, but she didn't. She just felt safer, as if the diamond bound her to the man who could keep her alive. Relieved, she let out a breath. "Whew. Okay, then."

Logan was leaning forward, his jaw flexing as he watched her. "You okay?"

She looked up, and her resistance melted away at the concern on his face. She fluttered her hand at him. "It's a big diamond. I feel like I landed a sugar daddy."

He grinned. "I'm definitely the sugar daddy type."

"I totally pegged you for that." She sat back in the seat, the tension easing from her body for the first time in hours. "This might be okay." The cold metal encircling her finger made her feel safe. It wasn't a reminder of her past, or a lie about her future. It was the truth that Logan was committed to protecting her.

"So, you're in?"

"Engaged to a sexy cowboy CIA agent from Wyoming who's my personal bodyguard and protector?" She smiled. "Now, *that* might be every woman's fantasy."

He grinned. "You think I'm sexy?"

Ah...that devastating smile and sparkle in his eyes was back. Her heart leapt, and she couldn't keep the smile off her face. "As if you didn't know that you're basically pure temptation all wrapped up in jeans and a sweatshirt."

"It's subjective, but I'm not going to try to talk you out of it." His smile was genuine now, amusement dancing in his eyes. "So it's a yes?"

She ran her fingers over the diamond. Was it a yes? She grinned. "It's a yes."

Operation Fake Fiancée underway.

CHAPTER EIGHT

BEING fake engaged to Logan felt great, for about thirty seconds.

Which was the point at which Skylar realized how great it really did feel.

The kind of great that made her realize that the hopelessly romantic dreamer inside her was taking it much too seriously.

As the plane cruised toward their destination, Skylar narrowed her eyes as Logan leaned back against the seat and closed his eyes. How could he sleep? He'd just proposed to her, and she'd just said yes.

But he hadn't. He'd proposed a plan to keep her from being murdered. Totally different.

But dammit if that little part inside her wasn't reacting as if it were real...as if she were really engaged to the man she imagined Logan to be. She already knew he was handsome. Big family. A protector. Kind. Loyal.

A man who would never leave her. Never cheat on her. Never rip her heart out and shred it in front of all the world.

"Skylar." Logan didn't open his eyes.

"What?"

"Would it work if I told you to relax?"

"No. I hate being told what to do."

He grinned, still not opening his eyes. "I'm the same way."

His smile made her relax slightly. "Is your family going to believe we're engaged?"

Logan's smile faded, and he opened his eyes to look at her. "I don't know."

"We have to lie to people you love." Calling her mom at one in the morning to tell her she was going off on a business trip to somewhere that didn't have cell service had been terrible. And that had been on the phone. What about in person? Day after day? To Logan's family. "I'm not a good liar."

He smiled. "That's okay. You don't have to say much. Just act like I irritate the hell out of you and you're not sure why you put up with me. That'll convince them. They all know I'm a pain in the ass."

She furrowed her brow. "I don't find you irritating."

He laughed. "Give it time. You'll come around."

She pursed her lips as the plane began its descent, making her ears pop. "What are we doing, Logan? This is ridiculous." She looked down at the ring on her hand, shiny and glittering. "Where are we going to sleep? Together? If we're engaged, they're going to expect that." She looked at him. "Unless your family is the no-sex-before-marriage type?"

Logan couldn't help but chuckle at the hopeful expression on Skylar's face. God, he couldn't believe how much she lightened the darkness that weighted him down so constantly. He hadn't expected to have any kind of reaction when she'd put the ring on, but the moment she'd settled it on her hand, something inside him had come alive. A fierce, unyielding possessiveness. Not of the ring. Of Skylar.

His response to seeing that diamond on her hand had been so visceral that he'd actually closed his eyes, trying to regroup, to remind himself of what mattered in his life and the promises he'd made to himself. Work. Protection. Focus.

He released a breath, focusing on Skylar's clear blue eyes as she waited for his answer on whether they would be sharing a bed. *Sharing a bed.* He hadn't given any thought to those details ahead of time, but now that she'd mentioned it? *Hell, yeah.* The idea was so compelling he couldn't stop thinking about it.

He cleared his throat. "I have nine brothers and one sister, and a dead father who knocked up eight different women to produce all of us, so yeah, not a lot of concern about premarital sex in my family."

Alarm flickered across her face, making him sit up. "We're going to sleep together, then? Share a bedroom? A bed?"

Protectiveness surged through him at her fear, protectiveness he hadn't felt in years, not since his younger brothers had grown up and his dad had died, ending the threat to all of them. But Skylar brought it all back, his need to keep someone else safe. His need to give every bit of his soul to safeguard her.

"I need to be with you all the time, Skylar," he said evenly. "On the slim chance Eugene finds us, if it takes even a second for me to get to you, that could be too late. So, yeah, we'll be sharing a bedroom."

"Shit."

He almost chuckled at her epithet. God, he loved how expressive she was, how she didn't hold back what she was feeling. But he did *not* like her being afraid of him. "I would never push myself on you. Ever. I swear it."

Surprise flickered across her face. "Of course you wouldn't. I wasn't worried about that."

He relaxed slightly, glad she realized that. "Then what makes you nervous?"

She chewed her lips. "Honestly?"

"Always." He was curious now.

She stared past him, focused on the window of the plane, clearly trying to figure out what to say.

He waited, his interest growing.

She finally sighed, and looked right at him, owning whatever she was about to say. "I'm super attracted to you, Logan."

Tension slammed into his gut, and all the sexual tension he'd been trying to keep at bay exploded through him.

He'd been attracted to Skylar since the first second he'd met her two years ago. Every single time he ran into her, he walked away with a hard-on. He'd fought it for a million reasons, and he'd proposed the fake engagement only when he'd made sure he could keep it straight in his gut that it was a business arrangement only.

But with her declaration hanging between them, all his best resolutions seemed to shoot out the window. He cleared his throat, and kept his voice neutral. "Okay." It was all he trusted himself to say.

Her eyebrows furrowed in that adorable way she had. "I don't want to get involved with anyone," she said. "But you make me dream of it. I don't know if I have the willpower to run around with your ring on my finger, being all cozy, and not fall for the guy I imagine you are."

Her words burned through him, temporarily rendering him speechless.

"I can't fall for the wrong guy again," she said. "I'd rather die a crazy cat lady with hair growing out of my ears than endure another heartbreak like I went through."

The wrong guy? She thought he was the wrong guy? That bit deep, but at the same time, he was glad she saw that about him, because she was right. He let out his breath and tried to deflect. "I thought I was the one who was going to have hair growing out of my ears."

She stared at him, and then threw her sweatshirt across the plane at him, smacking him in the face. "You're so irritating."

He caught her sweatshirt. "See? I knew you'd figure it out." He grinned, catching a whiff of her shampoo on the fabric. He loved that scent.

"Logan. I'm serious—"

"I know." He handed her back the sweatshirt. "Look, I'm not going to lie. I'm incredibly attracted to you as well."

Her cheeks turned pink. "How is that helpful?" She glared at him. "You're supposed to say that you find me so repulsive that I could throw myself on top of you stark naked and you wouldn't be tempted."

Heat shot to his groin at the vision of Skylar throwing herself on top of him naked. He'd seen her in shorts and a tank top enough times for him to get a pretty good idea of how incredible she would look naked. "Repulsive isn't a word I could ever associate with you." His voice was huskier than he intended, and he paused to clear his throat.

"Again, not helpful." She was hugging her backpack again, as if the bag could save them both from the sexual tension rising in the confined area.

He leaned forward, bracing his forearms on his thighs. "My job is dangerous."

Her eyebrows shot up. "Is it? I hadn't realized."

Damn, he loved her sass. "As you saw tonight, my job poses a risk to anyone who's close to me."

She wrinkled her nose. "I did notice that."

"When I made my career choice," he continued, "I promised myself that I'd never let the job endanger anyone I cared about. As a result, I've taken a number of precautions, including not forming close personal connections with anyone." He met her gaze. "That means I would never cross that line with you."

She stared at him, her lips slightly parted as she listened. "Really?" At his nod, she frowned. "So, there's never been anyone for you? No woman?"

"No one that mattered. I never let anyone in. Ever." The promise he'd made himself so easily ten years ago seemed to stick in his throat in a way it never had before. "I'm alone, Skylar, and that's the way I'll stay." He managed a small smile. "That means that when we're alone and have no one to impress, you're safe from my seduction, I swear it. I won't screw with your emotions."

She surveyed him, a thoughtful expression on her face that made him think she was seeing a lot more than he'd told her. "So, despite all this raving sexual attraction between us, we're going to be like brother and sister."

He snorted. "Shit, no. Just because I'm not going to make love to you doesn't mean I can think of you as my sister. More like the hot cheerleader who's so far out of my league that I don't even dare make a move."

She raised her brows. "Hot cheerleader?" she challenged.

He grinned. "Smart, successful, charming-as-hell architect who's off-limits for a bunch of reasons?"

"Better." She let out her breath. "All right, then. So, we're going to be a fake-engaged couple who entertain numerous sexual fantasies about each other, make out in public, lie to those we love, and share a bedroom, while maintaining a strictly professional relationship?"

His pulse quickened at the idea of making out with her in public. "Yeah. Pretty much."

"That sounds doable." She sighed and leaned back in her seat. "You definitely need to start shaving more closely, though. That stubble is literally begging me to run my fingers over it."

He laughed, and then leaned forward. "Skylar. There's something you need to know about me."

She let out her breath. "What?"

"I was born into a life of abuse." He ignored the concern that suddenly darkened her eyes. He kept going, not wanting to give her a chance to ask questions about his past. "Among other things, it taught me to be a protector of those who couldn't protect themselves. My younger brothers for a long time. And now, I protect the innocents who don't even know I exist. Protecting is in my nature, and you're in my circle now. I'll protect you. Not just your life, but your heart, your soul, and that adorable smile that lights up the world. I give you my word. You're safe with me."

She stared at him.

He frowned, waiting for her response. "Skylar?"

"That was quite a speech."

He shrugged. "It's the truth."

"I haven't felt safe in a very long time," she finally said. "The idea of being able to drop my guards is..." She stopped, and her eyes suddenly became shiny with unshed tears.

Something surged through him, more than the need to protect. Something deeper, more personal, more primal. "I won't let you down, Skylar. I promise."

For another moment, she said nothing. She simply stared at him.

He shifted. "Skylar—"

Before he could finish, she unfastened her seatbelt, walked over to him, and hugged him, burying her face in his chest.

He wrapped his arms around her and pulled her onto his lap. Her body was warm and alive against his, settling all the tension that seemed to always be rushing through him.

He brushed a kiss over the top of her head, and then froze at the intimate gesture, at his need to slide his hand under her chin, raise her face to his, and kiss her. For real. The way he'd always fantasized about doing.

Skylar went still against him. "Logan?"

"Yeah." Her hair was like silk against his jaw.

"I think hugging and lap-sitting in private should be off limits. Your abs are ridiculous, and you smell amazing."

He burst out laughing as she pulled back. "It's your hair that's unfair. It's pure temptation."

She retreated back to her seat. "I'll shave my head if you'll eat a lot of donuts and roll in horse manure. That should take care of it."

He grinned. "Deal." But even as he said it, he had a bad feeling he was in over his head.

That they both were.

And the cost of screwing up was her life. Her heart. And hell, maybe even his.

CHAPTER NINE

"WHAT DO YOU MEAN, it doesn't look like Mickey Mouse?" Chase Stockton leaned over the table, grinning as his four-year-old, J.J., pointed to the pancake.

"Those aren't ears, Dad."

"I think they're ears. Mira?"

His wife looked over from the sink, where she was wiping the face of a little boy named Alexander they were fostering. "Of course it's Mickey Mouse. Your artistic skills are perfect."

"Sarcasm is beautiful on you, sweetheart," Chase said with a laugh. "Alexander. What do you think?"

Alexander pulled away from Mira, ran across the kitchen and climbed onto his lap, tucking his little feet under him. Alexander was almost six, but he was small for his age and much too quiet.

Chase and Mira had been fostering him for only two months, and they were making slow progress with him. The most success had come with the horses, reminding Chase so much of his own past and how horses had helped him. "It looks like a ghost," Alexander finally said.

J.J. burst out laughing. "See? Not Mickey Mouse."

Chase threw up his hands in mock despair as the little boys giggled. His heart seemed to swell with happiness as Mira smiled at him. He sometimes couldn't believe this was his life. Married. With two kids he loved with all his heart. He'd thought he'd be a bachelor forever. That had been his goal. What he wanted.

And now, life had become so much richer than he could ever even have imagined, before Mira came into his life and changed everything.

Six of his brothers and his sister had moved back to Rogue Valley. They had spouses, kids, and a big Sunday morning Stockton brunch that had become chaos, craziness, and family. In two hours, Chase's family room, patio, stable, and newly installed in-ground pool would be overflowing with Stocktons. Including his brood, it was seven Stockton siblings, seven spouses, and ten kids. No, twelve kids, because Alexander counted, as did Liam Eaton and his grandfather, Frank, who had moved in with his brother Ryder and his wife Zoey.

And yet, with all those people, there was always an emptiness, because of those who weren't there. Logan. Quintin. And Caleb, who no one had heard from in almost a decade.

"Chase." Mira's hand slid onto his shoulder, drawing his focus back to the present. "That's your Sunday morning expression of melancholy," she said gently. "You've done so much, bringing everyone back together."

He put his hand on hers and looked up at her. "It's not enough, sweetheart. Not until everyone is home."

"They don't have to come home to be family."

"I know." He did know. But he also knew that for the Stocktons, family was all they'd ever had as kids, when life had been so brutal. He needed his brothers home, but more importantly, he knew all too well it was the shadows of their past that were keeping the last three away.

Until those shadows were healed, none of them would ever be able to truly live.

And they all deserved to live.

At that moment, he heard a car door slam.

"They're here already!" J.J. leapt off his chair and raced for the front window. Alexander scrambled off and followed his foster brother.

Chase glanced at the clock, and then frowned at Mira. "Did anyone tell you they were coming early?"

"No." She quickly wiped her hands off on a dish towel. "Why would anyone be two hours early? Maybe it's not the family."

"Or maybe something's wrong." Chase bolted to his feet and strode across the family room to the window that the boys were looking out of.

He frowned when he saw the truck. He didn't recognize it, but the truck was loaded with what looked like suitcases. "It's not family," he called out. "I don't recognize the vehicle —" He froze when he saw Logan walk around the back of the truck.

He froze. Logan had brought luggage. Enough for an extended stay.

Disbelief kept Chase anchored to the spot as hope shot through him.

"It's Uncle Logan!" J.J. shouted, jumping up and down on the couch. "Uncle Logan's here!" He leapt off the couch and raced to the front door, trying unsuccessfully to pull the heavy door open.

Alexander stood quietly, watching. He'd never met Logan before, and Chase picked him up, settling him against his hip.

Mira came up beside him. "Logan has bags?"

"It looks that way. Do you think...?" He couldn't even say the words.

But his wife understood what he hadn't dared say, giving

his hand a squeeze. "It's always possible. Who's the woman with him? Do you recognize her?"

"Woman?" At Mira's words, Chase dragged his stunned gaze off his brother long enough to notice a woman standing off to the side.

She was petite, with unruly blonde hair, and a curvy build. Her arms were folded across her chest, and she was periodically watching Logan and then scanning the ranch, as if she were trying to take it all in. "He brought a *woman* here? He's never mentioned a girlfriend. Or even a female friend. Ever." Any friend at all, for that matter.

As he spoke, Logan walked over to her.

She looked up at Logan, and he smiled at her.

Chase sucked in his breath at the expression on his brother's face. "Do you see that?"

"She means something to him," Mira said softly, her voice filled with excitement. "And look at the way she's watching him." Mira slid her hand into Chase's. "She can't take her gaze off him."

Holy shit. "You think he's brought her home? To stay?"

Mira squeezed his hand gently. "Chase, let them be as they are. Don't pressure them, or you could chase them away." She cocked an eyebrow at him. "I know it's tough for you, but try to be cool."

"I'm always cool."

Mira raised her eyebrows. "Cool isn't even in your vocabulary when it comes to your brothers. Other times? Yes, you're a total badass hottie. But when it comes to your brothers, you're all mush."

"I'm not mush."

"Mush."

Chase laughed softly and shifted Alexander to his left arm, so he could gather Mira against him with his right. "Have I told you lately how much I love you?"

Mira rested her head against his shoulder. "Not for at least ten minutes, but I can work with that."

"Dad!" J.J. was pulling on the door handle. "Open the door! I want to see Uncle Logan."

Logan and the woman were still talking in the driveway, standing intimately close to each other. Chase let out his breath. "Why aren't they coming to the door?"

"Who is that?" Alexander asked, his little arms wrapped tightly around Chase's neck.

"My brother, Logan," Chase said. "One who doesn't live in town." He looked at Mira. "Let's go find out what's going on."

She nodded. "Don't pressure him, Chase. You'll drive him away."

"I'll try." He tucked little Alexander more securely against his hip, then headed toward the door. He opened the door, and J.J. bolted out, running down the stairs and shouting for Logan.

His brother turned away from the woman and crouched down, opening his arms for J.J., who vaulted into them. As Logan picked him up, he met Chase's gaze.

Chase swore, reading Logan's expression immediately. All thoughts of trying to get Logan to move back fled from his mind, replaced with an instinct born of the childhood they all shared: a need to protect, a need to come together against the enemy, a need to make sure each and every one of the Stockton brothers survived yet another day.

"Something's wrong," he said to Mira. "Take Alexander. Something's really wrong."

He handed off his foster son, and almost sprinted down the front steps.

CHAPTER TEN

"HEY, LITTLE BROTHER," Chase said as he strode up to Logan and Skylar.

Relief rushed through Logan as he watched his oldest brother approach. The Stockton brothers were no longer kids, but they still had the same connection that had always bound them. The one that tightened whenever there was danger, or a threat to any of them. The moment he saw Chase's fierce expression, he knew he'd done the right thing bringing Skylar to Rogue Valley. "Hey, Chase. Surprise."

"Indeed." Chase's gaze flicked to Skylar as he held out his arms for his son. "Come on, J.J. Mommy needs you. I want to talk to Uncle Logan outside for a minute. Grownup talk."

Logan's nephew gripped his neck more tightly. "No. I want to see Uncle Logan. He's never here!"

Logan smiled at the feel of the little arms wrapped so tightly around him. He still remembered when Mira was pregnant, daring to come into their lives. He'd resisted, but now he loved his nephew and Mira more than he could ever have imagined. Which was why he'd made the choices he'd made. "I'll see you soon, J.J. I'm staying around for a while this time."

"Really?" J.J. screeched with delight, but Logan watched Chase's face. Hope flared in his blue eyes, a hope that made regret clamp around Logan's gut. He didn't want to hurt Chase by letting him get his hopes up.

"Yep, but not forever," he clarified. "Just a few weeks, then I have to go."

"You always have to go!" J.J. pouted. "When are you going to move back? Everyone else has moved back!"

Not everyone. There were still three of them left.

Chase's mouth tightened, and he gently extricated his son from Logan's neck. "Come on, hot shot. Go see Mama and Alexander." He set his son down as Mira leaned out the front door and called him.

"Hey, Mira." Logan waved at his sister-in-law, and she grinned at him before taking J.J. back into the house.

The moment the door closed, Chase turned to look at them. "What's going on?"

Logan took a breath, then held out his hand to Skylar. She hesitated for a split second, then she slipped her hand into his. The moment Logan felt her fingers wrap around his, rightness settled deep inside him. Her hand fit perfectly in his. *Perfectly.*

He squeezed gently as he tugged her close to him. "Chase, I'd like you to meet my fiancée, Skylar Jones." He expected to feel regret at telling his brother a lie, but to his surprise, the words didn't feel like a lie. They felt good. Right.

Shit. He was in trouble.

Chase's brows shot up, and he glanced down at the ring on Skylar's hand. He looked at Logan's face, then Skylar's, then shook his head. "Bullshit. What's really going on?"

Logan couldn't help but burst out laughing. "Hell, man. You never change, do you?"

"I'm the one who knew when Dad broke your arm, and you were afraid to tell anyone. I know you, and I know when you're in trouble." Chase shrugged. "You never could lie to me. None of you could."

Skylar wiggled her hand in his as if to get free, but Logan tightened his grip, not ready to let her go. "Mira and the boys will be watching us," he said to her. "We need to keep it up."

Skylar rolled her eyes at Chase. "Logan said that if I told everyone how irritating he was that people would believe we were engaged. I can see that's not going to be difficult."

Chase grinned, his gaze settling on Skylar. "Irritating as hell," he agreed. "Why don't you two tell me what's up, and we can figure out how to fix it."

Logan knew then that he was home. It was how they were. It was how they'd always been. Especially Chase, the big brother who had put himself in the line of fire hundreds of times to protect his little brothers. "I can't give you details, but—"

"Bullshit," Chase said. "This is the one place where you can talk about anything." He met Logan's gaze, those blue, unyielding eyes that had seen so much in their lifetimes. "Talk to me, little brother. Right now." He paused suddenly, looking at Skylar, then back at Logan, then at Skylar again. "Someone's after you," he said to her, understanding dawning. "Logan's trying to protect you."

Skylar glanced at Logan, the vulnerability on her face giving truth to Chase's conjecture.

Chase slapped his thigh. "Son of a bitch. You're doing the same thing I did with Mira." He met Logan's gaze. "We got your back, Logan." He shifted his gaze to Skylar. "Since you're with Logan, you've got all of us on your side, too."

"Thank you." Her voice was emotional, and her fingers tightened in Logan's hand as she spoke.

Logan looked over to see her eyes glistening with unshed

tears again. His chest tightened, and he released her hand to put his arm around her shoulders and pull her against him. He kissed the top of her head. Did he admit the truth to Chase? The whole truth? Tell Chase about the life he'd lived for the last decade, that he'd never revealed?

He hadn't planned on it, but the longer he stood there, the more he was realizing that it might be the path to take. He needed to tell Chase the truth. More than that, he wanted to.

Chase's expression softened. "Logan, my wife would be dead right now if I'd tried to protect her by myself. Instead of being our sister-in-law, Hannah would be in a coffin if Maddox had tried to defend her alone. But they both lived because we worked together. As brothers. That's what we do, Logan. Always. Forever. Don't take that chance with Skylar. She might not be your fiancée, but I know you care about her."

Logan looked over at Skylar. Her eyes were wide as she listened, her face stark with alarm. "Dead?" she whispered. "What happened?"

"Their past came after them," Chase said gently. "We were ready." He looked at Logan. "What's coming after Skylar?"

Skylar slid her arm around Logan's waist, tucking herself against him, waiting for him to decide how much to tell. He looked down at her, at her beautiful face, at her unruly hair, at the woman he'd held at a distance for two years to keep her safe.

It hadn't worked, and now she was in real danger. Would he break the rules to keep her safe?

She looked up at him, and smiled.

Yeah, he would.

Logan looked at his brother, who he'd worked so hard to keep at a distance since he'd left town. Suddenly, Logan saw him as he had when he was a kid again. His protector. The only one he could count on. The one who put every Stockton brother first, no matter what.

He could trust Chase. He could trust him with all of it.

Chase folded his arms over his chest. "I'll stand out here all day if that's what it takes, little brother. No secrets between us."

Logan let out his breath and nodded. "All right. Just you. Not the others." As he said it, the words felt good. It was right to let Chase in. Ten years was a long time to hide the truth from his own brother.

Chase nodded. "Inside? Want some coffee?"

"I don't want Mira or J.J. to overhear." He looked around at the ranch. The vast expanse of lands extended in all directions, as it had when he'd been growing up. But now there was a beautiful barn that Chase had built, an equine surgery facility they'd built for Steen's wife, Erin, the retreat for inner city kids that Zane and Taylor had opened, and other buildings, that each of the brothers had brought into the mix. "How soon until people get here for brunch?"

"Two hours officially, but it could be any time. I'll have Mira take the boys to the barn to see the foal." Chase started walking back toward the house, but his shoulders were tense and his gaze sharp as he, too, scanned his ranch for anything out of place.

Appreciation settled deep in Logan's gut as he and Skylar followed Chase. "Boys? You have another one?"

"Yeah. We're fostering a boy named Alexander. He's quiet. Try not to scare him."

"I never scare kids. They love me." Fostering a kid? It sounded right to him, offering a sanctuary to a kid who needed it.

Hell knew they all could have used it when they were kids.

Like he and Skylar needed one now.

He took Skylar's hand as they followed his brother up the front steps. At the top of the steps, he paused to survey the ranch once again for anything that didn't belong. He looked for the dust cloud that would indicate a vehicle approaching. He listened for the restlessness of nature that would indicate someone on foot.

Everything was normal. As it should be.

Then he looked over at Skylar, at her big, blue eyes as she watched him, and realized he was wrong.

Nothing was normal. Nothing at all.

CHAPTER ELEVEN

THE MOMENT SKYLAR stepped across the threshold into Chase's house, she felt like she'd come home. The home she'd yearned for. The one that had kept slipping out of her grasp, mocking her dreams, her needs, the call of her heart.

It was perfect and cozy, with wood beams, a massive family room with a huge stone fireplace, and floor to ceiling picture windows that looked out onto a huge backyard, endless fields, and a pool.

A woman wearing jeans and a pink, cotton tank top was standing in the kitchen, talking with two young boys. Her dark brown hair was in a loose ponytail and she wasn't wearing any makeup. But her smile was radiant, her eyes crinkling with warmth as she listened intently to the boys.

As Skylar and the men walked in, her gaze slid to Chase's face, then Logan's, and then Skylar's.

The moment her gaze met Skylar's, her face softened. She whispered to the boys, then hurried across the great room. "Logan. It's so great to see you." She gave Logan a smile of pure love, wrapping Skylar's reticent cowboy up in a huge hug.

Skylar was surprised to see Logan hug her back fiercely, as if this woman was part of the breath that gave his world life.

He cared about these people. The loner cowboy who had been so reluctant to smile or connect clearly cared so much more than she ever would have guessed.

The woman pulled back and smiled gently at Skylar as she held out her hand. "I'm Mira, Chase's wife. Welcome to our home."

"Thanks." Skylar shook her hand. "I'm Skylar Jones. I'm —" She hesitated. She couldn't make herself lie to this woman and announce she was Logan's fiancée, not with the warmth of her gaze wrapping about Skylar like a soft blanket meant to make her feel safe.

But then Mira's gaze fell on Skylar's left hand, on her glittering diamond. Her eyes widened, and her gaze shot back to Skylar's face, and then Logan's. "Seriously?"

Logan grinned one of his not-reaching-his-eyes smiles and put his arm around Skylar's shoulders. "Mira, I'd like you to meet the woman who has lived across the hall from me for two years. I think her name is Skylar, or something like that."

"You ass!" Mira smacked him in the chest, then held out her arms to Skylar. "Welcome to the family, girl!"

Skylar's heart turned over as Mira dragged her into a tight hug. She was appalled when tears filled her eyes, quickly trying to blink them back, but it was too late. All of the Stocktons saw the tears when Mira released her.

Logan swore under his breath, as he walked over to her and caught her hand. He lowered his head so his lips were a whisper from her ear. "What's wrong? How can I fix it?"

"I'm fine," Skylar said, wiping the back of her hand across her cheek, trying not to perseverate on how quickly Logan had come to her aid. "It's just been an emotional time for me." She smiled at Mira. "I wasn't expecting to be so welcomed."

"You weren't? What did Logan tell you about us?" Mira put her hands on her hips. "Honestly, sometimes these Stockton men can be so obtuse." She glared at Logan. "You didn't warn her about the rest of the family, did you?"

Still watching Skylar carefully, Logan shook his head. "Warn her about what?"

"Men!" Mira took Skylar's arm. "Look, the Stockton men seem tough, but they're the most loyal, most protective, kindest souls in the entire world." She smiled at Chase, her eyes filled with love. "They're worth every headache they give the women who love them."

Chase winked at his wife, and then bent down to scoop up the two little boys who were hanging on his legs.

Skylar looked over at Logan. "He does give me a lot of headaches," she admitted. Loyal? Protective? Kind? She believed that.

This time, Logan's smile was a little more genuine as he looked over at Skylar. "I'm sure I do," he said.

"But here's the thing," Mira continued. "In about two hours, a whole bunch of Stocktons are going to descend on this house, and every single one of them is going to claim you as theirs. That's the way this family works, so if I overwhelmed you with my hug, you're going to have to raise your game to handle what's coming for you." She raised her brows. "You okay with that?"

Skylar let out her breath. "Yes, of course." But as she said it, guilt cascaded through her. How could she fake her way through that?

Logan put his arm around her shoulders and pulled her against his side. His torso was warm and solid, and she instinctively wrapped her arms around his waist. "It'll be okay," he said, his deep voice resonating through her. "I'll stay by your side the whole time, I promise."

Skylar looked up at him, and her chest tightened at the

intensity of his gaze. He *would* stay by her side. Not only to protect her from his family, but from the man hunting her down. Either way, she didn't have to face anything alone right now. She smiled. "Thanks."

Logan grinned back, and she suddenly became aware of how close they were. All he would have to do is bend down, and his lips would be on hers.

Making out in public. That was part of the deal. Her heart suddenly started to race, and her breath caught as his gaze went to her lips. Oh, God. Was it going to be now?

Chase grinned. "Go ahead and kiss her, little brother. We don't mind."

"What?" Logan's gaze shot to Chase, clearly startled. He swore. "No—"

"No?" Mira put her hands on her hips. "Honest to God, Logan. Do you think any woman is secure enough to handle the man she loves refusing to kiss her?" She raised her gaze and turned to her husband. "Lay one on me, big guy. Right here. Right now."

Chase grinned. "Yes, ma'am." With a boy still on each hip, Chase walked over to his wife, leaned in, and kissed her like she was the sunshine he'd been seeking his whole life.

It was passionate. It was love. It was unconditional.

It was the most beautiful kiss Skylar had ever seen.

Chase finished by brushing his lips across his wife's forehead, smiling tenderly down at her. "Thank you for saving me," he whispered, for her ears only, but Skylar heard it. Saving him from what? Loneliness? Himself? Or the past that all the brothers had fought to overcome?

Chase and Mira looked over, both of them smiling with satisfaction. "That's how you treat your woman, little brother. Don't fuck it up before you even get started."

Skylar narrowed her eyes. Why was Chase pushing it? He knew damn well they weren't actually engaged—

Logan's fingers closed around Skylar's wrist, tugging her toward him. As she turned toward him, her heart started racing when she saw the intensity glittering in his eyes. "What—"

"Skylar." He released her wrist and framed her face with both hands, raising her face to his.

Holy shit.

"From the first moment I met you, I've dreamed of kissing you." His voice was rough and husky. Intimate. "And now I can."

He paused for a split second, giving her a chance to stop him.

She didn't even try. She couldn't have brought herself to stop him if her life depended on it. Instead, instinctively, she set her hand on his lean, muscular hip, feeling the warmth of his body through his shirt. She wanted this. This moment. This kiss. His kiss. "Me, too," she whispered.

A small smile flickered at the corners of his mouth, and then he bent his head and kissed her.

His lips were warm. His kiss tender. Kind. Beautiful. Magical.

More than she'd imagined, and she'd imagined it countless times.

He angled his head and deepened the kiss. She couldn't suppress the little whimper at the back of her throat, and when he slid his arm around her waist and pulled her against him, she knew he'd heard it.

His chest was solid against her breasts, his corded abs pressed tight against her belly. The kiss was searing hot, gaining steam, as if two years of waiting had unleashed a vortex of wanting and need that was getting hotter and hotter—

"Damn, little brother. I had no idea." Chase's laughter broke the haze of passion wrapping around them.

They broke the kiss at the same time, staring at each other in surprised silence.

What had just happened?

"Way to get Logan to step up to the plate, Skylar." Mira sounded thoroughly amused. "I think you're going to be able to handle him just fine."

Skylar cleared her throat. "Of course I can handle him. He's putty in my hands."

Chase coughed, and Logan's brows shot up. "Putty? You think I'm *putty?* There is literally nothing soft about me. I'm just...hard."

It was her turn to raise her brows. "I don't believe that, Logan. Not for a second."

Something flickered in his eyes, something that felt like longing, but it was gone before she could identify it. Swallowed up as he resumed his customary stoic expression. "Believe me when I show you who I am."

She lifted her chin. "I do."

He cupped the tip of her chin between his thumb and forefinger. "I don't think you do," he said softly. "I love that about you, but it won't end well if you can't see me for who I am."

"Oh, Logan." Mira interrupted. "None of you Stocktons see yourself the way you really are. It's only the women who see the truth."

"We see it eventually," Chase said. "It just takes time." He turned toward Mira. "Can you take the boys to the barn? I need to have a chat with Logan and Skylar."

Her gaze narrowed, and she gave her husband a hard look. "Be good, Chase."

"Always, my dear." He kissed her gently, gave each of the boys a secret handshake, and then stepped back.

"Okay, boys, let's go see baby Simba, and see if he grew

since yesterday." Mira rolled her eyes. "I tried for Pegasus, but who wants to name a horse after a horse, right?"

She gave them all a wave as she herded the boys out of the building, but her gaze lingered on Skylar a little bit too long, with a little too much thoughtfulness in her gaze. As the door closed behind Mira, Skylar looked over at Chase. "Do you think she knows we're not really engaged?"

Chase headed toward the kitchen and grabbed some coffee mugs out of the beautiful wood cabinet. "She might. If she doesn't, she'll have it out of me by the time we go to sleep."

Logan swore under his breath. "Chase, that's not cool. Our lives depend on this—"

"She's my wife." Chase picked up a coffee pot and began to pour. "I trust her with my life, which means I trust her with yours."

Logan swore and clasped his hands on his head. "It was a mistake to come here. I shouldn't have put you in this position."

"Bullshit." Chase handed Logan a steaming mug. "That's what we do, Logan. We have each other's backs. All the time. No matter what. You were right to come and you know it." He picked up another mug. "And now it's time for you to tell me what's going on. All of it." He met Logan's gaze. "Every last piece of it, starting with telling me who's after Skylar."

Skylar let out her breath as Chase's statement brought her back to the truth, that they weren't here for family bonding. There was literally an assassin hunting her at that very moment.

Logan was quiet for a moment, then he nodded. "All right, but if you decide it's a danger to Mira, you tell me, and we'll leave. Okay?"

Chase swore. "Logan—"

"Promise me."

Chase finally nodded. "I promise."

"All right, then." Logan gestured to the couch. "Let's sit down. It'll take a few."

Anticipation suddenly hummed through Skylar. Was this going to be her chance to find out more about Logan? Things she didn't know about? *Yes.* She wanted to know more. She'd been consumed by him for two years, and being around him wasn't helping cure her.

She was finally going to find out the secrets he'd been hiding all this time.

CHAPTER TWELVE

"COFFEE?" Chase held out a mug with the Stockton Ranch logo on it.

She eyed the mug suspiciously. "Coffee is on a time out for me right now."

He raised his brows. "Really?"

"It gets me shot at."

Chase looked from her to Logan. "Shot at?"

Logan cleared his throat. "It wasn't the coffee."

"It was." She walked over to the loveseat and sat down in the middle. "If I hadn't gone out for coffee, I would have been asleep at my desk, drooling all over my work, completely oblivious to the gunfight going down in my hallway. Which means that right now, I'd be having yogurt and granola in my own kitchen, having no idea what it looks like when a man is shot in the forehead right in front of me."

There was a long silence in the room, and Skylar felt her cheeks heat up. "Did I say that out loud?"

Chase sat down across from her. "Are you all right?"

"Physically? Yes. Emotionally?" She sighed. "I doubt it, but I'm too traumatized to be certain of anything right now."

Chase grinned, an understanding smile meant to comfort. "Well, you're in the right place. If there's anything we understand here, it's trauma."

She recalled Logan's comment that he was born into a life of abuse, and she looked at Chase more carefully. His sleeve was pushed up, and she could see little circular scars on his forearm. Cigarette burns? Did Logan have those? She'd never noticed. God, what had these huge, powerful, kind men endured before they were big enough to keep themselves safe?

"That we do. We have trauma parties every Friday night just to celebrate. It's fun," Logan said as he walked over. She saw his gaze go to the space beside her, which wasn't big enough for him. She had a split second of regret that she'd decided to sit in the middle, meeting his raised brows with a shrug.

He glanced at the armchair, then sat down beside her anyway, squeezing his muscular bulk between her left side and the arm of the loveseat. She scooted to the side, her heart fluttering as his shoulder and hip brushed against hers as he sat. Why did he get under her skin like this? It was distracting. And alarming, given that people in his life got shot at.

Logan turned to her, his dark eyes searching hers. "I'm deeply sorry to have dragged you into this." His voice was raw and rough. "I'll do whatever it takes to make it right."

His regret was so genuine, his anger at himself so bitter, that her walls softened. Instinctively, she touched his wrist, resting her fingers on his skin. "It's okay. Life happens. It's not anyone's fault." She managed a smile. "Who knows? Maybe I had to be there to save your life."

His dark eyes searched hers. "That's not your job."

"It's not a job. It's a gift when life gives us the chance to shine light into someone else's life, simply by being ourselves." The words she spoke were her dad's, surprising her when they tumbled off her lips. They wrapped around her like a hug, making her feel like he was there with her, back in her life, living the future they'd both dreamed of before he'd died too early, too young.

Her throat suddenly tightened at the memory of her dad, and she had to look away.

Logan took her hand, sandwiching it between his palms, his grip warm and solid as he grounded her. "You do that every single time I see you."

She looked back at him, trying to regroup. "What?"

"Shine light. That's what you do. You've always done that for me."

Her heart tightened as she stared at him, startled by the words from her reticent neighbor. "Really?"

He nodded. "But your light needs to shine, not be doused by me, and by the shit I rained down on you." The guilt and self-recrimination were bitter.

Was this the darkness she always sensed wrapped around him so tightly?

Chase cleared his throat.

She started, and saw by Logan's reaction that he'd also forgotten they weren't alone. Logan kept her hand as he turned to face his brother. "I don't want to bring that shit into your house either," he said. "I'd never forgive myself if something happened to Mira or the boys."

"Your problems belong right smack in the middle of your brothers' lives, so tell me what we're dealing with." Chase was leaning forward, his forearms braced on his thigh, his focus unwavering on the two of them.

Logan mimicked Chase's stance, but kept his grip on Skylar's hand, which meant she was pulled in toward him, her forearm tucked between his elbow and his waist, her hand between his knees. It was intimate and personal, but also casual, like it was simply a natural intimacy that Logan had done instinctively.

This from the man who had never touched her, ever, until that moment in his office.

She liked his touch. She didn't want to pull away, which meant she had to do so. She tried to tug her hand free subtly, but Logan didn't let her go.

Instead, he began playing with her fingers as he spoke to Chase. "When I left here, I joined the CIA."

Chase's eyes widened. "The CIA?"

Logan nodded, stroking his fingertips down the back of her hand. "I couldn't escape who I was, the past I had, that we all have. The nightmares. The violence. The things that would keep me from ever being...normal. I knew I couldn't leave it behind, so I wanted to force it into something useful. Save the world and shit like that."

Skylar could feel the tension in Logan's body as he spoke about his past. His references were vague, but enough to tell her that the boys in that picture had endured terrible things as kids. And Logan, the honorable man he was, had chosen to channel that into making a difference in the world.

Damn him for getting more appealing by the minute.

Understanding and regret flashed across Chase's face. "Did it help?"

"Yeah. It did. Sometimes, at least."

Chase nodded. "Sometimes is all we can ask for. How long were you in for?"

Logan paused, and looked down at his hands briefly before raising his gaze to his brother's. "I'm still in."

Chase went still. "It's been ten years since you left."

"Yeah." Logan kept playing with her fingers, restlessly, as if he couldn't keep himself still.

"You kept this from us for a *decade*?"

"Yeah."

Chase stood up and walked across the room to the picture window. He clasped his hands on top of his head, in the same pose Logan often used.

Chase said nothing, staring out at his ranch.

Guilt shot through Logan as he watched Chase turn his back on him. He knew the expression that Chase was hiding from him right now. Hurt. Pain. Betrayal. *Shit*. Logan cleared his throat. "I couldn't tell you. Any of you."

His brother didn't turn around. "Yes, you could have. You can tell us anything."

"It's the rules of the CIA, Chase—"

"Fuck the CIA." Chase spun around, his blue eyes blazing. "We're your goddamned family, Logan. Family is all that matters. Nothing ever comes between us. I'd give my life for you. We all would. Ten years. Ten years you hid this from us? What the hell? You told us you were in construction."

Logan met his brother's gaze. "The CIA is my life now, Chase. Not the ranch. I play by their rules." He kept his voice even and low.

Chase stared at him. "You've never played by anyone's rules. None of us have."

"I need the CIA," he said quietly. "It keeps the monster at bay."

Chase stared at him for a long moment, then his shoulders sagged in defeat. "If I could kill him again, I would. I'd kill him a thousand times for every nightmare he's ever given us, for every chance at happiness he's stolen from us."

Skylar stiffened beside him, and Logan swore. He couldn't imagine what she was thinking, listening to their discussion. He felt exposed and raw, but he knew it was for the best.

The kiss had been too intense. He'd felt her need for him, and his own need for her. He needed to find a way to keep it from going any further with them, and if it took this conversation, ripping the blinders off who he was, then he had to welcome it.

He took a breath, keeping his grip on Skylar's hand tight. "Killing him again wouldn't change anything."

"It changed a lot the first time I did it." Chase walked back over and sank wearily onto the couch facing him. "It freed us."

"Not all of us. Not completely." He paused. "Not me."

"*Fuck.*" The pain etched on Chase's face was visceral.

Logan never wanted to feel that pain. He kept his locked up, and that was where it would stay. Forever. No feelings were better than the expression on his brother's face.

To do his job, his emotions had been trained out of him, and he needed it to stay that way. Chase's pain was proof of that. "I love you, Chase. I love Mira, and the kids. Steen and Erin. Zane and Taylor. All of you guys. All the kids. I'd give my life for any of you in a heartbeat. But I can't live the life you guys have. I can't live a normal life. Not ever." He didn't look at Skylar when he said it.

Now that she was hearing this truth, he knew she'd never look at him the same as she once had. As if he had value. As if he were a good guy. As if he were someone who mattered as a human being, instead of simply a human weapon.

He was surprised by the depth of regret that swamped him at the thought.

So he didn't look at her.

But he didn't let go of her hand either.

"As soon as this is solved, I'm going back," he told his brother. "I'll always go back."

Chase braced his elbows on his knees and rested his forehead in his palms, saying nothing. He didn't need to say anything. The defeat in his posture said it all.

For ten years, Logan had dealt with the constant pressure from Chase to move back to Rogue Valley. For ten years, his brother had refused to give up on him. But right now, in this moment, he knew that Chase had finally given up.

Logan was stunned by the deep grief clogging his throat at the realization that his brother was finally going to let him go. He realized, too late, that Chase's constant harassment had been the thinnest filament keeping Logan bound to the humanity he couldn't be a part of. And he'd just severed it.

He swallowed. "I'm sorry, Chase."

Chase looked up, and his eyes were bloodshot. "Never apologize, Logan." His voice was rough with the tears he refused to shed. "There's only one fucker who owes us an apology, and he's dead. And it wouldn't matter anyway. The damage is done."

Logan nodded, his own throat tight. "That it is, but I am truly sorry that I can't be what you want."

Chase met his gaze. "It's not about what I want, Logan. It's about what you want. Is that what you want? That life? The CIA?"

"Yes." But as he said it, a silent scream welled up inside him, a voice that shrieked that he was lying, that he was always lying.

He ignored the scream. As he always did.

Chase took a breath, then nodded. "Okay, then."

Okay, then. It was over. The gossamer thread that led back to Chase was now gone.

Logan felt like he'd just pitched off a cliff and was freefalling into an abyss of the darkest night.

"Let's focus, then," Chase said. "Tell me what I need to know about you and Skylar."

And just like that, back to business. The way his whole life was. Always back to business.

CHAPTER THIRTEEN

SKYLAR FELT like her heart would shatter into a million pieces, listening to Logan and Chase talk. She'd lost so much, but nothing like what they had endured. She had baggage, but nothing like what haunted them.

She looked down at her hand, still entwined with Logan's. With each word he'd spoken, his grip on her hand had become tighter and tighter. His words had felt like a warning to get her to back off, but the way he held her hand was a desperate plea not to let him drown.

"I make enemies," Logan said, drawing her attention back to the present, to the issue they were facing. The issue of surviving.

I make enemies.

Those three words were so simple, but they sounded so terrible to Skylar. The way Logan said it made it seem like they defined him. *I make enemies.* What a terrible, lonely way to live. Instinctively, she squeezed his hand, but he didn't look at her.

He also didn't release her.

Chase frowned. "That's your life? I make enemies? And that's what you choose? That sounds good to you?"

Logan's grip tightened on her hand. "I make enemies of bad guys, because I'm one of the good guys. Do you know what an incredible feeling that is, Chase? To be a good guy?"

Chase sighed. "I do. Every time I look at J.J., or Mira, or Alexander, I know exactly what that feels like. There's no bigger miracle than for one of us to feel that way."

Logan nodded, and emotion squeezed Skylar's heart so tightly that she felt like she couldn't breathe. These men. God, these men. She felt like she'd been given a gift of this moment, a raw, unfiltered view into their very souls.

A view that they probably never gave anyone, except each other, and Mira, of course. She was sure Mira was inside that circle, holding it open for Chase, so he could find his way out whenever it tried to trap him.

Logan looked at Skylar, then back at Chase. "Skylar lives across the hall from me. Last night, two of my enemies found me. They used her to try to get to me. I killed one. The other got away, but Skylar saw him, and he knows that. He knows where she lives." He didn't say the rest, but he didn't need to.

Chase rubbed his jaw, not with weariness, but with focus. Adrenaline. Purpose. Skylar could feel the energy in the room shift from the agony of their shadows to purpose and determination. "Your team is searching for him while you get off the grid with Skylar?"

Logan nodded, absently bending and unbending her fingers, as if he were too restless to sit still, and it was her hand that he needed to ground him.

"Could they track you here?" Chase asked.

"Highly unlikely." Logan leaned forward again, moving her fingers back and forth restlessly. "Even if it's an internal leak, they won't find leads back to here. That's why I chose to bring Skylar here. I don't believe they would find us, but it's always possible."

Chase rubbed his jaw. "What about your emergency contact info? Death benefits? If it's internal, they could find us that way."

"No." Logan shook his head. "I didn't put anyone down. According to my paperwork, I have no heirs. No emergency contact. Nothing."

Chase frowned. "So, if you died, no one would tell us? You literally pretended that we don't exist?"

Logan stiffened. "I had to. It was the only way to keep you safe." He met his brother's gaze. "It was the right choice. I did it for you."

Skylar could see the depth of pain in Chase's eyes. The bond between the brothers was so apparent, and yet Logan had literally chosen to pretend they didn't exist. When he'd said he was alone, she hadn't realized how far he'd taken it.

Chase flexed his jaw, but he didn't take it further. Instead, he simply said. "Well, I'm glad you came home for our help." His voice was even. Measured. Hiding all the emotion that was roiling in his eyes. "What do you need? You want to stay here?"

"No. The ranch is in the Stockton name. I don't want to take that chance. What about the River House? Don't the Harts own it?"

Chase nodded. "Brody and Keegan Hart are there full time right now, and those men know how to fight. Ryder's there with Zoey as well. Plenty of room, and plenty of back up."

"Perfect." Logan grinned. "Those guys are tough."

"They are," Chase agreed. "We all are."

There was no mistaking the absolute confidence of the two men, in themselves and each other. Even with their difference in skin tone, they looked so much alike. Same focus. Same intensity. Same smile. But Chase was softer, warmer, as if Mira and his kids had broken down the walls that Logan kept wrapped around him.

"What do we tell them?" Chase asked. "The family."

"I can't tell them I'm in the CIA," Logan said. "But I want them to be ready for a threat."

Again, regret flickered in Chase's eyes, but he didn't argue. Instead, he glanced at Skylar. "How about a jealous ex-husband?"

Logan laughed. "How fast will it take for them to get online and look him up? They'll realize she hasn't been married before in about two seconds."

Skylar cleared her throat. "I've been married."

Logan looked at her in surprise. "Really? I thought you were just engaged."

"Nope. We were married." She tried to ignore the curiosity on Logan's face. "It's no big deal. It's fine." The same lie she'd been telling the world ever since it happened.

"Was he ex-military?" Chase asked hopefully.

Skylar laughed. "No, not even close. No one would believe he's not a great guy." No one, indeed. No one would believe any other side of the story.

Logan cocked his head, studying her more carefully, so she finally pulled her hand free of his and turned to face Chase. "What if I witnessed something? I can't talk about it, but it put me in danger."

Chase nodded, and looked at Logan. "I think that makes sense. Then there's less to tell, less to screw up."

"Works for me." Logan leaned back against the couch, his arms draped along the back.

His body language casual, but she could feel the weight of his gaze. Dammit. She didn't want to talk about her life. She didn't want his focus on her. Her problems were nothing compared to his. She felt stupid even having them.

"We need to tell them that the man is highly trained," Logan said. "They need to be ready."

Chase nodded. "Former military black ops?"

"That works."

She was being hunted by someone with former military black ops skills? Well, that was fun. Surreal.

This was real life stakes. Suddenly, the weight of everything seemed to crush down on her too much. Logan's pain of his past, of severing himself from the family he so clearly loved, her own issues, a freaking assassin hunting her.

"I need a minute." She stood up, walked to the window, braced her palms on the sill, and looked out across the plain, trying to pull herself together.

She'd fought hard to become resilient. To look at life with humor. To laugh even when things became tough. Her dad had taught her that. But right now, in this moment, she couldn't find the woman she'd fought so hard to become.

She took a deep breath, studying the vista before her, trying to find even a single good thing to focus on. Her gaze fell upon the pink wildflowers at the edge of the huge lawn. Bright pink, glimmering in the midst of the brown grasses of the fields behind them. Light. Laughter. What did they smell like?

She took a deep breath, feeling things begin to settle inside her. The landscape was so gorgeous. So free. So unfettered. "It's beautiful here."

Logan walked up behind her, pausing just behind her. Not touching her, but so close. "It is. I forget what it's like until I come back. It's always a surprise to me how it feels to be here."

"Wait until you see the rest of the place," Chase said as he walked up to stand beside them. "It's fantastic."

"I bet." Normal conversation about scenery. His home. It felt good. Grounding.

Logan looked over at Chase. "When will people be here? I want to talk to Ryder, Brody, and Keegan before we invade their place."

"No one's supposed to arrive before eleven, but I'm sure Mira has already made some calls." Chase grinned. "Everyone's going to want to meet your fiancée. I'm guessing we have about five minutes until people show up."

Fiancée? Skylar had totally forgotten about the whole "pretend to be engaged" thing. "How many people are coming?" The words were just leaving her lips when she heard a car horn out front, doors slam, and the sound of children shouting. *Crap*. She was not in the headspace to do this right now.

"A lot." Logan rested his hand on the back of her neck. "Don't look so worried. We'll pull it off."

She nodded. "Right. Sure. Okay." She looked at Chase. "Can I use your bathroom?"

"You bet." He pointed. "Down the hall. Third door on the left."

"Great." She ducked out from under Logan's arm, and hurried down the hall. Her chest was tight, and she felt overwhelmed. As she passed by the picture window, she glanced out. There were three trucks already parked outside, two more pulling up, and there were people piling out of them. All these people were his family?

She saw three men get out, men who had the same facial structure as Logan and Chase. Men who shared their terrible past, who had clearly fought for love and happiness that life had taught them they didn't deserve.

She watched as the brother closest to her put his arm around a woman with blond hair, both of them laughing as their kids shrieked and ran to see their cousins. Yearning rushed through Skylar, surprising her. She pressed her palm to the window, watching their smiles as they greeted each other.

Family.

How could she lie to these people? Good people who believed in family and each other. People who had suffered. "You know what? I don't think this is a good idea. Let's just tell people we're friends..."

"Skylar." Logan's hands settled on her shoulders as one of the children saw her through the window and pointed.

Everyone immediately turned to look at her.

Dear God. How could they possibly pull off a fake engagement? "I can't do this, Logan."

He wrapped his arms around her waist, rested his chin on her shoulder, and waved at the little boy. "Yes, you can."

Dammit. His body felt far too warm and reassuring. Strong. Protective. Like a safe haven. She wanted to turn around, wrap her arms around his waist, and bury her face in his chest. "They're your family. They'll see right through me—"

"We're not like any family you've ever met. Trust me when I say it'll be okay."

"I know you're not like any family I've ever met. That's the problem."

He stiffened. "I know you don't want to be tangled up with us. With me. It's ugly here. Ugly inside me. Ugly inside my brothers." His voice was cool. Distant. Pulling back. Thinking he was too much for her.

"No." She spun around in his arms and glared at him. "Don't do that. Don't be an ass, Logan."

His eyes narrowed. "Don't do what?"

"Don't put that on me. Just because you see yourself as a damaged monster doesn't mean I do. Don't put that on me. I see exactly who you are, and your brothers. I'm not afraid of it. I just feel bad lying to people who have been through so much, people who are going to be crushed when they find out you haven't actually found your Mira."

He stared at her, clearly stunned. "But—"

"I know it's for my safety. I know that. But unlike you, I'm not used to turning off my emotions, so it's going to be a little difficult for me." She heard footsteps on the front porch. "I need a moment. Go away." She took off before he could stop her, and didn't stop until she made it into the bathroom and shut the door.

Then she leaned back against it, let her head fall back, and let out a long breath. She couldn't do this.

And it wasn't simply because she didn't want to lie to them.

It was also because this family, this huge, loyal family was exactly what she wanted. If they welcomed her the way Mira had, she was going to fall in love with all of them, with this life, with their world.

And then she was going to have to leave it. Them. Chase. And, most importantly, Logan.

She hadn't been lying to Logan when she'd told him her heart couldn't take being shattered again. But what other choice did she have?

She literally had nowhere to go. The moment she'd locked eyes with Eugene, he'd taken all her options away from her.

She wanted to live. Even broken, vulnerable, and fragile, she wanted to live.

Which meant she had to stay here. They had to stay. They had to do whatever it took.

With a groan, Skylar pushed away from the door, walked over to the sink, and rested her palms on the counter. She stared at herself in the mirror.

She was still wearing her sweatshirt and leggings from when she'd run into Frances and Howard on her way to getting coffee. Her hair had lost its fluff. She had no makeup on. She had bags under her eyes from a night without sleep. She looked strung out, scared, and stressed.

A bag of dirty laundry would be a vast improvement. Frances would be horrified...which made Skylar start laughing.

This was her life. Bags under her eyes. Assassins hunting her. Wearing an engagement ring that wasn't hers. Making out with a man who was insanely tempting but completely off limits. Having her heart bleed for a family she'd just met.

It was insanity.

But was it better than the alternative? Working hundred-hour weeks, afraid to live, broken, numb, and alone?

She looked at herself more closely, and noticed, for the first time in a long time, there was life in her eyes. Spark. Anticipation.

She breathed deeply, realizing that she felt alive. Out of her depth, sure. A little traumatized? Absolutely. But most importantly, alive, with a chance to try on a life and see how it felt.

Maybe walking into that gunfight hadn't been to save Logan.

Maybe it had been to save herself from the quicksand that she'd allowed herself to drown in.

The CIA could have decided to stash her in a safe house somewhere. Instead, she was in Wyoming, on a huge ranch, with a bunch of people who had the skills and desire to keep her safe. Good people who had faced the worst and figured out how to thrive. Beauty. Family.

And Logan. *Logan.*

They weren't complete, she and Logan. That kiss had been something else. Skimming the surface. He was broken. She was...not broken...but in the process of it, for sure.

But when they were together...there was something between them.

And she wanted to pursue it. Him. This temporary life.

This temporary family. This opportunity for them both to finally heal what was holding them back.

Voices echoed through the house, and this time, she smiled when she heard someone say her name and ask where she was. If there was one thing she'd learned from her dad, it was that life offered chances all day long, and only fools turned them down.

She had three weeks. Or less. Or more. What was she going to do with it?

Mope around? Or try to use the chance to begin to move past the demons that had held her captive for so long and get busy living?

She stared at herself in the mirror. "Get busy living, of course."

One of her biggest demons was trust. Logan had a lot of issues, clearly, but trustworthiness wasn't one of them. Maybe he could teach her to trust again, and in return, she could help bring a smile back to his face. He'd sworn he'd stay by her side to make sure she was safe, and she believed him.

And the fact Logan was hot, tempting, and distracting? Completely irrelevant.

Skylar let out her breath. She could do this. Stay chill. Enjoy the ride. Make the most of the opportunity. Refuse to allow a professional killer and other fun stuff to haunt her.

She splashed some water over her face and took a deep breath. "I got this."

She took one last look at her face, grinned at the sparkle in her eyes, and then went out to meet her future in-laws.

CHAPTER FOURTEEN

SEVERAL HOURS LATER, Logan stood at the edge of Chase's yard, watching the chaos.

It had been a long time since he'd been in town for a Stockton family brunch. It used to be whatever brothers were in town. Him. Chase. Maybe Travis or Ryder. Brothers who carried the curse of their piece-of-shit father like a poison in their blood. Brothers who had sworn a lifetime commitment that they would stand by each other no matter what, that no one else would ever be invited into their world.

Now? He didn't know where that poison had gone for his brothers, because it seemed to have vanished.

Kids everywhere. Wives. Brody and Keegan Hart, who were brothers of Maddox's wife, Hannah. Even the colors had changed. As a kid, he and his brother Quintin had been the only ones with skin that had any hint of brown. Now? Almost half of his nieces and nephews were assorted shades of brown, many adopted. In fact, as far as he knew, he could think of only one or two of his nieces and nephews who were biologically related to both parents.

It didn't surprise him. The Stockton boys had so many

different mothers that they'd learned early on that family had nothing to do with blood, and everything to do with the soul. It made sense that as adults, they'd add kids to the family no matter where they came from.

It felt right, for the Stockton name to be expanding like it was. But that didn't change the fact that so many spouses and kids created a circus. Not a bad circus. Just one Logan didn't fit into anymore, not that he ever did. Everyone there was his family, but he didn't even know how to talk to them.

The one that he couldn't wrap his head around the most was Zane. His brother had been a recluse. And now? He was at the pool, swimming with his two sons, as well as Chase and Mira's kids. Holding the two little boys of Chase's, his huge, rebel brother looked like a complete contradiction.

Logan watched Zane's face as he played with the kids. His brother was happy. There was genuine joy in his smile, in his eyes. There was so much laughter. Joy. Things that had never been a part of their childhood, or their lives.

Envy flickered through Logan. He was always so deeply submerged in his life that he never thought about whether he was happy or not. But as he stood there, watching his brothers, he knew he never smiled the way they were—

He heard Skylar's laughter, and his gaze shifted to her, as it had every few seconds throughout the morning. She was only a few yards away, talking with a couple of his sisters-in-law. They were clustered around her, laughing, chatting, drawing her into their family, exactly as he'd known they would.

He watched as Taylor said something to Skylar that made the women burst out laughing.

He found himself grinning as he watched Skylar. Unlike his family, her brightness held his demons at bay, pushing them into the vault he tried to keep in. Skylar seemed to fit him, and she also fit his family. He didn't understand how that was possible, but it appeared to be the case.

He was glad she was smiling. The shadows in her eyes were haunting him something fierce. He didn't like that he'd dragged her into his hell.

And she'd been married? He wanted to know more. He *needed* to know more.

The sunlight was glinting off Skylar's hair, making it shimmer and glisten. She'd ditched her sweatshirt for a tank top, her leggings for shorts. Her legs were curvy and tempting. Her body---

Shit. He dragged his gaze off her and stared out across the yard. What the hell was he doing, fantasizing about her? He glanced at her again, and this time, she was watching him. She held out her hand to him, inviting him into the circle, but he shook his head.

He had no idea how to jump into a circle of women and talk, even if they were his family.

His place was on the edge, in the shadows. It was where he belonged. It was where he needed to be. In his work. In his life.

Not in the sunlight.

Never in the sunlight.

～

Chase looked like his soul had shattered in half, and that was not all right with Mira. "Zane? Can you watch the boys for a bit? I need to chat with Chase for a few minutes."

Her brother-in-law nodded. "We're good. Got a good game of pool ball going."

"Great!" She waved at Alexander and J.J., then turned and jogged across the yard to where Chase was leaning against a tree, his arms folded across his chest, alone. Her husband was never alone at their family functions. He was always in the middle of everything, feeding off the joy of the big family that he'd brought together.

His gaze shifted to her as she walked up. Determination settled in her when she saw the pain in his eyes. Whatever demon had dared to wrap its nasty little claws around her husband's throat was going to get its ass kicked right now.

"Hey, love." She held out her hands, and smiled when he reached for her. She kissed him lightly, but she could feel his attention was trapped by shadows. "What's going on?"

He shook his head once. "Later."

"Nope. Now." Still holding his hand, she started backing toward the barn.

He smiled. "We have guests." But he followed her.

"They aren't guests. They're family." At her words, the smile faded again. "Come on. I'll race you." She dropped his hand and took off in a sprint toward the barn.

"Mira—"

She ran harder, grinning as she did it.

He swore, and then she heard him start running. He was fast, but she had a big head start. As she neared the barn, she heard him closing in, and she pressed as hard as she could the last few yards—

He burst past her and slapped his hand on the door of the first stall, laughing. "You'll never beat me."

She hit the wall, and stopped, gasping for air as she laughed. "I let you win. Your male ego is so fragile."

Their newest horse, a midnight black beauty named Snowflake, popped her head out of the door, her white-tipped ears curious. She'd been in such tough shape when she'd arrived, but she was already filling out, and her wounds were healing. Mira had already decided to keep her. She was too sweet to let go.

Mira opened Snowflake's door and slipped inside. "Come

on, Chase."

He followed her, latching the door behind him as they headed toward the back corner of the stall. The shavings smelled like freshly cut wood, and the hay was vibrant and aromatic. The minute they were on the other side of Snowflake, Chase caught Mira around the waist and pinned her up against the wall.

She grinned and draped her hands behind his neck as he bent his head and kissed her. The kiss was intense and passionate, as it always was. Time had only increased their need for each other, not lessened it.

He leaned into her, his corded body hard and familiar against hers. For a moment, she settled into the kiss, in the tenderness of his lips, in the fiercely protective way he held her hips. Always safe with him. Always loved. And always needed.

"Chase," she finally whispered against his mouth. "What's wrong?"

He paused the kiss and rested his forehead against hers. "Logan."

She'd suspected as much. "You don't like Skylar? She seems lovely. And the way they look at each other makes it clear how much they care about each other. I'm sure you guys will all be able to keep her safe." Chase and Logan had called all the adults in for a meeting when everyone had arrived, leaving the older kids to watch the younger ones. It had been agreed to have Skylar and Logan set up at the River House, but everyone was on alert.

Chase pulled back. "I know we'll protect them."

She frowned. "Then what's wrong?"

He sighed and brushed the hair back from his face. "Logan. He's not coming back. Not ever. I can see it in his eyes. He told me things today..." He met her gaze, his eyes filled with such anguish that Mira felt her own heart break for him. "He's too broken, Mira. He can't get past it. I see it now. He's in the CIA, and he said it's the only thing that helps him. Killing bad guys, I guess helps."

Mira let out her breath. The CIA? She so wanted to explore that, but it wasn't the issue that was breaking her husband. "All of you Stocktons believe you can't be saved. Until you meet the right woman, none of you have hope. But he's got Skylar now. Love heals, and she isn't afraid of what he is."

"They're not engaged."

She blinked. "What?"

"Not even dating. She's his neighbor. He got her shot at accidentally, so he feels obligated to keep her safe while his team hunts down the assassin." He looked at her, his eyes dead with the loss of hope that had driven him for so long. "He'll never try, Mira. He'll never let a woman in."

Mira thought about that, and then she looked up at her husband. "That's what he believes. Don't get sucked into his negativity."

"You weren't there. You didn't hear him—"

"I *was* there. I saw the way he kissed her. I saw the way he couldn't take his gaze off her, the way he followed every move she made as you guys were talking."

Chase frowned. "Because he's protecting her."

"With his kiss? In our living room?" When Chase continued to frown, she sighed. "I also saw the way she leaned into him. She watches him equally as closely. For heaven's sake, did he really have to decide that being engaged was their best cover?"

"No," Chase said slowly. "He didn't."

"Right?" She cocked her head. "How long have they known each other? Two years?"

Chase nodded. "That's what he said."

Mira grinned. "Well, I think that despite his best efforts,

Logan *has* let a woman in, but he's not willing to admit it. And he's going to run from it as soon as he can." She gently poked him in the stomach. "I seem to recall another Stockton who took some convincing that the woman he'd decided to protect was the woman who could save his soul."

A small smile finally quirked at the corner of his mouth. "It did take some convincing."

"It took me living down the hall from you, sharing your house, and being my charming, adorable self in every inch of your life." She raised her brows. "And now Logan is here, needing to play protector to the woman who might save him. I think we can make sure they get stuck together a lot, don't you? Make the most of this opportunity while we have it?"

Chase stared at her, and then his smile widened. "You think we should play matchmaker?"

"He already played matchmaker." Mira grinned. "All we need to do is treat them to the Stockton magic."

"You think it'll work?"

Mira wrapped her arms around his waist and grinned up at him. "Love always wins."

"What if it's not love?"

"And what if it is?"

He smiled. "If it is, then he's a lucky bastard." He smiled, and now, finally, the smile reached his eyes again. "Have I told you lately how lucky I am to have such a manipulative, interfering, plotting wife?"

She smiled. "Not for at least five minutes." She stood on her toes and kissed him. "Let's go recruit some assistants. This is going to be fun—"

"So is this." He caught her around the hips and lifted her up, a mischievous gleam in his blue Stockton eyes. "Five minutes, baby. That's all I need."

It took a lot longer than five minutes.

And it was worth every second.

CHAPTER FIFTEEN

LOGAN STOCKTON WAS dangerous in all sorts of ways.

Skylar leaned back in her seat, hiding behind her sunglasses as she watched Logan show his brother Maddox the "best" way to grill hot dogs.

Logan had been so tense at the start of the brunch, but Chase had suddenly appeared and dragged him to the patio to help grill with his brothers. Once he'd gotten the grill tools in his hand, Logan had become more relaxed. Still tense. Still watching her all the time. Still keeping a distance from his family. But she could tell how much he loved being with his brothers.

How could he deprive himself of a life and a family he so clearly loved? She didn't understand. She would give anything to have her family back together again.

His laugh was deep and beautiful, making her want to laugh along with him.

And his kiss...she could still feel his lips on hers.

She wanted more. Of the kiss. Of his smile. Of the secrets he kept locked away so deeply.

"If that isn't a look of pure yearning, I don't know what

is." Mira suddenly appeared and sat down next to her. "Logan's a sexy devil, isn't he?"

Skylar felt her cheeks heat up, embarrassed to be caught ogling Logan. "That he is."

Mira leaned forward and rested her chin on her hands, her eyes dancing. "Any woman who gets to take a Stockton to bed is one lucky gal. Welcome to the exclusive Great Sex for Life Club."

"Right?" Another woman plunked herself down. Her blue eyes were sparkling with mischief. "I'm Taylor, Zane's wife. The first time I met Zane, he climbed naked into my bed. Scared the shit out of me, but also, let's be honest, a gift from heaven, right?"

Skylar raised her brows. "He climbed naked into your bed?"

"He still maintains he didn't know I was in the bed at the time, but I find that hard to believe." She winked. "The man still can't keep his hands off me, and I wouldn't have it any other way."

"So, tell us, Skylar." Yet another woman pulled up a chair. Skylar was pretty sure her name was Erin, and she was married to Steen. She was wearing cute pink shorts and a sweatshirt with the words "Spread Love" across the chest. "Did you know he was the man for you instantly, or did it take time?"

Skylar looked around at the table full of women, all staring at her expectantly. They were all so nice and welcoming. She loved them all already. *Go with it, Skylar*.

She took a deep breath and decided to stick with the truth. "Well, I think it was from the first moment I saw him. It was the day I moved in. I was standing in the hall, trying to get my key to work in the lock, and he walked out of his condo, which was right across the hall."

All the women leaned forward. "Was he shirtless?" Mira asked. "Shirtless always works with the Stocktons."

She shook her head. "He was heading out to catch a flight. He smiled at me, and introduced himself. He had the most beautiful voice with this hint of western drawl." She paused, remembering that moment. "He had kindness in his eyes. He looked at me with *kindness*. I was so desperate for kindness that I almost started crying right then. He said to knock if I ever needed anything, no matter what time of day. If he was home, he'd help."

The women nodded in unison. "That's how the Stocktons are," Mira said. "They have the hugest hearts."

"I could tell." Skylar looked around at the table. "I could tell he meant it, and that felt like the greatest gift anyone had ever given me. That little moment gave me the hope not to give up. I held onto that exchange in my darkest moments, as proof that there was goodness in this world, in my life."

The women collectively sighed, and Mira's gaze flicked behind Skylar. "Did she ever tell you that, Logan?"

Heat flared in Skylar's cheeks, and she spun around. Logan was standing behind her, a plate of hot dogs in his hand, a look of absolute surprise on his face. "No." His gaze quickly scanned the table. He nodded a hello at everyone, then he focused on Skylar again. "I had no idea."

Skylar shrugged, embarrassed. "I didn't know you then. It would have been stalkerish to tell you." She barely knew him now. It still felt stalkerish to tell him, but hey, if a girl couldn't stalk her own fake fiancé, then who could she stalk?

"Do you remember that moment, Logan?" Mira asked.

Skylar felt like sinking into her chair. Of course he wouldn't remember. She hadn't showered in three days. She'd been a wreck emotionally. Barely coherent.

"I do." His voice was low and rough as he set the food down. "You were wearing those light blue leggings with the rainbows on them, and that gray sweatshirt with the frayed cuffs. Your eyes were this gorgeous, stark blue, huge and scared. Your hair was in that crooked ponytail, and I wanted to reach over and tug it straight. Not to fix it, but just to see if it was as soft as it looked."

Skylar stared at him in shock. She had been wearing that outfit. It had always been her comfort outfit, and she'd needed it that day. "You remember?"

"Yeah." He leaned on the back of her chair. "I remember every conversation we've had," he said. "The day you got promoted to senior associate and you were dancing in the mailroom? The song was *Live Like Sunshine*. The anniversary of your dad's death, when you were crying in the elevator? March 14. The time your mom sent you those huge tomatoes from her garden? Her own variety of Chocolate Stripe. I picked some up a few weeks later to see what they tasted like."

Skylar was wordless, stunned into silence.

The other women were silent too, everyone staring at Logan.

He looked around the table, and then his cheeks flushed. "So yeah, I guess we were both stalkerish," he muttered.

"No." Mira smacked her palms on the table, making everyone jump. "It's not stalkerish. It just means that the two of you felt that connection from the first moment. We can't help what our heart sees and remembers, sometimes before our mind catches up. I think it's incredibly romantic." She elbowed Taylor. "Isn't it romantic?"

Taylor cleared her throat, as if she'd been caught in a daze. "Hell, that's not just romantic. That's heart-melting." She looked back and forth between them. "You guys were meant to find each other. It's so obvious."

"Definitely obvious," Erin said.

"Completely obvious," Mira agreed. "Right, Logan?"

He was looking down at Skylar, his dark brown eyes focused on her, and her alone. "Obvious." His voice was husky, that same tone he'd had before he kissed her earlier.

Erin started banging her fork against a glass that was on the table. "Kiss her!"

Embarrassment flooded Skylar. "This isn't a wedding—"

"You're engaged, so it's close enough!" Erin continued to make the glass ring. "Kiss her, Logan!"

Mira immediately grabbed a knife and started tapping it against Erin's glass, too. "Kiss! Kiss! Kiss!" she started chanting.

"Kiss! Kiss! Kiss!" Taylor picked up a spoon and start dinging it against the crystal. She was joined by a few adults at the next table, and then Chase started tapping the barbeque tongs against the grill. Louder and louder, and people were all chanting for them to kiss. Even children's voices were raised with glee.

Logan raised his brows in apology, but he was smiling now. "I told you, my family's different." He held out his hand. "They won't stop until we satisfy them."

Her heart pounding, Skylar set her hand in his, and let him tug her to her feet. He slid his arms around her waist, amusement flickering in his eyes. "My family is a bunch of sex addicts. We need to make this good."

Oh, God. "You're kidding, right?"

"I never joke about sex." But he chuckled as he pulled her against him, leaned in, and kissed her.

Her stomach jumped the moment their lips touched, and need roared to life inside her. She wrapped her hands around his biceps, kissing him back. He deepened the kiss almost immediately, a perfect, sensual, delicious seduction that made her want to crawl into his arms and never leave.

His kiss was tender and scorching at the same time. The way his arms locked around her, holding her against him like he was her protector was insanely hot and deliciously addict-ing. He tasted like mint and temptation, and he kissed her like she was the only woman on earth he ever wanted to kiss again.

Gradually, the sounds of cheering broke through the haze of his kiss, and she realized that his entire family was hooting and hollering. How long had they been kissing?

She pulled back, but Logan's arms tightened around her for a split second before he swore under his breath and released her. She stepped back, embarrassed to have gotten so caught up in a kiss that was supposed to be fake.

And then she saw the expression on Logan's face. Pure intensity. Raw desire. Unstated passion. He clearly wanted more. Not for show. For real.

Her heart started to pound. "I can't," she whispered.

He let out his breath, and replaced the need on his face with a reassuring smile. "It's okay, Skylar. I won't take it further." He held out his hand to her as everyone continued to cheer. "Come."

Reluctantly, she put her hand in his, her breath catching when his strong hand closed around hers. He tugged her against him, and draped his arm over her shoulder as he turned them to face his family, making sure to tuck her protectively against his side. He raised his hand in a wave and bowed, making people burst out in more cheers and laughter.

"How is he, Skylar?" One of his brothers yelled. "Worth keeping?"

Heat flared in Skylar's cheeks, but she nodded. "Gold star," she announced. "Definite keeper."

Everyone cheered, and laughter fueled the air as people returned to their conversations.

Skylar let out her breath as people turned away. Logan's body was hard and tempting against her side. Too tempting. Too good.

Mira folded her arms across her chest and leaned back in her seat, beaming at them. "Now, *that* was a kiss."

Skylar nodded. "It was." On so many levels.

"I think we should ask for another one," Taylor said, holding up her fork. "What do you guys think?"

Oh, God. Not another one.

Logan bent his head, his breath warm against her neck. "You okay?" he whispered.

She nodded, watching as more of his family started to head toward them, mischief evident on their faces. "Maybe we can step away for a few?"

He nodded. "How about I show you the horses?"

"Perfect."

"Let's do it." He took her hand and nodded at the table. "I'm going to sneak my girl off to the barn for a little privacy. We'll be back in a few."

Mira's smile widened. "You do that. We'll be here." She winked. "We'll make sure the kids stay here so they don't walk into anything untoward."

Skylar groaned inwardly. "We're not going to have sex in the barn."

"Don't knock it 'til you've tried it, baby," Erin said with a grin. "It's a little tricky now with all the kids around, though. The campers are working on the Fourth of July float in the indoor arena, so keep your clothes on around there."

Before Skylar could protest, Logan tugged her away. "We won't traumatize any of the kids, I promise. Be back shortly." He got her away from the table. "Now, run," he whispered. "Before they stop us."

Skylar started giggling as he broke into a jog, tugging her with him. "They're going to think we're sex obsessed."

"Which is perfect. What else do newly engaged people do, but have sex?"

"In barns with a dozen kids around?" She couldn't help

but laugh as they jogged out of the yard and around the side of the house. "They weren't serious, were they?"

"I don't know. I don't spend that much time around all these married people." He looked over at her. "But if we were actually engaged, I'd definitely be wanting to get you naked as often as possible."

Her jaw dropped. "Logan!"

He had the grace to look appalled. "Sorry. I didn't mean to say that out loud."

"Did you mean it?" The question burst out before she could stop it, and she grimaced, afraid of the answer. Afraid he'd say yes. Afraid he'd say no.

He glanced over at her as they continued to jog. "I'm not sure you want to ask me that when I'm fresh off a kiss with you."

That was a yes.

Definitely a yes.

CHAPTER SIXTEEN

Y ES.

Yes.

Yes.

Logan was thinking about seeing her naked. What the hell? That was so unfair. The idea made chills race down Skylar's spine.

She was so freaking attracted to him. She'd always been attracted to him, but it had been safe. He was a stranger. She was committed to being single. Nothing would ever happen from it.

But now he was a temptation that was becoming increasingly difficult to resist, even though now she knew enough to know what a bad idea it would be. For a million reasons.

"Skylar." Logan caught her wrist as she tried to duck around a corner. "Wait a sec."

She took a breath, then turned to face him. She was out of breath from running to the barn, and then continuing to run to the next barn, and then the further one. Just trying to put distance between them.

He was too fit and stubborn to be left behind.

She put her hands on her hips. "What?"

His dark brown eyes searched her face. "Talk to me."

"I am talking to you."

The corner of his mouth quirked. "You're running from me."

"I'm practicing for when Eugene shows up to kill me. I like to be prepared. I'm pretty sure that's a good plan." He was too close, so she backed up until her butt hit a horse blanket hung up on a rack behind her. Damn wall.

Logan grasped the bars of the stall on either side of her head, his gaze searching hers.

He was so close to her that she could smell that faint, delicious scent she associated with him. She wasn't sure if it was his soap or his shampoo, or simply his skin, but it didn't matter. She loved the scent. It made her feel safe and protected, like she had that day she'd met him, and he'd promised to help her if she needed it.

"Why are you running from me?"

She wrinkled her nose. "I just said—"

"I'm a trained operative. I'm pretty certain I can tell when you're lying to me." He cocked his head. "In my line of work, details can be the difference between life and death. I need to know what's going on with you."

"Besides the fact you basically admitted that you want to get me naked?"

His face went blank. "I didn't admit that."

"Oh, my God." She shoved at his chest, but he was a solid wall that didn't move. "Stop! Just stop! I'm not some stupid work assignment. Don't treat me like one! I'm me!"

His brow furrowed. "I'm not treating you like—"

"You are. You used to see me. Or at least, I felt like it. But now, it's all like 'hey, I'm a CIA operative. I can see through your lies.'" She felt like she was panicking, and she closed her eyes. "Go away."

Logan didn't move.

"I said—"

"I know what you said, but I need to protect you."

"Right. It's about protection." Dammit. She knew that. "I know that. I know. I just—" Argh. She felt like screaming. She opened her eyes and glared at him. "You know what? Forget it." She ducked under his arm. "Isn't that float with the kids around here somewhere?"

She didn't wait for him. She just started walking. She needed to get away from him. Calm down. Get her equilibrium back.

Logan fell in beside her, matching his steps with hers, letting her lead the way. "Skylar."

"I don't want to talk about it." She didn't even look at him.

Frustration shot through Logan. He had no idea what had happened to shift the mood. The naked comment? "I'm sorry I mentioned seeing you naked."

She spun toward him, her blue eyes blazing. "It's not the naked comment!"

Logan felt completely lost. "Then what is it?"

"You!" She poked him in the chest. "You and your family and your kisses!"

He stared at her. "What about them?" He wanted to understand. He was surprised how much he needed to figure out this woman standing in front of him. He'd worked so hard not to care about anyone, and even to keep his brothers at a distance, but Skylar was different.

Skylar got to him. He wasn't capable of letting this go, of ignoring her emotions, and forgetting about her stress. "Let me help, Skylar. I want to help you."

She whirled around, her hands on her hips and glared at him. "This is what I'm talking about. God, could you be more difficult?"

For a long moment, they stared at each other, and then he started to smile. A smile that started deep inside him and seemed to come alive.

Her frown deepened. "And that freaking smile. It should be illegal. Why on earth does a man who carries a gun for a living get dimples? And why are you laughing at me?"

His smile widened. "Trust me, I'm not laughing at you."

"Then what's so funny? That I'm upset?"

"No." He took her hand and rubbed his thumb over her palm. "I'm smiling because I care that you're upset."

She didn't pull away. "That doesn't make sense."

"I've spent my life turning off my emotions," he said, continuing to draw circles on her palm. "It was the only way to survive my childhood. It was hell, and I wasn't interested in drowning in it."

Empathy flickered in her eyes. "Logan, I'm sorry—"

He touched his finger to her lips to silence her. "No need to be sorry. My life made me strong. I'm damn proud of the fact that I don't feel much these days. It makes me successful at my job. It makes it easy to do what I need to do. It makes it easy to put distance between myself and my past. To keep away from my brothers."

Skylar cocked her head, listening to him now. "So, you're numb emotionally?"

"Yep."

"And that's good."

"Isn't it?"

Pain flickered in her eyes, pain that he wanted to know more about. "I guess it can be," she said.

"I consider it good." He took her other hand, rubbing circles gently on both her palms. "But the one thing I could never figure out is why I felt better after I saw you. Why the darkness seemed to leave me for a little bit. I felt less numb, but in a good way. Like my head became clearer. Quieter. Brighter, even."

She said nothing, but her gaze searched his.

"It's because you make me care about something deeply enough that I can't shut it down. That's what makes me feel alive. Caring. It sounds simple, but I just figured it out, right now." He grinned. "I care about why you're upset. I need to know. And that feels good."

She narrowed her eyes. "Dammit." She pulled her hands free and started to walk away again.

Logan caught her wrist. "Why are you so upset, Skylar? I want to know."

Skylar didn't turn around, but he saw her look down at his fingers around her arm. Finally, she looked back over her shoulder at him. "You," she said softly. "This. You. All of it."

Emotion was thick in her voice, settling deep in his gut. "Okay," he said, as gently as he could. "Which part is the worst?"

She still didn't turn around, but she met his gaze. "You."

"What about me?" He didn't like being the cause of her stress. In the line of executing his job, he was the cause of many, many people's stress, and he always shrugged it off. It didn't matter. It couldn't matter.

But Skylar? It made him feel like shit.

She finally turned to face him. Her hands were on her hips, her chin raised. "It's not your fault," she said. "It's my fault. Don't worry about—"

"I'm worrying about it. I'll keep worrying about it, and that's going to distract me from keeping you safe." That was total bullshit. He couldn't allow anything to distract him from keeping her safe. He was aware of every sound around them. Every shadow. He'd checked every footprint on the way to the barn. He was in hyper-alert mode. But he *was* going to keep obsessing about her well-being until he got some answers. So he needed the answers. Now.

"I don't want—"

"Come. Let's walk." He put his arm around her shoulders. For a split second, she leaned into him, and then she pulled away. He decided to focus on the fact she'd leaned into him instinctively. "The indoor ring is back this way."

They passed by a few stalls with horses, but many were still empty. He was amazed at how big the stables were now. His brothers had invested so much money in the place. It was incredible what the barn had become.

"My ex-husband had an affair for three years before I found out," Skylar said suddenly.

Logan jerked his gaze to Skylar, but she wasn't looking at him. She was staring blankly down the aisle as they walked. "I'm sorry—"

She held up her hand to silence him. "I don't talk about this, so I'm saying it once, and we're not talking about it again. He doesn't get the right to affect my emotions anymore. I deserve more than that."

"You sure do."

She still didn't look at Logan. "He was taking her as his date to spouse events at his work. To dinner parties with our friends. He told them all terrible stories about me, and they all told him he was doing the right thing by stepping out on me. They all told him what a good guy he was for continuing to stay married to me and support me financially despite what an albatross I was."

Logan swore under his breath. "Your friends knew?"

"Yep. I would run into them at the store, and they'd smile and be nice. I had no idea." Her voice was brisk, cool, edged with emotion she had reined in with ruthless focus. "Then one day, I had a meeting with a potential client for my firm."

Her voice got stronger, and Logan could feel the sheer willpower it was taking to hold off the emotions.

He silently slipped his hand around hers, half-expecting her to pull away. But she didn't. She gripped his hand like her very soul depended on it. "What happened?" he asked.

"She walked into my office, sat down, and then announced she was tired of my husband refusing to marry her because he had to take care of me. She told me to stop pretending I didn't know about her and to just let him go." Skylar finally looked at Logan. "It was like getting hit in the face with a cement block."

"I bet it was." He could see the pain in her eyes, but more than that, he could see her absolute determination not to give them the power to take her down. Fuck, he admired her. "What did you do?"

"I let him go."

He laughed softly. "That's my girl."

She stopped walking and turned to face him. "He's an ass. I get it. I don't want him back, obviously. But the thing is that I completely trusted him. I worked long hours, and I never thought he'd be using that time to cheat on me. I trusted my friends. I trusted his colleagues. I trusted him. They were *all* lying to me. They *all* believed I deserved it. The level of betrayal was beyond words."

Logan finally understood. He knew the source of the pain in those blue eyes the day he'd met her. He understood why she kept herself at a distance. He understood why he'd always sensed such a core of strength deep within her. "I can arrange for them to disappear."

She stared at him, then burst out laughing. "You could, couldn't you?"

He grinned. "I could, actually, yeah." God, she was beautiful. Able to laugh even when she was reliving hell. "Want me to?"

"No. I'm good." She took a breath. "Here's the thing. I'm fine, right? I have a great career. I have plenty of money. I'm good." She met his gaze. "Except I don't believe I will ever trust again. Not a man. Not a friend. Not anyone."

Logan couldn't imagine feeling like that. He might keep his distance with his brothers, but he always, *always* trusted them. He'd trust them with the little things, the big things, and everything in between, which is the reason he'd brought Skylar home to them when her life was at risk.

She took a breath. "I find myself wanting to trust you, Logan."

His pulse quickened. What a statement, coming from her. He was honored. "You can trust me. I'll keep you safe."

"I know, but that's not what I'm talking about." She paused, then held up her hand with the ring on it. "I want to trust you with my heart, Logan. My heart is starting to believe in you, in your beautiful family. My heart wants to open to you, and I can't do that." She whispered the last words. "You're going back into your hiding place when this is over. Guns. Death. Violence. You'll be taking your family with you, away from me. All this—" She gestured expansively to the ranch. "It'll be gone, and my heart will..." She paused. "I can't do that," she whispered.

He was stunned by her admission. *Stunned.* "I'm not like your ex," he said. "My loyalty is forever. I swear it. If I give it, you can stake your life on it."

"That's the thing. You're not going to give it to me," she said. "Not your heart. Your heart is with your job." She sighed. "I might want to trust you, but the truth is that even if we got together, I'd be one of those bitchy, jealous, insecure women that would drive you away. If you're out of my sight for a month on one of your missions, I'll accuse you of cheating on me. I won't be able to trust you, and that would destroy what little chance we had. It won't even matter if you're cheating or not. I'll probably believe that you are." She tapped her chest, over her heart. "This is broken now, Logan—"

He caught her hand. "It's not."

"It is—"

"It's not." He searched her gaze. "My father beat the shit out of all of us when we were kids. My brothers and I have seven different mothers. It was hell beyond what I can afford to revisit long enough to tell you about it. We were *all* fucked up beyond words. The shadows remain, but we're all doing all right. You can get past it if you want to. You can."

"Maybe I don't want to. Maybe it's safer to be alone. Like you. You've chosen to be alone, and you actually have people you trust and love." She met his gaze. "We're not different, Logan, except that I'm in danger of falling for you. Hard."

He felt like he'd been gut-punched. "You're falling for me?"

"Don't say it like that's a good thing—"

A loud crash suddenly echoed through the barn, followed by the sound of children screaming.

Logan was running before the first shrieks had faded from the air, his gun in one hand, and Skylar's hand in his other.

CHAPTER SEVENTEEN

LOGAN AND SKYLAR burst through the double doors to the indoor ring. Half a dozen campers were clustered around a parade float shouting, but Logan did a quick, careful scan of the entire interior, looking for a gunman or other threats. Ceiling. Walls. Corners. Clear.

He was still running toward the kids, his gun by his side, ready. "What's wrong? What happened?"

"The horse fell off!"

"It landed on Leila!"

"It broke!"

It landed on a kid? Logan swore and sprinted toward the float, Skylar right beside him. "Where? Where's Leila?"

"Over here," one of the girls shouted. "On this side!"

"He has a gun!" Everyone screamed suddenly and ran for the door, shrieking like the devil himself had found them.

"He's on our side," Skylar yelled, but the kids were already gone, running for their lives back to the main house.

Skylar and Logan ran around the float, but he moved carefully, keeping Skylar behind him as he checked to make sure no one was waiting for them on the far side. But when they saw a pair of bare legs and sneakers sticking out from under a massive, fake horse, they both dove for the girl.

Fear gripped Skylar as she bolted around the horse, terrified of what she might find. She fell to her knees beside a girl who looked to be around sixteen. "Are you all right?"

The girl looked over at Skylar, her eyes wide with panic. "I'm stuck. I can't get it off me."

"It's okay. We'll help." She took the girl's hand and pressed it between her palms. "Logan? Can you get it?"

He was already grabbing the horse's butt, his muscles flexing as he tried to move it. "It's heavy. Shit—"

Male shouts suddenly filled the arena, and Skylar looked up as Logan's brothers and the two Harts rushed in, all of them armed and fierce-looking. Good heaven. They *all* had guns?

"Where's the gunman?" Chase shouted. "The kids said there was a gunman!"

"It's me!" Logan yelled. "The horse fell on Leila. Help me get it off!"

Logan's brothers ran to his side, but the two Harts fanned out, their guns ready as they stood guard, protecting the others.

Together, the men easily lifted the horse off Leila. Skylar grabbed her under the arms and dragged her out from under the horse. The girl scrambled back, and Skylar was relieved to see her using her legs normally. She helped Leila get to the side while the men righted the horse.

Skylar crouched in front of Leila, her heart breaking when she saw tears filling her eyes. "Where are you hurt?"

Leila shook her head. "I'm not hurt. I'm fine."

"You're sure?"

She nodded, but the tears were flooding down her dark brown cheeks. "I'm fine. Did any of the kids get hurt?"

"No. They ran out of here screaming when Logan showed his gun."

"Logan?"

The rescuer in question crouched next to Skylar. "Yeah, I'm Logan. How do you feel?"

Leila tried to catch her breath, but Skylar could tell she was about to fall apart. "I'm fine. I'm okay. The kids are okay? Really?"

"Fine." Chase was the one who answered, from over at the float. "They just freaked out about Logan waving his gun around."

"Okay. Okay." Leila looked around. "Are Zane and Erin here? They'll be so mad." Tears filled her eyes again.

"Zane and Erin are with the younger kids," Chase said as he helped try to get the horse back on the float. "They're fine. He won't be mad. You're sure you're okay, Leila?"

Leila nodded and stood up. Her hands were shaking as she wiped the dirt off her shorts. "We need to get that fixed. The Fourth of July parade is in two days."

Skylar frowned as Leila hurried back toward the float, almost frantic. "Maybe you should take a break, Leila."

"I can't. It's fine. I got it." The teenager was already back on the float, telling the brothers where to put the horse, even with the tears on her cheeks and her hands shaking.

Skylar stood up, frowning. "Why is she panicking? It's just a float."

Chase walked over to stand with them. "She's been working almost around the clock on the float for weeks. She wanted to make the horse's head bob, but she couldn't get it to work. I think maybe the adjustments she made weakened it. She feels like the younger kids are counting on her, and she doesn't want to let them down."

Skylar put her hands on her hips, watching Leila frantically work on the horse. Her shoulders were hunched in exhaustion, and the tears were real. She watched Leila kneel next to the horse and pick up its head, which was no longer attached.

She had a sudden memory of working on projects with her dad. With his construction background and her design skills, they'd had the best time creating projects.

It was a long time ago, but some of the best memories of her life.

She walked over to the trailer. "Leila? I'm a design whiz. Mind if I help a bit?"

Leila looked over at her, a look of such gratitude on her face that Skylar smiled. "That would be amazing."

"Great." Skylar hoisted herself up on the trailer. "I'm Skylar. Why don't you fill me in?"

Skylar was incredible.

Logan leaned against the trailer, watching as Skylar and Leila crouched next to the horse's front leg, examining the mechanisms that the two of them had built. It was almost midnight, and they hadn't stopped all day, except when Logan had forced them to break for food.

Assorted campers had popped in to help put finishing touches on the float, but it was clear that Leila was the heart and brains behind the mechanics. The teenager was a whiz, and Logan was impressed with her mind and her skills.

And Skylar...impressive didn't even begin to describe her. Logan had never been around her while she was working before, and he was grateful for the opportunity to watch her work. He'd already realized she was smart and successful, but her mind was literally brilliant. Her vision was incredible, and the speed at which she could process each step and redirect their plan was staggering.

She was in her element, working out problems and creating solutions. She had absolute faith in her abilities, and that confidence had translated to Leila. Spending the day with Skylar had already changed Leila's posture. The teenager was speaking up, seeing possibilities, and becoming more confident.

Skylar had even gotten some smiles out of her.

Logan had helped with the heavy lifting, but other than that, they wanted no part of him. It was their project, and he loved watching them work together.

While she was working, the fear that haunted Skylar had vanished. She was confident and happy. Her eyes were sparkling, and her laughter was infectious. He could tell she loved what she was doing, and her joy lifted up everyone around her.

He was surprised to find out how much he'd enjoyed the day. Just hanging out with them. Being their muscle. Listening to their laughter. Watching them bond. It was the simplest day he'd had in a very long time, and the most satisfying he could remember.

Zane walked up and leaned on the trailer beside him. "It's great to see Leila happy," he said. "Skylar has a connection with her that the rest of us haven't been able to form."

Logan looked over at his brother. "What's her story?" Skylar and Leila were at the other end of the trailer, out of earshot.

"She's been a camper for two summers. She turns seventeen at the end of August. She'll age out of foster care on her eighteenth birthday," Zane said. "I think she's worried about what will happen to her. We've told her she can come work for the camp full time, but I don't think she believes us."

Logan sighed. "Good things don't come to people like her," he said. He understood that, because that was what he and his brothers believed for a long time.

"That's what she believes." Zane sighed. "Honestly, she should be going to college, not working at the camp. Her grades are shit but it's easy to tell she's brilliant." He looked over at Logan. "It's tough. I want to give forever homes to all the kids in our program. We've started the process to adopt the twins, but they're both so young. We can't take on more than that."

"Julia and Sophie?" Logan had seen the two little girls hanging on Taylor at the brunch earlier. "They have beautiful accents. Where are they from?"

"Haiti. Both their parents have passed away, and they have no local family." Zane glanced over at Logan. "I'm not gonna lie, Logan. Working with these kids has made me even more aware of how lucky we were to have each other growing up, and to have each other today. Taylor saved me, and I didn't even know I needed saving. I'm glad you found Skylar." He grinned. "These women sneak up on us, don't they? Steal our hearts and heal our souls before we even know what's happening."

Logan leaned on the trailer and watched Skylar hunched over with Leila, studying the horse's knee joint. "Yeah, they do."

"You guys going to move back here?"

Logan stiffened. "No."

"Why not? Because you think life is better away from us? I used to think that, too, and I was wrong. Family kept us alive for a reason, Logan. It's because it's our lifeline. We're meant to be with family."

Logan looked over at his brother. "My job makes it impossible for me to move back here."

Zane shrugged. "Find another job."

"My job matters to me."

"There are a lot of jobs out there. You've only got one family."

Logan ground his jaw. "I know that."

"Then think about it." Zane grinned. "You really going to deprive Skylar of us? We're the best in-laws on the damned planet."

They both looked at Skylar, crouched beside Leila as they peered intently at the knee joint of the horse. "Skylar already loves you guys," Logan admitted quietly.

"Smart woman." Zane set his hand on Logan's shoulder. "Either way, glad to have you back, buddy." Before Logan could answer, Zane moved away from him. "Leila. It's time to call it a night, sweetheart."

"Five more minutes," she protested. "Skylar and I almost have this finished." She grinned. "Its legs are going to move. It's going to look like it's running. How cool is that?"

Zane grinned. "I'm impressed." He smiled at Skylar. "Thanks."

She beamed at him. "This has been the best day ever, right, Leila?"

The teenager grinned at Skylar. "Totally."

Logan watched the three of them talk, a faint tinge of jealousy echoing through him at the way Skylar and Leila were beaming at Zane and each other. They were connected, the three of them. And it was beautiful. "I'll walk Leila back to her room when they're finished," he said. "Skylar and I will stay with her."

Leila shot him an appreciative smile, then looked at Zane. "Please?"

Zane pretended to grump. "Fine, but no more than fifteen minutes. You guys can finish tomorrow."

"Perfect!" The women went back to work.

Zane looked over at Logan. "It's good here on the ranch. It would make you happier than you think."

Logan let out his breath. "Let it go, Zane."

"If I did, I wouldn't love you." He patted the trailer. "Good night, ladies. See you at breakfast, Leila."

"Of course." She didn't even look up as Zane left.

Logan walked over to the engineers. "Can I help with anything?"

Skylar looked up and smiled at him, a genuine smile that made his gut turn over. "Actually, yeah." She grabbed his hand and pressed it to the horse's knee. "Hold that right there while we..."

Her voice trailed off as she and Leila studied the paper she'd sketched the design on.

They were perfect together, the two of them.

The moment was perfect.

And he loved being a part of it.

CHAPTER EIGHTEEN

IT WAS ALMOST two in the morning by the time Logan drove up to the River House. Skylar hadn't stopped talking the whole way there. She was so animated about the horse, detailing every idea she'd had and how they'd worked through each failure.

She was pure joy and animation, and Logan loved listening to her.

He couldn't remember the last time he'd been around such radiant exhilaration. She was just so happy and energized. Logan could tell she'd totally put aside her vulnerability with him and her worries about Eugene. She was in the moment, fully embracing the joyful day she'd had.

How did she do it? How did she embrace the good so completely, even when there were such shadows dancing around her? She was incredibly strong and determined, and he admired the hell out of her.

Almost wishing that the drive had taken more than fifteen minutes, Logan pulled into the five-car garage, beside the four cars already in there. He hadn't even put the car in park when Brody and Keegan Hart walked out of the house, clearly waiting for them. Regret flickered through Logan. He didn't want to share Skylar or end her rampage of delight.

But Skylar fell silent, watching the Harts. "They're still up?"

"Apparently."

"Because of Eugene?"

"That's my guess." He put the car into park and turned to face her, needing to tell her how special the day had been, but before he got a word out, Brody knocked at his window. *Shit.*

He opened the door. "Thanks for waiting up."

Brody nodded. "We got things set up to maximize security." He looked past Logan. "Evenin', Skylar."

She waved. "Thank you for everything. It's incredibly nice of you."

Brody grinned. "You're family now, Skylar. We take care of each other no matter what."

Skylar's smile faded, and she glanced at Logan, wariness back in her eyes.

Shit. He didn't like that being treated well made her unhappy. He needed to fix that. Later. Not now. Right now, he needed to focus. "Thanks." He opened the door and indicated for Skylar to get out.

Keegan was already beside the car, and he opened the door for her. "Welcome, Skylar. We're glad to have you."

As Skylar climbed out of the big pickup truck, she couldn't help but feel safe. The three men were all big, muscular, and clearly highly competent. She didn't know what Brody and Keegan's training was, but they'd both had handguns when they'd charged into the indoor arena, holding them like they'd been carrying them their entire lives.

She grinned nervously as she stepped down. "I'm glad you guys are on my side. I'd hate to be an enemy of this family."

Brody shrugged. "We don't have enemies. We just protect our own. There's a difference."

Skylar glanced at Logan, who clearly lived a very different life than the Harts did. "I like that approach. Who needs enemies, right?"

"Enemies are bad vibes," Keegan said. "It keeps you focused on them, instead of on yourself and making your own life better. We have no room for that." He glanced at Brody. "Brody taught us that when we were little. Still stands today."

"Sure does." Brody nodded at the bed of the truck, where their bags were stashed. "These all yours?"

"Yep," Logan answered. "But I can get them—"

"Teamwork." Brody grabbed a few bags, Keegan grabbed several, Logan picked up the rest, leaving only Skylar's backpack for her.

She swung it over her shoulder and yawned, suddenly tired, now that her adrenaline was wearing off. She realized she'd been up for almost two days straight, except for the brief nap on the plane.

Logan waited for her, flashing her a private smile. "Hang on there a little longer. You can crash in a few."

"I'm good." She followed Brody and Keegan through the interior garage door into the house, aware of Logan right behind her. She was flanked by the three men, and she knew no one would be able to get to her.

They emerged into a mud room. Racks of men's outdoor gear, boots, and life jackets were hung, along with a small blue life jacket and a pink one. There was a pair of flowered flip-flops and a small pair with robots on them. She smiled at the sight, at the reminder that there were real people living here. Ryder and his wife, and the little boy and his grandpa who they had claimed as family. "Are Zoey and Liam here? Or did they move out because of us?"

"They're here." Brody grinned at her as he led the way into the kitchen. "We can keep everyone safe. It's good."

Relief rushed through her. If they were letting Zoey, Liam

and his grandpa stay here, that did mean that they all truly believed she would be safe.

She was safe.

"You want us to show you around?" Brody asked. "We can show you what we've set up."

As he spoke, Keegan punched in an alarm code, and the lights turned to red. "We're secure for the night. Don't open any doors or windows or it'll set it off. We have the air conditioning running so we don't need to open windows." He handed a piece of paper to Logan that had about twenty-five digits on it. "Memorize the code and then toss it."

Logan looked down at the sheet of paper for about an eighth of a second, then handed the paper back. "Got it."

Skylar stared at him. "You memorized it already?"

"It's what I do." He put his hand on her back. "Let's get Skylar settled, and then we can talk. She's beat."

She yawned again. "I'm fine. I can stay up with you guys."

"No need. Let's go." Logan nodded at the Harts, who both indicated their agreement.

Brody led the way to the staircase, giving Skylar only a limited chance to check the house out.

The kitchen was huge, with a center counter, a table big enough for a dozen people. It led into a big family room. The entire side of the house was lined with big windows. The house was rustic, but warm. There were flowers on the counter and the table, and kid's shoes had been kicked off in the family room. A few sweatshirts were askew on the back of the couch, along with some throw blankets, which made it seem like more than a few movie nights had happened in that room.

She could imagine what movie night with the Stocktons and the Harts would be like. Loud. Boisterous. Laughter. Food.

It would be fun.

She sighed, catching Logan's attention. He raised his brows at her. "You all right?"

She smiled. "Just hitting the wall," she lied.

"Just a couple minutes, and you can crash."

She nodded as they followed the Harts up a central staircase. They reached the second floor, which was a long hallway with rooms on either side. "We're putting you in this room." Brody opened a door on the right and set the luggage inside. "It's between me and Keegan, so we're close if anything happens."

Logan nodded his approval. "Sounds good."

Brody pointed to another door that was closed. "That leads to the third floor. Ryder and his family are all up there. We figured that was safest. If your man shows up here, he won't make it to the third floor." He grinned. "The old man wanted to sleep in the living room and be the first line of defense. He said he was great with a gun."

Skylar's throat tightened. "Seriously?" Someone she hadn't even met yet wanted to be her front line of defense? What was with this family?

"Yeah, but I think he just didn't want to move to the third floor," Keegan said with a grin.

"He had to give up his room?"

Keegan raised his brows. "Don't even start with that guilt, Skylar." His voice was gentle, but also unrelenting. "There's no room for that. When one of us has a need, we all pitch in. Everyone needs help at some point. You don't do anyone any favors by feeling bad about it."

Logan put his hand on her back. "Thanks, guys. Let me get Skylar settled, and I'll meet you downstairs."

Brody nodded. "Keegan will come up and stay with her while I'm filling you in."

"I don't need Keegan," Skylar protested

"Yes, you do." Logan's gaze was unyielding, and she felt

like she was in the hands of an operative again, pink flip-flops in the foyer notwithstanding. "Give us fifteen minutes, okay?"

The Harts nodded. "I'll be back to spell you," Keegan said as he set the bags inside the room.

"Thanks." Logan gave each of the brothers a hard clap on the shoulder, and then nodded to her. "Wait here a sec." Before she could answer, he disappeared into the room with her bags, leaving her alone with the Harts.

"You don't need to wait," she said.

Brody laughed, leaned against the wall, and folded his arms across his chest. "You don't know how to accept help, do you?"

"I—" She didn't know how to respond to that. Finally, she shrugged. "I'm used to being independent."

"I can see that." Brody considered her. "You can be both. Independent and able to rely on others for help."

"I know, I'm just not used to it." She paused. "I have trust issues."

Brody smiled. "We *all* have trust issues. It's human nature." He nodded at the door. "Even Logan. I suspect he understands yours, doesn't he?"

She looked at the room where Logan had entered. "I don't know."

"Give him a chance." Brody paused. "I see the way he looks at you. He's fighting to be ready for how he feels about you. He'll make it."

She stared at him. "What do you mean?"

Before he could answer, Logan came out of the room. "It's secure. You guys did great." He smiled at her. "Come on, Skylar. Time to crash."

She wanted to ask Brody more questions about Logan, but she bit her lip. "Okay." She paused to smile at Brody and Keegan. "Thank you."

"Our pleasure. See you in the morning." The Harts each

gave her a quick hug, surprising her, then they headed downstairs, their boots thudding on the carpeted steps.

Logan gestured to the room. "After you."

"Thanks." She took a breath, then headed into the bedroom she'd be sharing with Logan. The first thing she noticed was that there was one bed. No couch. No cot. No carpet on the floor.

Just one bed.

She shot a look at Logan as he closed the door behind her and locked it. "One bed?"

He paused, glancing from her to the bed, as if it hadn't occurred to him that would be a problem. "Are you not comfortable with that? I'm sure I can grab a sleeping bag—"

"No. It's fine." She let out her breath. She might not trust him with her heart, but with her body? He'd protect her with his life. "It'll be fine." She grabbed her smallest bag and headed toward the bathroom. "I'll just be a minute."

As Skylar closed the bathroom door, she expected to dissolve into some melodrama about sharing a bed with Logan, but the minute she was alone, exhaustion flooded her, and all she could think of was getting into bed. It took only a few minutes to brush her teeth, wash her face, and pull on her sleep shorts and tank top, and even then, she felt like she was going to pass out on her feet.

When she opened the door, Logan had turned the bed sideways across the room, so that the side of the bed, instead of the headboard, was against the wall. The other side was facing the room, so by sleeping on that side of the bed, he would be the first line of defense regardless of whether someone came in the window or the door.

It was an awkward place for the bed, and realizing why he'd done it made fear trickle down her back. "I thought we were safe here."

"Just a precaution." He pulled down the comforter. "Climb in you. You look like you're going to pass out."

She set her bag down and ducked past him, crawling onto the soft sheets. She snuggled down under the blankets, tucking herself against the wall, trying to make herself as small as possible. She watched Logan as he moved their bags to the side, under the window, making that access more difficult. He moved with quiet, confident precision, and she could see the operative that he was in every line of his body.

"Logan?"

He didn't look over. "Yeah?"

"Is there a chance he's going to find us? That he might kill us?"

Logan looked over at her, and his face softened. He walked over to the bed, climbed on, and stretched out on his stomach so his face was even with hers. "I will do everything in my power to keep you safe," he said. "I'm very, very good at what I do. My brothers and the Harts are solid backup."

She nodded, tucking her hands under her chin while she pulled her knees up, making herself into a ball. "Okay."

"But I have to be honest. As long as Eugene is alive, there's a chance he'll find us, however slim. He's also very good."

Fear clamped down on her spine. "Okay," she whispered.

Logan put his hands over her fisted ones, dwarfing hers. "If he comes," he said, meeting her gaze. "I will stop him before he gets to you. I swear it."

Some of the tightness gripping her eased at his intensity. "Okay."

He smiled and brushed her hair back from her face, his touch tender and gentle. "I know it's tough to relax, but try to get some sleep. I promise you I'll be watching out for you the whole time."

She met his gaze, and something inside her finally let go.

She believed in him. She believed in this man who had sworn to keep her safe. A faint smile curved her lips. "If you mess up and I get killed, I'll haunt you for all eternity."

He didn't smile. "Yes, you would," he said in complete seriousness. "I'd never get over it, so let's not have that happen."

Her belly tightened at the intensity of his voice. "I thought you were trained not to let things like that get to you."

"I am." He paused. "But all the training in the world hasn't prepared me for you."

Her heart started to pound. "Is that bad?"

The corner of his mouth lifted ever so slightly. "Absolutely *nothing* about you is bad, Skylar. *Nothing.*"

He was so close to her. If she leaned forward just a tiny bit, she could kiss him. Would he kiss her back? Her heart beat even faster. "There are a lot of things about me that you don't know."

His gaze went to her mouth, and then back to her eyes. "I'm aware of that. I want to learn about each and every one."

Her breath caught. "Logan—"

There was a light knock at the door, and Keegan called out. "I'm here. Take your time."

For a moment, they simply stared at each other, and she found herself wishing desperately that he'd kiss her. That he'd break all the rules she'd laid out for him, gather her in his arms, and kiss her like his soul depended on it.

"Logan?" Keegan sounded tense. "Is everything all right?"

"Yeah, coming!" Logan brushed a kiss over her forehead. "I'll be right back, Skylar. I'm going to have Keegan wait in the room with you, but you don't need to talk to him. Just go to sleep. Trust us."

She sighed. No kiss. Which was definitely the right choice, even if it felt like a total disappointment. "Okay."

He leaned in, and before she realized what he was doing, gave her a quick kiss on the mouth. It was over in a split second, but the feel of his mouth lingered. He paused, and when she smiled, he grinned at her, his eyes crinkling with warmth. "I'll be back soon. Don't wait up."

"Hurry back." She smiled to herself and closed her eyes as he got up, the bed shifting under his weight. She heard him open the door, and the sound of the two male voices conferring quietly seemed to wrap around her like a warm blanket.

She fell asleep almost instantly, feeling truly safe for the first time in years.

Because of Logan.

CHAPTER NINETEEN

Two hours later, Logan leaned back against the bedroom door as he locked it behind Keegan.

He was tired as hell, but he didn't move to go to bed.

Instead, he watched Skylar sleep.

She was still tucked in a ball against the wall, her hands clasped beneath her chin. She looked tiny and vulnerable, but from her deep breathing, he knew she had fallen asleep, trusting him and the Harts enough to let down her guard.

Her hair was spread over the pillow, a glorious array of silken strands.

He'd been looking forward to getting back to the room the entire time he'd been with Brody. Security was his thing. It was part of his job. He loved focusing on details like that. And yet, tonight, his mind had kept drawing him back to the woman waiting for him.

And now he was back, about to climb into bed with her.

He let out his breath. When was the last time he'd fallen asleep with a woman in his arms? He honestly couldn't remember. Maybe never. Spending the night was an intimacy he could never afford, one he would never risk.

And now... Now he had Skylar. The engagement ring sparkled on her hand, and his gaze settled on it.

What would it feel like to put that on her hand for real? For that diamond to tell the world that this woman was his, forever. And just as importantly, that he was hers forever.

He thought about it for a moment, thought about Zane's words earlier in the evening. What would it take for him to make that choice to be with her?

He'd have to quit his job.

His job took him away, off the grid, for weeks and sometimes months at a time. No contact. And each time he left, there was a decent risk he'd be killed. He wouldn't do that to her. Hell, he wouldn't do that to himself. Leave her for months at a time and throw himself in front of a bullet with the same lack of fear that had defined his career?

No chance.

But he had no idea how to survive without his job.

She stirred, and her eyes opened slightly. She saw him, and smiled. "Logan." She sleepily mumbled his name, then her eyes closed again.

He closed his eyes and leaned his head back against the door, letting the moment fill him. The way she'd said his name. Welcoming. Warm. Trusting. Gentle.

No one ever spoke to him like that. Like he was a giant teddy bear that brought beautiful things into people's lives.

Fuck.

He liked it. A lot.

Her eyes opened again, this time with a little more wakefulness. "What's wrong?"

"Nothing. Nothing at all."

"Then come to bed." She sleepily stretched out her arm, resting the back of her hand on the pillow. Her fingers moved, beckoning. "Come."

Come to bed. Anticipation rushed through Logan, and he

let out his breath. How on earth was he going to climb in there and not kiss her? Every single part of his soul was leaning toward her, needing her. Her kindness. Her warmth. Her humor. Just...her. "I'll change. Give me a sec."

He grabbed his bag and headed into the bathroom.

When he was on a high-risk assignment, he always slept in his clothes, in case he needed to get up in a hurry.

When he was home, he slept naked.

Tonight, neither of those felt right. There was no chance he was climbing into that bed in jeans. Naked? As much as the idea tempted him, there was even less chance of that.

He settled for boxer briefs and a tee shirt.

Logan left the bathroom light on dim, then stepped out into the bedroom. Skylar had moved toward the middle of the bed, her arm stretched across his spot. Her eyes were closed again. Had she fallen asleep?

His heart literally started racing as he walked across the room, which made him laugh. He could hunt down the world's nastiest criminals without even breaking a sweat, but climbing into bed with Skylar was rattling him to his core.

"You're getting to me, sweetheart," he whispered as he flipped back the covers and slid beneath them.

He had to move her arm to get in, but the moment he was under the covers, Skylar snuggled against him, her face pressed into the crook of his neck, her hands tucked against his side, her feet wrapped around his calf.

Logan settled his arm around her shoulders, pulling her more closely against him. Then he lay there, staring at the ceiling, listening to her breathing. He was viscerally aware of her bare feet against his leg. Of her breasts against his ribs. Of her breath brushing over his neck. Of her hair tickling his shoulder.

Hell.

This moment felt...perfect. Peaceful. Right. Like his body

and his mind could finally settle. Like if he let down his guard, the nightmares wouldn't come. He could simply...relax.

His job kept him so focused that the darkness couldn't come. He'd thought that was relief.

But Skylar made him so peaceful that the darkness didn't come. It didn't want to come. It was as if she soothed the darkest part of him, simply by her presence. Did Skylar take away the need for his job? Did she allow him to feel? To slow down? To simply...be?

He laughed softly. Maybe for a moment. Maybe for two. But in the end? The darkness always came for him.

"Logan?"

He closed his eyes, his heart turning over at the sound of her voice wrapping around his name. "What's up?"

She didn't answer.

He frowned. "Skylar?"

"I want you to kiss me."

CHAPTER TWENTY

REFLEXIVELY, Logan's arm tightened around Skylar. "I want to kiss you, too." He waited. There was no way in hell he was going to make a move on her after he'd promised he wouldn't. It had to come from her.

"I'm falling for you." Her voice was small. "I don't know how to handle this."

Logan rolled onto his side so he could look at her. Her eyes were open and vulnerable, her gaze searching his. "I don't know how to handle it either," he said honestly. "But... yeah...I'm falling hard for you, too."

Her eyes widened. "What does that mean?"

"I don't know. I just...I don't have experience with how you make me feel. It's new to me." He wanted to trace his fingers along her jaw, but he didn't. He made himself stay where he was. But it was incredibly difficult not to reach for her. "I will always give you the truth, Skylar. I can't make any promises about a relationship or a future. But...you're making me think of things I haven't thought of in my entire life. That's not a promise. That's nothing. Just wanting you to know that you're that special of a person."

She smiled. "You're so careful with me."

"I don't want to hurt you."

"I appreciate that." She put her hand on his chest, flattening it over his pec. "Your heart is racing."

He laughed softly. "That it is. That should tell you something. I'm pretty unflappable."

She took his hand and laid it over her heart.

"Your heart's racing, too." Her tank top didn't protect her skin from his touch entirely. His thumb was on her bare skin, on her sternum. His fingers were also touching bare skin at the front of her shoulder. Her skin was soft. Silken. Warm. Alive. Human. *Her*.

She nodded. "What if we..." She stopped.

"What if we...what?"

She met his gaze. "What if we...go with it?"

He raised his brows, absolutely refusing to make assumptions. She had to be clear, crystal clear before he would make any moves. "Go with it? What does that mean exactly?"

She let out her breath, and he could feel her heart speed up even more. "I'm afraid of men, right? Of trusting?"

He nodded. "I know," he said softly.

She met his gaze. "I trust you," she whispered.

At those three words, something turned over inside him, something glorious, something that rendered him speechless.

"I need to learn to trust again," she said. "You make me *want* to learn to trust, to come out of my little shell I've been hiding in." She traced her finger along the collar of his shirt. "I know that we probably don't have a forever," she whispered. "Maybe that makes this easier. Less scary. Less at stake, you know?"

He caught her hand then, and pressed a kiss to her fingertips. "What do you want from me, Skylar?" He knew what he wanted from her. He wanted everything. He wanted to heal her, honor her, treasure her. He even wanted her to save him.

But there was no way he'd ever put that gargantuan, unmanageable burden on her beautiful shoulders.

She took a breath. "Can we...can we make this..." She waved her diamond ring at him. "Can we make this real while we're in Rogue Valley? In private as well as in public. Just...go all in. Let us heal each other, maybe, a little, if that's possible?" She touched his jaw. "I think you could help me heal, Logan, and I'm pretty sure I can help you."

He froze at the hope that leapt through him. His throat got tight, and suddenly, he couldn't breathe. Was there hope for him? To become like his brothers? To be able to live in society? A life that at least had a semblance of normal?

Embarrassment flooded her face. "Never mind. It was stupid." She started to scoot away.

"No." Logan rolled on top of her. "It wasn't stupid." He kept most of his weight off her, not wanting to crush her, but their bodies were touching from chest to toes. He could feel her ribs moving against his with each breath. Her breasts sandwiched against his chest. Her thighs between his.

She looked embarrassed. "You didn't respond—"

"I was too stunned by the idea that there might be hope for me."

Her face softened, and she looped her arms around his neck. "There's always hope, Logan. For you. For me. Without hope, we have nothing."

"Then I've had nothing." He said it without thinking, then swore. "I didn't mean it like that. I have a great life. I have everything—"

"Shh." She put her finger on his lips to silence him. "Shut up and kiss me."

He didn't move. He was afraid to move. Afraid to unleash the need fighting so hard to get free. "Are you sure?"

"Oh, for heaven's sake. Sometimes women have to do

everything." She tightened her grip on his neck, pulled herself up toward his face, and then kissed him.

Her kiss wasn't tentative. Her kiss was certain, passionate, and raw, everything that was coalescing inside him. With a low groan, he kissed her back immediately, a kiss that spun into a raging torrent of need so quickly that he could barely keep up.

She grabbed his shirt, and he pulled back long enough for her to tug it over his head. She looped it behind his neck with a mischievous sparkle in her eyes. "You're seriously the hottest guy I've ever met."

"I moonlight as an Instagram model. It helps pay my bills." He let her tug him down to her, and kissed her. Deep. Hot. Demanding.

She wrapped the shirt around her fists, locking his head down to where she could reach him without sitting up. He loved that she was taking control. He knew he wouldn't be kissing her that intensely if she wasn't driving it. There was no way he was going to take the chance of accidentally convincing her to do something she didn't want to do.

But if she were driving it? He was all in. *All in.*

Her feet were locked over his thighs, holding him tight against her as she started to move her hips. Desire poured through him, a thunderous torrent of need that seemed to consume him. His muscles literally started shaking with his need for her, and her name kept going through his mind, again and again, and again until—

Swearing, he broke the kiss and rolled onto his back.

Skylar sat up, her brow furrowed. "What's wrong?"

"I want to make love to you," he said, his voice raw and rough. "You awaken need inside me that's so strong, so powerful..." He swore again. "It might be best if we stop. I don't want to tempt you to make a choice you'll regret in the morning." Sweat was beading on his brow. "Go to sleep, Skylar."

She didn't go to sleep.

Instead, she rolled on top of him, sat down on his stomach, and braced her palms on his shoulders. Her hair fell forward, framing her face like a halo. "Logan."

"My dear, sweet Skylar." He reached up and trailed his finger through the golden locks. "It's as soft as I imagined." He watched the ends slide across his hands. "You're like an angel."

Skylar's heart ached at the look of reverence on Logan's face as he played with her hair. It made him look younger. Softer. Vulnerable. Like he'd forgotten to keep up the shields he always wore. He didn't look like an operative. He looked like a man who had a heart so big that it could encompass the world.

Her heart turned over, and she knew she wasn't simply falling for him. She had fallen for him. The whole way. With all her heart. With all her soul. She knew there was no certainty of a future with him. In fact, probably the opposite. She knew she could never be with him and have him gone so much, risking his life, and all that came with his job.

But right now, tonight, she needed what he could give her: a feeling of safety. A circle of protection where she could feel again. Trust. Maybe Logan wouldn't be hers forever, but he would *always* protect her. *Always.* "Logan."

"Skylar."

She smiled at the way he said her name, with that western drawl. With that reverence that always felt so good. "I don't want to go to sleep."

His gaze moved from her hair to her face.

"I want a night of intimacy. Passion. Lovemaking. I want to feel your hands all over my body. I want to lose myself to you, to turn my entire being over to you for safekeeping. I want the whole nine yards with you tonight." She smiled when his eyes darkened. "No regrets in the morning, I promise. I just want you. And if you ask me if I'm sure again, I *will* punch you, so just kiss me, consume me, and lose yourself in me. Got it?"

A slow grin spread across his face, reaching those beautiful eyes of his. "Yes, ma'am. Cowboys are known for their manners, so what choice do I have, but to give you want you want?"

"Exactly."

CHAPTER TWENTY-ONE

LOGAN'S HANDS went to Skylar's hips, to the hem of her tank top. "This needs to come off."

Her pulse quickened as he slowly, deliciously slid it up her ribs. His palms were rough and deliberate as they eased along her skin, following the path of the shirt up her sides, over her arms and then over her head.

He set the tank top on the pillow beside his head, and then put his hands on her hips, his gaze drinking her in as if he were starving for her. She smiled, watching the reverence on his face as he looked at her body.

"You make me feel beautiful," she whispered.

"You are beautiful." His voice was filled with awe as he traced his fingers along her ribs, over her belly, and then gently cupped her breasts. "I feel like this moment is the gift that the universe knew I'd been craving my entire life, but I didn't know it was even possible."

Tears filled her eyes at the wonder in his voice. "How can you make me feel like this?"

"You deserve to feel like you're everything. My every-thing." He sat up, tunneled his fingers through her hair, and then kissed her. A nibble at the corner of her mouth. A kiss at the other corner. A seductive, playful temptation that promised everything she wanted so badly. She wrapped her fingers around his strong wrists, kissing him back, basking in the roughness of his stubble, the warmth of his mouth, his adoring, thorough exploration of her lips.

She expected him to toss her on her back and get down to business, but he didn't. He continued to kiss her as if he had all the time in the world, as if there was nothing he wanted more than to taste her lips, play with her hair, and breathe her in.

The pace gave her space to feel safe. To lean into it. To build trust.

With a contented sigh, she slid her hands down his arms, over his biceps, across his broad shoulders, and then looped them behind his neck. She pulled him in, so her bare breasts brushed against his chest. They both sucked in their breath, then laughed at the same time.

"You make me feel like this is my first time," she admitted. "Being with you feels so electric."

"Back at ya, sweetheart." He kissed the tip of her nose, then drew her in again, kissing her like he never wanted to stop. This time, when her nipples brushed his chest, neither of them laughed.

They just held each other tighter, and the kiss became deeper, more insistent, more consuming.

Need began to pool in her belly, a yearning that echoed his name, again and again, reaching out for this incredible man in her arms.

He locked his arm around her lower back, supporting her, and then kissed her jaw, her neck, along her collarbone. She leaned back into his arm, trusting him to hold her up as his kisses moved across her chest, over the swell of her breasts, toward her nipple.

The moment his lips closed over the peak of her breast, she gasped and gripped his upper arms as sensation rippled through her like a river gaining current. She closed her eyes, surrendering herself to him, to his kiss, to his seduction.

Soon...or maybe it was later...she didn't know. She lost all track of time. They were tangled up with each other, both of them naked, legs entwined, hands, lips, mouths exploring each other. Laughter. Intimacy. Giggling. It was everything. It was perfect.

Logan kept saying her name, whispering it again and again as he worked his way around her body, making sure to kiss every part of her, leaving no part of her untouched, unloved. She'd never been cherished and adored the way Logan loved on her. It was like the blossoming of her own soul into his protective embrace, breathing and expanding in a way she'd never felt safe to do before.

The moment he slid into her, completing the bond between them, Skylar was completely lost to him. Not just in that moment, but forever. She leaned her head back on the pillow, arching into him as he moved inside her, slow, seductive, stoking the flame between them like he was born to be a nurturer of the magic that seared her very soul.

"Skylar." Logan's voice was rough and low, and she opened her eyes.

His hands were braced on either side of her head, his gaze fixed on her face, as if he were etching the moment into his brain for all eternity. She reached up, laying her palm on his cheeks. "My prince," she whispered. "So handsome. So beautiful, in every way."

He turned his head and pressed a kiss into her palm. "My sweet angel."

She could tell he meant it. Words that reached inside her heart and wrapped around her soul, pouring love into the wounds that had been so deep for so long.

Silence fell between them as he quickened his pace, his thrusts becoming deeper, hotter, more consuming. Need began to take over her body, stealing her control away from her mind and sweeping it up into a tornado of passion.

Heat coiled tighter and tighter inside her, gathering strength and fire, until she could barely breathe, barely think. She gripped his shoulders, desperate for him, for more, for the final freefall into his soul---

The explosion was sudden and glorious, hurling her over the precipice into arms that would never fail her. Logan held her tight as he joined her, their bodies and souls melting into a single, blazing inferno together.

The moment it let them go, he collapsed on top of her, burying his face in the crook of her neck, his arm tight around her, as if he would never release her.

Skylar wrapped her arms around his upper back, never wanting to let go. He was heavy on top of her, a glorious, protective weight that cocooned her between his body and the mattress.

"Perfection." His whisper was low, his lips right next to her ear.

She smiled at the reverence in his voice. "I agree. We'll never top that."

He lifted his head and grinned at her. "I'm sure we can top that with enough practice. Just because we're starting off at the top doesn't mean we can't go up from there."

Her smile widened. "You want more?"

His smile faded. "Sweetheart, I want it all."

Her pulse quickened. "What does that mean?"

"I—" He cut himself off, then shook his head. "I don't know."

Her heart dropped, but she managed a smile. "I know. It's complicated. What time is it? Time to get some sleep, don't you think?"

She tried to roll away from him, but he caught her jaw and turned her head toward him. "Skylar."

"What?"

"Don't give up on me. Not yet."

She shrugged. "It's fine, Logan. I know the situation. How could it work? I mean, there's just too much, right?" She managed a smile. "When we were making love, I was thinking, maybe it would be worth it. To have you for a week here or there, in between your assignments. Like whatever I could get would be worth it. But I think..." she took a breath. "I think it would break me in a way I've never been broken before."

He swore under his breath. "Skylar—"

"Not because you're a bad guy, but because I've never loved anyone like I love you. Not even close."

His eyes widened. "Skylar—"

Crap. She hadn't meant to say that! "No." She put her hand on his mouth. "Please, don't say anything. I didn't mean to say that. Just...this is about the moment, the present. It's not more. I know. Please. Let it be. Promise?"

He shook his head in refusal. "Skylar—"

"Dammit, Logan! Can't a girl just fall in love and not have it be a big deal?" She grabbed a pillow and covered his face with it. "Don't say anything. No matter what you say, it will be wrong."

His body started shaking, and she could feel him laughing.

She jerked the pillow away. "You're *laughing* at me right now?"

"I'm laughing because you're fantastic." He grabbed her hands and braced them above her head trapping her. "I have news for you, babe. I'm not that guy that you can boss around. And I'm definitely not that guy who will sit here and nod and say thanks when you announce you love him."

She glared at him. "Seriously, Logan. Shut up. I'm sorry I

messed up our perfect moment by getting squishy, but we can pretend I didn't. Move on."

"No, we can't."

She narrowed her eyes. "Go away."

"No."

"Now."

He started laughing again. "No." He kissed the tip of her nose. "Double no. Triple no. Not until you let me respond to your jaw-dropping declaration."

She paused. "It was kind of jaw-dropping, wasn't it?"

"Yes, ma'am, it was."

She studied his shit-eating grin. "If I let you talk, are you going to give one of those awkward speeches that's supposed to let me down easily, and just winds up ripping out my poor little heart? Because I'll pass on that."

"I'm never awkward. I wasn't even awkward as a teenager."

"And my heart?"

"It belongs where it is, in that beautiful body of yours."

She narrowed her eyes. "If you feel like you need to be a gentleman by giving some acknowledgment of my emotions—"

"I've never been a gentleman. Not even once." He kissed her, a playful, smiling kiss that finally got her to smile.

She sighed. "Fine. Have at it. But note that I'm probably still very fragile and you're stuck with me for the foreseeable future. If you mess this up, it's going to make things incredibly uncomfortable."

He grinned, his eyes sparkling. "All right, then. Don't interrupt me until I'm done. Unless you have questions. Or compliments. Or applause."

"I can't give you a standing ovation because you're on top of me, but other than that, I make no promises." She was getting curious now. He looked so freaking happy that she couldn't believe he was going to eviscerate her heart. He was definitely too nice to delight in raking her soul through the embers of hell. "Talk."

He let his weight settle more deeply on her. "Here's the thing, Skylar. I do believe in love. I've loved my brothers since I can remember. And now my sister. They're my everything."

She nodded. "I know."

"I have also seen them fall in love with their wives, or husband, as in the case with my sister. So, I know it happens."

She bit her lip. "Okay."

"But the love I feel for my siblings...it's not the same thing as a normal, healthy romantic relationship. I don't know how to be like they are. I don't know how to be normal." He paused. "I don't want to feel what's inside me. It's not pretty."

She nodded, her heart sinking. "I understand."

"But with you, I feel, and it's good stuff. I wouldn't ever call anything about me pretty, but how I feel about you?" His smile faded. "It's fucking glorious."

Her heart leapt, but she didn't say anything.

"I won't bring you into my world, into my life and my job," he said. "And I don't know how to leave it, or even if I'd be okay if I lost the protections from myself it gives me. I don't have these answers. I don't know how to solve it."

She pressed her lips together and nodded.

"But I will tell you this," he continued. "I love the living hell out of you, Skylar. I have since the day I met you. It just took this long to figure out what I was feeling, because, as I said, I try like hell not to feel anything. I don't know what to do with the fact I love you, but yeah, you're not alone. I love you right back, probably a hell of a lot more. Where do we go from here? I don't know."

There was no way for Skylar to keep the tears from filling

her eyes, and spilling down her cheeks. His announcement was so unexpected she could barely process it. "Did you just say you love me?"

He grinned, his face softening. "I sure did. Crazy shit, right?"

She started laughing through her tears. "It's ridiculous. We have no business falling in love with each other. We barely even know each other."

"First, that's bullshit. We've known each other for two years, plus we're engaged. So I think love is very reasonable." He paused to kiss her, a thorough, sassy kiss that made her heart want to dance.

"What's second?" she asked when he finally pulled back.

"Second?" He put his hand on her breast. "That's second. Did you learn nothing in middle school?"

"Not second base." She burst out laughing and slapped his hand away. "You said, 'first, that's bullshit.' What's second?"

"Oh, right." He propped himself up on his elbows. "Second, you're absolutely right. It's ridiculous, but pretty fucking awesome, don't you think?"

She nodded. "I was ready for you to let me down easy and give me the friends speech."

He smiled. "We were friends first. Lovers second. Who wants to go backwards to just friends?"

"I don't," she whispered.

"I don't either." He kissed her again, this time more slowly and thoroughly. "But, my dear, sweet Skylar, I meant it when I said I have no idea where to go from here." He pulled back. "I don't know what to do with this unexpected development." He raised his brow. "Any suggestions?"

She shook her head. "No. I don't see how it can work."

"Me either."

For a long moment, they stared at each other, then Logan sighed. "Well, you're smart as hell. I'm resourceful. We're stuck with each other until Eugene is found. That gives us time." His smile gentled, and he tucked her hair gently behind her ear. "Time to figure it out. To get this right."

Get it right? What did that mean? What did *he* mean? She took a breath. "If you could have anything you wanted, Logan, what would it be?"

"With us?"

She nodded.

He shrugged. "That's easy. I'd want this moment to last forever."

She laughed, her heart dancing. "You're such a romantic."

"Who knew?" He raised his brows. "What about you? If you could have anything you wanted, with us, what would it be?"

Her delighted laughter faded, and she bit her lip. God, what a question. Two days ago, she would have said, nothing, nothing, *Nothing*. Ever. Not with him. Not with anyone. All she'd wanted was to be safe in her little workaholic cave, numb and alone. But now? With his family? His kisses? *Him?* She didn't know anymore. Could she go back to her cave? She didn't feel like it. Could she truly open herself to him? She didn't know if she could, or if she were brave enough to even try.

Logan touched her cheek. "Skylar?"

She shook her head. "I don't know anymore, Logan. I...I don't know what I want, and I don't know if I could do it, even if I knew. I feel like...I don't know."

He smiled gently, empathy in his beautiful, dark eyes. "It's all right, sweetheart. We'll figure it out. We have time." He snuggled up beside her and tucked her against his body. "In the meantime, sleep with me. We both need sleep, and I can't think of anywhere I'd rather sleep than with you in my arms." He kissed the top of her head. "I love you, my sweet Skylar."

Tears filled her eyes as she held onto his arms, where they

were wrapped around her so tightly. "I love you, too, Logan," she whispered.

She could tell he fell asleep almost immediately.

She didn't.

Because all she could think about was his statement that they had time. Because they didn't know that. He could get a call in thirty seconds that said Eugene had been caught.

And then they would be out of time.

CHAPTER TWENTY-TWO

LOGAN AWOKE FIRST, tempted into consciousness by the feel of Skylar in his arms.

She was nestled against him, her hair flung across his chest, her breathing deep and even.

Instinct made him want to reach for his phone, to check and see if anything had happened that he needed to know.

But Skylar kept him still.

He wanted to absorb this moment. Examine it. Explore it.

Waking up with a woman wasn't something he thought he'd ever give himself the luxury of doing. And now that he was in that moment...

It felt good.

Really good.

He opened his eyes and stared at the ceiling. Skylar. He'd said he loved her. He would have bet a year's salary that he wouldn't have known love if it hit him in the face. That he couldn't have felt love, other than for his family. He probably would have been willing to stake his life on it, which wouldn't actually have been a big loss.

He'd never considered his life worth all that much. Never

worried much about when his time would come. That was part of what made him good at his job. Wanting to survive, but not worrying about the day when his luck ran out.

But right now, he cared.

He wanted more time with Skylar.

He wanted more mornings with her.

He wanted to keep feeling the way he felt when he was with her.

Quit his job.

He'd have to quit his job.

But...then what? How did he survive that?

He waited, but there were no more answers than there had been last night. A road never travelled was difficult to find.

But he realized he wanted to find it. He fucking wanted to find it. He would find it. He'd find a way—

"Logan?"

His heart leapt at the sound of her voice, and he smiled. "Yes, sweetheart."

"Last night was too much. All of it."

He smiled at the tremor in her voice. He was too well trained in people not to know that she didn't mean it. She was just terrified. "It wasn't," he said gently. "I still love y—"

She put her hand over his mouth and sat up, her blue eyes wide. "I'm freaking out this morning," she said. "I can't get back into a relationship. I can't fall for you. I don't want this. I don't want us." She climbed over him and hurried out of bed. "I dreamed that you left me, and that your family all hated me, and then you got shot and killed by Eugene, who then came after me. My mom had to go to my funeral alone, and she was the only one there, because the CIA had to pretend I wasn't actually dead. She was crying, Logan. All alone. Just like when my dad died, but worse because I wasn't there, and you weren't there, and no one was there."

He swore under his breath. "Listen—"

"No." She grabbed a stack of her clothes from her suitcase. "Look. I love you. I do. But I can't do this. Let's just go back to the original plan." She paused in the doorway to the bathroom, her clothes clutched to her face. Her eyes were wide and scared, like a fawn ready to bolt.

He was halfway out of bed, planning to go to her, but when he saw the fear on her face, he stopped where he was, realizing how close she was to being spooked. "It's okay, Skylar," he said softly. "I won't hurt you."

"I know. I just... Please. Okay?" The panic in her voice made him freeze. "I can't do this again," she whispered. "I can't fall for you and change my life for you. I can't put myself in your hands. I *can't.*"

Son of a bitch. She was absolutely terrified. The sassy, spunky woman who made his heart sing hid a woman who lived in more fear and darkness than he'd ever imagined. What had she been like before her ex had eviscerated her? *Bastard.*

Logan had a sudden, dark desire to go after Skylar's ex. To hurt him. To make him suffer for what he'd done to Skylar. He knew how to make a man feel pain, physical and emotional. He could do more to that man than he could ever imagine coming for him, and the bastard would deserve every second—

The depth of his sudden anger stunned Logan. Use his training against a civilian? Derive satisfaction from hurting someone?

What the *hell?* He sat back down on the bed, shocked by the roiling darkness inside him. Darkness that was like the violence that had ruled his brutal childhood. Jesus. Was he still like his father? After all the work he'd done to move past it? Had allowing himself to love Skylar unleashed the very monster he'd fought against his whole life?

Skylar frowned. "What's wrong?"

He held up his hand as he fought to take a breath. To lock down the beast that had sprung to life so unexpectedly. What the fuck had just happened?

She took a step toward him. "Logan? Are you all right?"

"I don't know." He pulled himself together enough to meet her gaze, giving her a reassuring smile. "I think it's not a bad idea to take a step back."

The words bit at him as he said it, and more anger roared through him, but it wasn't anger at her ex. It was anger at his father for making him who he was and forcing him to step back from the woman who had just won his heart, so he could keep her safe from him. Anger at himself for being so weak that he couldn't defeat the darkness.

Skylar's forehead was furrowed with concern as she watched him, but she nodded. "Okay, then. Agreed." She paused. "Breakfast? I'm starved."

"It's lunchtime, but yeah, we'll go downstairs and eat." He still didn't move. Skylar was too perceptive. She knew damn well he wasn't okay, but instead of calling him out on it like she used to, she was letting it stand.

He missed her challenging him. Making him be better than he was. He missed *Skylar*.

"Okay." She started to close the bathroom door, then stuck her head back out. "Are you sure you're all right? You don't look okay."

And there it was. The Skylar he loved. He raised his gaze to hers. "I'm not okay. At all," he said honestly. "I don't want to talk about it. But I still love you, and that won't change, so you don't need to question that. Ever."

Her face softened, but she shook her head. "You're incorrigible. You need to stop."

"Loving you? You want me to stop loving you?" He

couldn't keep the incredulity out of his voice. "Because that's impossible."

"No. Stop telling me you do. I need to go back into my cave." Desperation tinged her voice. "Please, Logan. Let me."

He held his palms up in surrender. He wanted to go to her so badly right now. Pull her into his arms. Fix what was falling apart between them. But he couldn't. Not until he knew who he would become if he let himself love her and all that accompanied it, like quitting his job, which he *had* to do if he went all in on this. "All right," he said, somehow managing to keep his tone even. "Space it is."

"Okay." She pressed her lips together, hesitating, as if she wanted to say more. But she didn't. She just closed the door, leaving him alone.

He didn't leap to get dressed.

He just bent his head, rested his forehead in his palms, and cursed his legacy.

～

Skylar was trying.

She really was.

But it wasn't working. An hour later, Skylar could no longer deny the truth that sleeping with Logan and trading "I love yous" with him had not only messed up her relationship with him, but it had also affected her interaction with his family.

Ryder and Zoey were teaching young Liam how to paint, while Frank, Liam's grandfather, still recovering from a broken leg, sat at the breakfast table, chatting with Brody and Keegan. Logan was cleaning up from lunch. Everyone was being nice and friendly, but the tension in the room was palpable, no doubt feeding off the tension between her and Logan.

She was such an idiot. How could she have messed this up? She watched Logan at the kitchen counter scrubbing the frying pan he'd used to grill her a sandwich. He kept looking out the window, and she knew he was surveying the landscape to make sure they were safe.

She wanted to go to him, to hug him, to bury herself in his arms, to let him make her feel safe again. To hear him say the words she'd banned him from saying.

But every time she thought about doing it, tension gripped her. She was so on edge.

"Hey, Keegan," Logan said suddenly. "You still having issues with the design of the bakery?"

Keegan, who had just come in from a tour of the outside of the house nodded. "We fired the architect. He just wasn't getting it right."

Logan nodded at Skylar. "My fiancée is a brilliant architect. Why don't you have her look at the plans? Maybe she can see something."

His fiancée. The words turned over in her belly.

"Damn. Why didn't I think of that?" Keegan looked at her expectantly. "Would you take a look at the plans? That would be great."

Skylar felt herself relax slightly. This was a world she felt comfortable in. "Yes, sure. I'd be happy to."

"Great. I'll be right back with the plans." Keegan jogged out of the room.

Brody started clearing the large dining table. "Let's spread them out here."

Skylar jumped up and started clearing placemats, while Ryder and Zoey moved Liam's painting gear to the family room area. Logan moved the bowl of fruit off the table and wiped it down. His hip bumped hers as he wiped it, and her heart leapt at the touch.

He said nothing, but his hand brushed across her lower

back as he walked past, an intimate touch that was too subtle for it to be for public consumption. It had just been for her.

A few minutes later, Keegan was back, and the plans were out on the table. As soon as Skylar saw them, her focus kicked in. She leaned on the table between Brody and Keegan, listening as they explained their goals, what they'd done so far, and what the problem was.

The plans were good, but she could quickly see the issue they'd run into. She bent over, explaining to Keegan and Brody, when she felt Logan's gaze on her. She looked up, and saw him leaning against the opposite counter, arms folded, watching her with a smile.

She realized then that he'd suggested showing the bakery plans intentionally, knowing that doing design work would help her settle, like it had yesterday with Leila. She smiled. "Thank you," she mouthed to him.

He nodded and tapped his heart with two fingers.

Heat flushed her cheeks, but before she could start to freak out again, Keegan asked her a question, drawing her attention back to the designs. She shot one last glance at Logan, then let herself be drawn back into the discussion, into the world that she knew, in which she felt in control, at peace, and competent.

And happy.

Design work hadn't made her feel happy in quite a while, but standing there in the kitchen with Keegan and Brody, helping shape their dreams felt deeply satisfying. This was why she'd become an architect. To bring dreams to life. Not to design impersonal office buildings.

This was what she loved. And Logan had given it to her.

What was she going to do?

CHAPTER TWENTY-THREE

LOGAN WAS LEANING against the stove, studying Skylar as she went over the designs with the Harts. She clearly wasn't relaxed, but she was focused and calmer. Her work did the same thing for her that his did for him. Took them both away from the baggage that haunted them.

No wonder she worked all the time. It was the same reason he did. Because being focused on work was better than dealing with life.

"You look cranky." Frank, Liam's grandpa limped over to him, his cane the only legacy from the car accident that had broken his leg not too long ago. "Jealousy's not a good look for a marriage, Logan."

He smiled at the older man. "I'm not jealous. I'm glad they're helping her relax. I'm just thinking."

Frank leaned against the counter and folded his arms. "No good thoughts make a man have that expression on his face. What's going on? Trouble already?"

He glanced at Frank. The older man's gray hair was a sharp contrast to his dark skin, and the wrinkles around his eyes were ones of a lifetime of weariness, not laughter. "No trouble. Just the complications of life."

"We make life complicated," Frank said. "But it's pretty basic. Comes down to one thing, really."

Logan raised his brows. "What's that?"

"Love."

"Ah. Love. Seems like that's pretty complicated actually."

"Not so much." Frank braced his hands on the counter, letting it take some of the weight off his injured leg. "When you get a chance to love, you love with all your might until it's gone. Then you love what you still have."

Logan recalled that Frank's son, Liam's dad, had been killed in the military. As far as he knew, it was only Frank and Liam. He didn't know what had happened to Liam's mom, or if Frank had ever been married, but he knew that right now, Liam was all Frank had. "Liam's a good kid."

They both looked over at Liam as he worked with Ryder and Zoey. "That he is. He's my shining light." Frank's voice was rough and emotional. "And now we've got Ryder and Zoey. And the Harts. And the Stocktons." He glanced at Logan. "The day my wife died, I thought I couldn't go on, but I had a son to raise, so I focused on him. When my son was killed, I had Liam."

Logan met his gaze. "I'm deeply sorry for your losses, Frank."

"Thank you." Frank inclined his head. "But I'm all right. Love keeps us going, and makes us whole again."

Logan's gaze returned to Skylar. "That assumes you were once whole to begin with."

"I know about your past," Frank said softly. "Ryder's told me about it."

Logan's jaw flexed. "It's fine. It's in the past."

"Yes, it is. You gotta let that shit go and stop letting it define you."

"It's not that easy."

"Nope. But all you need to do is decide you deserve it. If you never decide that, you'll never be free."

"I'm free when I'm working." Logan watched as Skylar laughed at something Keegan said. God, she was beautiful.

"You're not free until you can sit in the moment with someone you love and let yourself be happy. As long as you keep running, you're not free."

"I'm not running. I like my job. It fulfills me." He paused. "I need it, like Skylar needs hers."

Frank grunted. "Do you think you deserve to be happy, Logan? To sit in the moment and be happy?"

Logan looked over at him. "I tried that, and it let the monster out."

Sadness flickered in Frank's eyes. "Emotions don't make you a monster, Logan. They make you human. Even ones that scare you."

He thought of the anger he'd felt over Skylar's ex. Frank was right. It had scared him to feel that much anger, to feel like he could be his father. "You know us. My brothers. Our history. You know the poison that he poured into us. You know that, right?"

Frank nodded. "I do."

"If you had a daughter, would you let her fall in love with one of us? Even knowing what you know?"

Frank met his gaze. "If I had a daughter, there's no one I'd rather have her fall for than a Stockton man."

Logan was stunned by Frank's words. He could tell the older man meant it. A man who'd seen so much, lost so much, loved so much, would trust his own daughter with a Stockton. "Thank you," he said gruffly. "I can tell you mean that."

Frank smiled. "You Stocktons are good men. I've always known that."

Logan folded his arms over his chest, watching Skylar.

What if he was good enough for her? What if he did deserve her? What if he was who she needed?

I want that. I want her. I want forever with her.

The realization settled in him with complete rightness, and he knew suddenly, with absolute conviction what he wanted. He wanted the life he'd never let himself yearn for, and he wanted it with Skylar. But... "How do I do it?" he asked. "I don't know how to be normal, to function without my job." He paused. "To be enough for her. To get her to trust me. To be worthy of that trust." He paused. "To heal her heart again."

Frank smiled. "As long as you want to, you'll figure it out." Frank clapped him on the shoulder. "Love, my boy. Follow love and you'll be all right."

Love. Logan grinned as he watched Skylar. *Love.* He'd never thought it would be for him, but it felt right. So right. They both had barriers, big ones, but he was a master strategist. He could find a way. He *had* to find a way.

At that moment, his phone dinged. He glanced down and saw a text. *Call me. Now.*

Adrenaline pulsed through Logan. "I'll be right back." He was already dialing as he strode out of the room. He stopped in the front hall, out of earshot, but still able to see Skylar. The phone rang twice before Director Hamilton answered. "What's up, Sir?" Logan didn't bother with preamble.

"Skylar's work computer system was hacked. Her mother's address in Vermont was accessed."

Alarm shot through Logan, and Skylar looked up at him suddenly, as if she felt his tension. "Get her mom out of there. Now."

"I called the local police. They have her at the police station."

"She's not safe there." Logan swore, and Brody and

Keegan both looked up, their eyes narrowing when they saw him pacing.

"I know. I have a team going into collect her—"

"How do you know they're safe? There might be an internal leak." Logan swore again, trying to think. They needed to get Skylar's mom out of there and safe. Where was safe? He looked across the house at the Harts watching him, and he knew where safe was.

Safe was with him. "Hang on." He gestured at Brody. "I need you."

Brody immediately headed over, but Keegan and Skylar followed right behind him. Shit. He didn't want to bother Skylar, but he didn't have time to argue. He gave up trying to be secretive. "Brody, how fast can you get your plane to Vermont?"

"Vermont?" Skylar's hand went over her heart. "Is my mom okay?"

"She's fine." Logan put his arm around her to reassure her, but he needed to focus on solving the problem first. "Brody?"

"We were planning to leave today, so she's all fueled up and ready to go. Why?"

"Skylar's mom's address has been compromised. We need to get her out of there. I want to bring her here."

"I'll go." Keegan was already pulling out his phone. "Brody, you stay here. I'll get Skylar's mom. What's her name?"

"Abby Jones. But—"

"I'm sending a plane," Logan told his boss. "It's leaving in —" He raised his brows at Keegan.

"Thirty minutes. What airport should we land at?"

Logan handed his phone to Keegan. "Talk to my boss directly. It's faster."

Keegan took the phone and turned away, while Logan

turned to Skylar, whose face was ashen. "They have her at the police station. They'll keep her there until the plane arrives."

"The police station?" She frowned. "Will she be safe there?"

He couldn't lie to her. "Probably."

"Probably." She stared at him. "Logan, she's all I have—"

Keegan handed the phone back. "We're all set." He grabbed his keys. "I'll be in touch. Be back soon." He gave Skylar a quick hug. "She'll be fine, Skylar. I've called a friend I have in the area. He's going to meet her at the police station and make sure she's safe. He'll take her out of there if he thinks it's not." He met her gaze. "He's ex-military. He's very, very good."

Something turned over inside Logan, an unexpected appreciation for the help. He knew the Harts considered themselves family now, but it still was unexpected. "Thank you." His voice was gruffer than he intended.

Skylar clung tight to Logan. "Yes, thank you, Keegan. I appreciate it so much."

"We got this. Family sticks together." He winked at her. "I'll be in touch." Then he grabbed his car keys and literally sprinted out the door. Logan could hear him running to his truck.

He took his phone back. "Is my identity compromised?" he asked his boss.

"Not that we know of," his boss said. "But stay on alert. I expect he'll go after Skylar's mom first as a hostage. I'll be in touch."

Logan hung up, his adrenaline racing. He had contacts he could call, but he didn't dare. He had no idea who was secure. He could only hope that Keegan's friend was as good as he'd said.

"I know who he called," Brody said. "No one will get to your mother, Skylar. He'll take her off grid if he needs to."

She nodded, but she looked like she was going to be sick. "Okay." She took a deep breath. "Should we go back to the drawings then, Brody?"

Brody raised his brows in surprise, but nodded. "Sure, let's do it."

Logan frowned as he watched the two of them return to the table and start talking about the plans for the bakery. Skylar was tense, and her hands were shaking. She was trying to lose herself in work, but there was no way she could focus.

Work could help only so much.

How could he help her?

Ryder came up beside him. "What's going on?" he asked quietly.

Logan filled him in, finishing with, "It's going to be a tense few hours for her until we get her mom in the air and on her way here."

"Yeah, it will be." Ryder watched Skylar. "I would lose my mind if Zoey were in danger and I had to sit around and wait."

"Yeah." Logan was feeling pretty stressed even though it wasn't Skylar. Her mom was her world, which made her that important to him.

His phone rang again, and he swore. Brody and Skylar looked up sharply as he pulled it out. He looked at the caller ID. "It's Zane," he said. But he didn't relax. Was something happening at the ranch? "What's going on?"

"Leila's having a tough morning."

It took Logan a moment to focus his brain on the teenager that Skylar had spent the day working on the float with. "What's wrong?"

"I'm not sure. She won't talk to us." Zane paused. "You think Skylar would want to come by? Hang out with her for a bit? Skylar seems to help her."

Logan looked at Skylar's trembling hands, and suddenly,

he knew what to do. He knew what had helped him, and his brothers, as kids, when nothing else would. There was only one thing that ever truly took away the darkness, a solace he'd walked away from so long ago, and forgotten about. Would it help Skylar and Leila? It might. "Actually, I have a better idea."

He told Zane what he was thinking, and his brother agreed. "It's perfect. I'll make some calls." He hung up and Ryder was grinning at him.

"It's a great idea. Horses are magical."

"You think?"

"Yeah. It'll be good. You want us to come?"

Logan appreciated the offer. "No, I want it to be just us today. I think it's what we need."

"You got it." Ryder headed back to his family as Logan walked back to the kitchen table, where Skylar and Brody were watching his approach. "Zane called. Leila's having a tough morning."

Skylar's brow furrowed in concern. "She is? What's wrong?"

"She won't talk to anyone. Zane asked if you could come by and hang out with her."

"Of course." Skylar put down the plans, then frowned. "Is it safe?"

"We'll make it safe."

"All right, then. Let's go." She smiled, but it didn't reach her eyes. The only thing in her eyes was fear. Fear for her mother.

He was going to try to change that.

He was going to see if either of them had a chance to survive outside the numbness of their work. Not just her. Him as well. Because if he couldn't, there was no future for them...and he knew it would break him to lose her.

This had to work. For her. For him. For them.

CHAPTER TWENTY-FOUR

CHASE HAD six horses saddled in front of his house when they pulled up. All of the horses were loaded with saddlebags. Five had no riders, but there was a cowboy with a hat on the sixth one.

Logan swore under his breath. "Son of a bitch. I can't believe he's here."

"Who is that?" Skylar asked. He was too far away to see clearly, but he looked familiar.

"My brother." Logan parked the truck and the cowboy rode up to the window.

He leaned down and grinned, flashing Logan and Skylar a smile that looked stunningly familiar, because he looked almost exactly like Logan. He had the same Stockton jaw and cheekbones as all the brothers, but this man had the same skin tone and dark eyes as Logan.

"Heard you needed a little backup."

"I do." Logan got out of the truck and clasped Quintin's hand in the kind of handshake that was more like a man hug than an actual handshake. He was grinning broadly. "When did you get here?"

"About twenty minutes ago. Chase gave me a heads up." He grinned at Skylar as she got out of the truck on her side. "And you must be the woman I'm hearing about. You really think this guy's worthy of your time?"

She smiled at the warmth in his voice. "I do. You must be Quintin."

He tipped his hat. "Last time I checked, that was how it seemed." He nodded at Brody as the Hart brother got out of his truck, which he'd parked behind Logan's. "Good to see you, Brody."

"Always a pleasure." Brody reached up to Quintin and they did the same handshake. Powerful. Bonded. "You coming riding with us today?"

"Riding?" Skylar raised her brows. "We're going riding?"

"Yep. Riding was our only salvation most days," Logan said. "I thought it might help Leila." His gaze settled on her face, and she saw the concern in his eyes. "And you."

She managed a smile. "I'll be fine when my mom is safe."

"She's safe," Brody said. "Our friend will make sure of it. He'll escort her all the way here." He handed her his phone. "Check it."

She looked down and saw a text. Logan leaned over her shoulder, reading along with her. *Got her. Police station wasn't safe. Will keep her off the grid until plane arrives.* While she was reading it, another text came in. *If her daughter is half as hilarious as she is, I'm going to marry her daughter when I get to Wyoming.*

Skylar burst out laughing as tears suddenly filled her eyes. "If my mom's giving him shit, she's all right." She handed the phone back, her heart feeling much lighter. "Who is the guy who has her?"

"A friend with skills." Brody started to tuck his phone in his pocket, but Logan held out his hand.

"Can I borrow that?" Logan asked.

Brody grinned. "Be nice."

"I'm always nice." Skylar leaned in, watching as Logan typed. *She's already marrying someone else, but you will definitely get an invite to the wedding for keeping her mom safe.*

She started laughing as Logan handed the phone back. "Male posturing in the middle of a crisis?"

"It's not a crisis," Logan said. "We have it covered. Just wanted to make sure he doesn't get the wrong idea." He looked past Skylar. "Here comes Leila. You guys ready?"

Skylar looked over as Leila approached. She was walking beside Zane, but her head was down and her shoulders were slumped. She was wearing a red cowboy hat, jeans, and red cowboy boots that were well-worn. She looked like she belonged on the ranch...the ranch that didn't belong to her.

Skylar's heart turned over at her visible dejection. "Leila!"

The teenager looked up, and her face brightened. "Skylar!" She looked at Zane. "Is she coming? You didn't tell me she was coming."

"It was a surprise." Zane's voice was gentle, but Skylar knew his truth. He'd been afraid to get Leila's hopes up in case Skylar hadn't come.

She bunched her fists in determination. She wasn't going to be one of the people in Leila's life who let her down. "Do you know how to ride?" she asked. "I haven't ridden in years."

Leila's smile lit up her face as she ran toward them. "I've been learning."

"Well, let's go!" The men all mounted up, after making sure Skylar and Leila were all set.

"You've got enough food for all day," Chase said as he stepped back. "Enjoy."

Logan grinned as he rode up beside them. "You guys good?"

"Wait!" Mira came running out of the house with an off-white cowboy hat. "It's a sunny day. You'll need protection."

She handed the cowboy hat to Skylar. "Now you look like you fit."

Skylar grinned as she settled the hat on her head. She was wearing hiking boots, but the hat made her feel like she matched her escorts, all of whom were pure cowboy. "Perfect."

"Let's go, then." Quintin turned his horse toward the west, and set off at a slow lope.

"Yay!" Leila beamed at Skylar, and then headed out after him.

Logan raised his brows. "Do you need a refresher?"

"I got it." She patted her horse, and then urged the mare forward. The palomino responded, moving into a lope that was so comfortable it felt like she was riding on a couch. Logan immediately fell in beside her, and Brody pulled up the rear, staying about twenty-five yards behind. "What's my horse's name?"

"That one is named Meg, I think."

"Meg?" It was perfect. She leaned down and patted Meg on the neck. "Let's go, girl."

Once they were clear of the farm, she opened up the mare's strides, catching up to Leila. "You ready?"

"Yes!" Leila was beaming at her, her face flushed with delight. "Let's do it!"

The two of them took off with a whoop. Still in the lead, Brody looked back over his shoulder at them, waved his hat, and then increased his pace. He moved off to their right, and Quintin drifted to the left, flanking them from a distance. She could see the glint of sunlight off Quintin's gun, and she assumed Brody was also armed.

Three cowboy bodyguards. Empty plains as far as she could see. She was safe right now, she realized. Truly safe. And now that the Hart's friend had taken her mom into hiding, her mom was safe, too. She could relax.

Logan rode up beside Leila, grinning. "It's glorious, isn't it?" he shouted over the pounding hooves.

"Amazing!" Skylar had ridden around a ring at a neighbor's barn. She'd taken a few trail rides through the woods. But she'd never had the experience of riding across open plains that seemed to last forever. She held out her arms and raised her face to the sky. "Freedom," she shouted.

Leila laughed and did the same thing. "Freedom," she screamed. "I'm free!"

Skylar couldn't believe how amazing it felt to be riding. To feel the power of the animal beneath her. The pounding hooves on the plains was like a mantra of power and peace, of freedom and speed, of glorious connection with the earth and nature.

"Freedom," Logan bellowed, raising his arms like they had.

For a moment, the three of them rode side by side, arms out, heads back in unison, breathing in the moment.

It was perfect. Skylar had never felt so free, so happy, so at peace.

"This is the best," Leila said as they raced across the plains. "Zane and Taylor never let me go this fast. I'm always in charge of the younger campers."

Skylar smiled. "I like speed. I won't stop you."

Leila's gaze slid to Logan, clearly wondering if he was going to tell her to slow down, but he grinned. "I need this as much as you do, Leila. Today is about no rules. You lead the way. It's your day."

She shrugged. "I don't know where to go."

Logan got a thoughtful look on his face. "I have an idea. You guys up for an adventure?"

Leila's face lit up. "Yes!"

Skylar grinned. "Of course."

"Then follow me." He raised his hand, gesturing to Brody

and Quintin. Their bodyguards immediately turned to the south. Quintin took off in a gallop, riding on ahead, while Brody stayed with them. "Quintin's going to make sure it's clear." His gaze landed on Leila. "I think you'll like this."

She smiled up at him, the faintest bit of hero worship gleaming in her eyes. "I can't wait."

Logan smiled over at Skylar, and her heart leapt at the warmth on his face. He was so handsome. And he looked so happy. True happiness. She'd never seen that look on his face before. "You look happy," she said.

He looked surprised at her comment, then a thoughtful expression came over his face. "You know, I am." His smile widened. "Let's go! Follow Quintin!"

And off they went.

They rode for almost an hour, slowing down to a more leisurely pace to rest the horses from time to time. Leila had cheered up, and the vibrance of her soul was riveting. She was so smart, so talented, and funny.

Skylar adored her, and Logan was wonderful with her. The two of them already had a bond as well, and she could almost see Leila sitting taller and shining brighter as the ride went on.

It was glorious in all ways.

"Here we go!" Logan reined in, and Skylar and Leila stopped beside him. They were on a hillside above a river that was wide and slow, drifting gently. Quintin was riding toward them along the opposite riverbank. "You guys ready?"

"Are we going swimming?" Leila asked.

"Not us. Come on." Logan led the way down the embankment, and Skylar gestured for Leila to go next. She followed behind them, her mare picking her way down the slope with easy surefootedness.

Logan reached the edge of the river, but he didn't stop.

He and his horse plunged right in, spraying water everywhere. "Come on!"

Leila shrieked with joy and urged her horse in. The bay trotted right in without hesitation, the water splashing up around his hooves.

Logan was already up to his horse's fetlocks in the water, a huge grin on his face. Excitement rushed through Skylar, and she urged Meg into the water. The palomino nickered with delight, tossing her head as the water splashed. The water swished all around them, and Skylar laughed as Meg put her head down to drag her nose through the river.

"Keep the horses moving forward," Logan said. "Sometimes they like to roll in the water." As he said it, Skylar saw the legs of his horse buckle. "Logan—"

He jumped off a split second before his horse hit the water, snorting with delight as he rolled onto his back, kicking his feet in the air. Leila shrieked with laughter as Logan grabbed for the reins, trying to stay out of the way of the flailing hooves, clearly not totally trying to make his horse stop.

By the time he got his horse back on his feet, Logan was completely soaked. Water was dripping from his hat, his shirt was plastered to his body, and his face was glistening with water. His saddle was drenched, and his horse was delightedly wet.

Quintin was laughing at him. "You've lost your touch, bro. I don't think we can call you a cowboy anymore. You're a city slicker."

"Never. I was distracted by these two amazing gals." He swung back into the saddle, a huge grin on his face. "I was always the one who let my horse roll. Ol' Skip used to always give me grief for coming back with a wet saddle."

"Chase will yell at you," Quintin said.

Logan laughed. "No, he won't. He'll hope that it was so fun that I'll never leave the ranch again!"

Skylar's heart caught at his words. Never leave the ranch? "You mean move here? To Rogue Valley? Would you do that?"

What if he moved back here? And she was stuck in Boston? She'd never see him again. There would be no time to see what could happen with her across-the-hall neighbor when this was over and they were back home.

Leila's face lit up. "You'd move back here? Really?"

Logan's smile faded as he looked at both of them. "No, I —" He stopped suddenly, a surprised look on his face. "I don't know."

He might. He might move back. Skylar could see it in his eyes. He was thinking about it.

Suddenly, the joy of the day was gone.

Logan met her gaze, and he frowned. "You want to ride upriver?" he asked Leila.

"Yes!" She turned her horse and started walking.

"One word of warning," he said. "Don't come out here alone. This river is prone to flash floods, and not all parts of it have a sandy bottom that the horses can navigate easily. Ask one of us to go if you want to come out here."

Leila nodded. "Sure." She clucked to her horse and they headed upriver.

Up on the banks, Quintin and Brody followed along, being their guardians.

As Leila moved ahead, Logan fell in next to Skylar. "What happened to your smile?" he asked. "Not having fun?"

She bit her lip and focused on her mare's head. "Would you...would you really move back here?"

"I don't know. I'm happy today, and that feels good."

She nodded.

They rode in silence for a few minutes, until he spoke again. "Would you consider living here?"

Her heart leapt, and she looked over at him. "Are you serious?"

"Dead serious. I love you, Skylar. I want to find a way to make this work. This. Us. Life. I need to know if you would ever consider living here."

She looked toward the teenager riding ahead. To Brody and Quintin on the banks. To the man riding next to her. "Give up my job? My life? To move here?"

He nodded, watching her face.

A part of her yearned to say yes, to throw herself into this magical world of horses and family. "I'm scared to even date," she said. "But to give up everything to take a chance on us?"

She wanted to be that woman. She wanted to be that brave. But what if she did, and then everything fell apart? If she moved out here, she would be completely dependent on Logan and his family. She would have nothing left of her own. All she had would be his to take away whenever he felt like it.

She looked over at Logan, at his beautiful, dark eyes watching her so carefully. God, she was head over heels for this man. So lost for him that it was so tempting for her to throw everything into him and go all in...but she couldn't. Even if he was the man she thought he was, trustworthy with all his heart, she never wanted to be so lost and without anything of her own ever again. "I can't," she finally said. "I just can't. I'm sorry."

Regret flickered over his face, but he nodded. "I understand. Stop for a sec."

They both reined in their mounts. The moment they stopped, he moved his horse closer to hers and leaned over, kissing her softly. "I love who you are, Skylar. Never apologize."

His kiss was beautiful and perfect, and she leaned into him, needing him, his kiss, his love. She knew how much he loved her. She could feel it in his words, his kiss, and his touch.

But the shield around her heart wouldn't come down.

"Oh, come on," Leila shouted. "Stop kissing! Let's go!"

Logan pulled back with a grin. "Kids," he teased, brushing his thumb over Skylar's cheek. "We never get a moment alone anymore. It's tough being parents." He winked at her, then raised his voice. "Coming, Leila!"

Skylar watched him as he rode ahead, then laughed when he leaned down, dragged his hand through the water, and then splashed Leila.

She shrieked with laughter, then splashed him back. "Come on, Skylar! Let's team up against him."

Skylar made a decision. Maybe they didn't have a forever. Maybe she was too broken to take advantage of the gift that the universe was trying to give her. But they did have this moment, this afternoon, this oasis of laughter, fun, and togetherness.

She wasn't going to ruin it with "what ifs." She was going to live to the fullest that she could, just like her dad had always taught her. "Coming!" She urged Meg forward as Logan leaned down to use his hat to scoop up the water. "Logan, you are so going down! Girl power will triumph—"

Logan caught her square in the face with a blast of water from his hat.

Leila doubled over with laughter. "Make him pay for that," she shouted.

Skylar grinned and whipped her hat off her head. "The game is *on*."

It was the best day of her life.

CHAPTER TWENTY-FIVE

SKYLAR WAS STILL FEELING happy when they rode back to the barn and took care of the horses. Logan and Leila showed her what to do, and by the time she finished taking care of Meg, she was completely in love with the mare. Quintin and Brody were charming, and it was an amazing time. Brody had kept her updated when her mom had boarded the Hart plane and gotten safely airborne, so her heart had been light all day.

After taking care of the horse, when they walked out of the barn, Skylar saw a blue pickup truck in front of Chase's house. It looked familiar. "Is that Keegan's?"

"It is," Brody said. "I told him to meet us here."

"Keegan's here? *My mom's here?*" As Skylar spoke, the passenger door to the truck opened, and her mom stood on the running board and waved, a broad smile on her face. Her gray hair was in two braids, and she was wearing her favorite Vermont sweatshirt.

"Mom!" Tears burst free and Skylar broke into a run.

Her mom leapt down and caught her in a hug and Skylar clung to her mom, unable to stop crying. She'd thought she was being strong, but seeing her mom made all her defenses crumble. "I was so scared I'd never see you again," she whispered. "I thought I was going to die and then I thought you were going to die and—"

"Shh!" Her mom stroked her hair, as she used to do so many years ago when Skylar was a little girl. "It's okay, sweetheart. Everything's okay." She pulled back and smiled at Skylar, brushing her thumbs over her cheeks to wipe away the tears. "We're good, baby."

"I know." She took a deep breath, trying to gather herself. "You're okay? Everything went okay?"

Her mom grinned. "It was the most fun I've had in ten years. The police show up at the farm, throw me into the squad car, and whisk me off to the station. Then a handsome young man with more guns than you can shake a stick at literally kidnaps me out of the station." She beamed at her. "Then I get to ride a private jet back to Wyoming with two armed escorts? It made me realize how damned boring I'd let my life get!"

Skylar stared at her mom in surprise. "You weren't scared?"

"Sure, I was. That was the fun part." As her mom spoke, Keegan got out of the truck.

The back door of the cab opened, and a man Skylar didn't recognize got out. He was well over six feet, with beautiful brown skin and a predatory grace that made her glad that he was on their side.

Her mom beamed at him, trotted over to him with more pep than she'd had in years, and tucked her arm through his. "Skylar, I'd like you meet Falcon." She winked. "He has an actual name, but he claims he has forgotten it over the years."

Emotion clogged Skylar's throat. When her dad died, a part of her mom's spirit had died along with him. The light had left her eyes for so long that Skylar had thought she'd never get her mom back...but the woman grinning at her was the mom she remembered, the mom she used to have.

Falcon grinned at Skylar, his face breaking into a smile that was much warmer than she would have expected. "I hear you're already getting married, so I'm going to marry your mom instead. Hope that's okay."

"What?" Skylar's mom shrieked. "You're getting married?"

Skylar grimaced. She'd forgotten about that. "Ahh..."

Logan stepped up beside her and put his arm around her shoulders. "Logan Stockton, ma'am. I love Skylar with all my heart, and I'll spend my life making her happy."

"Oh..." A knowing look came over Abby's face. "You're the man who lives across the hall from her. When did you two start dating?"

"Recently," Logan said. "But it's been a long time coming."

"It sure has. It's about damned time. Skylar would glow and get all giggly every time she ran into you."

Skylar felt her cheeks heat up. "I didn't get giggly."

"Of course you did." Skylar's mom beamed at Logan. "My name is Abby Jones. I can't even tell you how delighted I am that you got through Skylar's walls." She held out her arms. "Lay one on me, Logan!"

Logan grinned and walked over to Abby. Her mom swept him up in her arms, and held tight.

After a brief hesitation, Logan hugged her back just as fiercely. When Abby finally let him go, he pulled back only slightly. "I swear to you I'll take care of her."

Abby's face softened and she patted Logan's cheek. "I can tell. Welcome to the family." She beamed at Skylar. "Where am I staying? I want to unpack. Falcon snuck me home to get my stuff. You won't believe how capable he is. It's so impressive."

"I'll take her back to the River House," Keegan said. "All her stuff is already in my truck."

"Hang on!" Chase walked out his door. "It's dinnertime. Why don't you all stay? Ryder and Zoey are already here." He walked up to Skylar's mom. "I'm Logan's brother, Chase. I'd like to welcome you officially to the family, Abby."

Her mom smiled. "Well, thank you."

Chase held out his arms. "Hug it out?"

She laughed and let the cowboy hug her. "I like this family, Skylar, but you're in so much trouble that I had no idea you and Logan had gotten past gawking at each other in the elevator."

Skylar released a long breath. It was fantastic her mom was so happy, but she hated that it wasn't real. Would she lose her mom again when Abby learned none of it was real? The stakes were getting higher and higher.

"May I escort you inside?" Chase held out his arm, and Abby laughed and set her hand in his elbow.

"You'll have to fight me for her." Falcon held out his elbow for her other hand, which she tucked into the crook of his arm. "I saw her first."

Abby's laughter echoed like music as she disappeared into the house with the men.

Skylar stared after her. "I haven't heard her laugh like that since my dad died. It's incredible. I thought...I thought I'd never have my mom back again. Not like that."

Logan put his arm around her. "She reminds me of you. That sparkle in her eyes is vibrant. I can see where you get your sass."

"She's amazing," Leila whispered, her voice awed. "She's just like you."

Skylar turned to see Leila with her arms wrapped around her torso. "She's pretty special."

Leila looked over at her and seemed to pull herself back. "Okay. I gotta get back to the dorm. Thanks for today. It was fun." She turned and started trudging back toward the barn.

Skylar glanced at Logan, who was frowning. "Leila," he called out. "Come join us for dinner."

She looked back at him. "I can't. I have to do camp stuff."

"Hang on." He pulled out his phone and dialed. "Zane? I want Leila to join us for dinner at Chase's. Cool?" He paused. "Perfect." He hung up. "It's all set."

Her face lit up. "Really?"

"Come on," Brody said. "I'll take you in." He held out his arm to escort her, like Falcon and Chase had done with Abby.

Leila grinned. "Well, all right then." She put her hand through his arm, and then started giggling when Keegan jogged over and held out his other arm. She put her hand through his arm, and was still giggling as they escorted her up the stairs into the house.

Skylar started to follow them, but Logan caught her hand. "One sec?"

Her heart leapt at the feel of his hand around hers, and she let him turn her back. "What?"

Logan gently tugged her closer to him, then slid his hand behind her neck and kissed her.

Skylar sighed and leaned into him, unable to stop herself from breathing him in. She loved his kisses so much. The kiss quickly turned hot, and she melted into him, loving the feel of his body against hers.

He grinned and pulled back. "I've been wanting to do that all day. When this is over, I'm taking you back to that river alone, and we're going skinny dipping."

Desire rushed through her at the idea, but she tried to ignore it. "When this is over, we're going back to Boston. Me to my job, you to yours. There won't be any more rivers."

"Maybe."

She frowned. "Maybe to which part?"

"Not sure yet." He kissed her again. "But I'm getting

more clarity. Come on. Chase is a fantastic chef. Whatever's on the menu is going to be great."

A part of her wanted to make him stay outside and talk about them, their future, or their lack thereof. But fear kept her silent. She was afraid that he wanted a forever. Afraid he didn't. Afraid of what she wanted. Afraid of what she needed.

So, she said nothing. She just let him take her hand and lead her inside, to the family who thought she belonged to them.

CHAPTER TWENTY-SIX

SEVERAL HOURS LATER, Logan was leaning against the kitchen counter, watching everyone play charades.

Charades. He was at a *charades* game with two of his brothers, their wives, two Harts, Falcon, Leila, two gray-haired seniors, three kids, and Skylar.

And he fucking loved it.

He. Loved. It. And he knew it was because of Skylar.

He grinned as he watched Skylar acting out something. Abby was sitting on the couch next to Frank, and the older man had a smile on his face that Logan had never seen before.

Frank was watching Abby with an interest that Logan recognized. It was the same way he used to look at Skylar, when he'd been envisioning what it would be like to be with her, and Abby had the same sparkle in her eyes every time she looked over at Frank.

"I think there's some romance afoot," Chase said as he leaned on the counter beside Logan.

Logan nodded. "Frank and Abby would make a good couple. I'd love to see them happy."

"I meant you and Skylar."

Logan looked over at his brother. "I love her." Saying the words aloud felt glorious. It made them true, made them real. "I love the hell out of her."

Chase smiled and clapped him on the shoulder. "I'm so happy for you. How does she feel?"

Logan grinned. "She loves me," he admitted.

Chase gave a little fist pump. "Mira saw that in you guys. She'll be so thrilled she was right. What are you going to do about it?"

Logan said nothing. He watched as Skylar and Leila burst into hysterics about something, and he smiled. Today had given him the clarity he needed. He had no doubts anymore. "I need to quit my job. I can't be married and do that work. It's not right."

"Okay."

Logan almost laughed at his brother's non-committal response. Chase was trying so hard not to push. "I think..." he paused. "I think I'd like to move back to Wyoming. I was thinking of volunteering for search and rescue. And working with the horses again. Not sure in what capacity, but it felt right being out there today. If that's okay with you."

Chase said nothing, so Logan looked over at him.

There were tears in his brother's eyes.

Logan's throat immediately clogged up. "Cut that shit out," he muttered.

Chase suddenly turned toward him, grabbed him and hugged him.

Logan hugged him back just as fiercely, holding on tight to the brother who had somehow kept them all alive and together through their brutal childhood. "Thanks, Chase," he said, his voice rough. "Thanks for everything. None of us would be here if it weren't for you."

Chase let go and nodded, emotion etched on his face. "I'd have given my life for any of you. I still would."

"I know, but you don't need to." Logan cleared his throat. "I need to convince Skylar now. She's scared. She's been badly burned."

Chase nodded. "Let me know how we can help. Want Mira to talk to her?"

"No. It's gotta be me." Logan let out his breath. "I'm going to talk to her when we get home."

"No. Do it now. Never wait to tell someone you love them. Never."

Logan knew Chase was right. And he didn't want to wait.

Chase saw the decision on his face and clasped his hands. "Time for a break," he called out to the room. "Who wants dessert? I made three pies."

As the crowd moved toward the kitchen, Logan paused to tell Leila that he was going outside with Skylar for a minute and to wait for them, then he wove through the crowd to where Skylar and Abby were talking. "Abby? Do you mind if I steal your daughter for a sec?"

Abby lit up. "Take her away, Logan. She's all yours. Frank's waiting for me anyway." She hopped up and headed off toward Frank, who was leaning on his cane, waiting for her.

Logan held out his hand. "Skylar?"

Skylar's heart started to pound at Logan's serious expression. She couldn't quite read it, but she knew he had an agenda. "Is everything all right?"

"It is." He folded her hand in his and took her out through the glass doors to the patio. He pulled out a chair for her at a nearby table, then took the seat next to hers.

They were still within view of the gathering, and she saw Brody, Quintin, and Falcon slip out the door and melt into the shadows at the edge of the patio, keeping vigilant.

Reminding her of the threat that was still hunting them.

Logan took her hands in his and leaned forward. "Skylar."

She dragged her gaze off their bodyguards. "Logan."

"What do you think of my family?"

She couldn't help but smile. "They're wonderful. Keegan and Brody want to hire me to design the bakery. They even made an official offer that's a little outrageous, honestly."

His brows shot up. "Really? That's fantastic. It looked like you were having fun working on that."

"I was." Excitement bubbled through her. "I became an architect so that I could design the houses my dad was building. But while I was still in school, he got sick. I got a job at a firm so I could send them money to help them out while he wasn't working. Then he died, and I never left the firm. I kept doing it to help out my mom, and I'm good at it, but—" she paused, trying to think how to phrase it.

"But there isn't magic."

She met his gaze. "Exactly. Working on the bakery was magical. Their passion is contagious. It was like working with my dad again. I loved it so much."

Logan smiled. "Did you tell them you'd do it?"

Her smile faded. "I can't do it. I have to go back to my job."

Logan let out his breath. "You don't."

"I do—"

He pressed a kiss to her knuckles. "Skylar." His voice was rough, incredibly sexy, making goosebumps pop up on her arms.

"That's my name." She tried to keep her voice light.

"You know I love you."

She nodded. "You mentioned that."

He kissed the ring on her finger, the engagement ring. "I've got a shitty past. A lot more than you know, but it's pretty ugly."

Her heart turned over. "I know a little bit of it."

He was watching her, those dark eyes so intense. "I went to work for the CIA because I wanted to use that anger inside me to do good. It turned out that when I was focused on my job, the monster was quiet. I became dependent on that work to keep my mind off the darkness."

He was rubbing his thumbs over her knuckles again, in that way he had. It was so sweet and tender, an absentminded gesture of intimacy. She nodded. "I used my work the same way after my dad died and I left my marriage." She smiled. "I understand you."

"Then do you also understand that you've changed me? That you make me feel again. I feel pain, and it scares me, but I also feel happy. I feel love. For my family. For you." He met her gaze. "Especially for you."

She bit her lip. Her heart wanted to lean into him, to open to him, to bring her deep inside her soul...which terrified her. "Logan—"

"I want to hear what you have to say, but I'd like to finish first. Okay?"

She nodded.

"I want to be this man that you've unwrapped. I'm not sure exactly how to do it, but being out on the range with you and Leila today sealed it for me." He took a breath. "I want to move back here. Quit my job, move back here...and do it with you."

She stared at him, her heart thundering. "What are you saying?"

He kissed the ring. "I want this to be real, Skylar. I want to marry you."

She pushed back and stood up. "We barely know each other. You can't know that—"

He rose slowly to his feet, as if he didn't want to spook her. "We've known each other for two years. How many hours have we spent talking in the hallway? Thousands?"

"I knew my ex for three years before I married him. Three years, and look what happened! Everyone was lying to me! I lost everything!" Tears started running down her cheeks, but she couldn't stop it. "I already love your family. And I'd love the job working with the Harts. What if I come out here? And I give up everything to do it? And then you and I don't work out? Then I lose them, too. I'll have nothing. At least in Boston, I have my job and my mom and—"

"Skylar." He caught her wrists, his grip gentle, but enough to draw her attention. "First of all, the Stocktons are forever people. Loyalty is everything to us. *Everything.*"

"So, they'll be on your side—"

"Baby." He put his finger over her lips. "There are no sides here. When I commit to you, like I'm doing right now, that's forever. That means that I will do whatever it takes to keep our relationship healthy, thriving, and beautiful. I won't walk out. If something's wrong, we'll fix it."

She shook her head. "You don't know that. What if something happens in ten years? Or fifteen? Or—"

"I won't leave. I won't ever leave you. I don't leave the people I love."

"You left your family." The minute she said it, she regretted it, especially when she saw the guilt flash over his face. "I'm sorry, I didn't mean—"

"It's okay. But I didn't leave them. I was *always* there for them. I came back when they needed me. Always. Yeah, I moved to Boston, but they were still the most important part of my life. And you can have family and move away. But you can't move away from your partner. It's different."

Skylar looked around at the beautiful house, at the gorgeous ranch. She looked through the glass doors at the people milling about. She saw her mom beaming at Frank. It was everything she wanted. "I couldn't go halfway with you," she whispered. "I couldn't hold myself back."

He smiled. "That's good."

"It's not. I couldn't protect myself." She stepped back, out of his reach. "You don't understand how broken I was," she said. "I gave away everything to him. I trusted him, and all our friends."

"I'm willing to do whatever it takes to build that trust between us," he said. "Whatever it takes."

She pressed her hands to her forehead, trying to control the panic rising in her. "Logan, I can't do this. I can't. I'm not ready. I won't ever be ready."

"It's okay," he said gently. "You're okay. Breathe, sweetheart."

She tried to take a breath, but her chest was tight. "I can't—"

"Do you love me?"

She scowled at him. "Logan, stop."

"Skylar." He walked over to her and took her hand. "Do you love me?"

"That's not the point," she said, pulling her hand away. "It's not so much about you, and whether I trust you. It's about me. I don't trust myself anymore. I can't trust myself. I made a mistake before, a terrible, terrible mistake that went on for years. If I couldn't see what was happening then, how can I possibly trust my judgement again? The fact I love you and your family and this whole life out here makes it even more impossible to trust my ability to see clearly."

Logan ground his jaw. "It's all right, then. I'll go back to Boston with you. We'll take it slow—"

"No," she whispered. "Don't you understand? There is no slow for me when it comes to you. You've been my sunlight for so long that I can't hold back with you. I'd be all in with you. And I can't do that."

"Skylar—"

"No." She held up her hand as he tried to talk. "No more. Just...please...stop. I'm going inside. Please, just let it be, okay?" She pushed past him, hurrying by. He didn't move as she passed, letting her go.

She didn't turn as she ran inside, but she felt him behind her following closely. She waved at everyone as she stepped inside. "I'm going to run to the bathroom." She ducked down the hall before anyone could ask and practically dove inside the same bathroom she'd hidden in when she'd first arrived.

She didn't bother to look at herself in the mirror this time. She just sat on the edge of the tub and hugged herself. Why was she so broken? Why couldn't she take a chance? If it didn't work, it didn't work. Plenty of people recovered from broken hearts. Why was she so pathetic?

She didn't want to be like this. She hated being afraid and pathetic. But her hands were shaking, and she felt like she was going to throw up.

There was a light knock at the door, and she squeezed her eyes shut. There was no way she could talk to Logan right now. "Go away."

The person at the door knocked again.

CHAPTER TWENTY-SEVEN

"Skylar?"

Her mom. It was her mom at the door, not Logan. Disappointment and relief rushed through her, and Skylar rested her forehead on her knees. "I'm fine, Mom. I'll be right out."

"I hope you're not naked, because I'm coming in and there are kids out here." The door opened before Skylar would have had a chance to get dressed, and her mom poked her head around the door. When she saw Skylar hunched over on the edge of the tub, her face softened, and she walked in.

She shut the door behind her and sat down on the floor at Skylar's feet. "My baby girl," she said gently. "What's going on?"

"We're not really engaged," Skylar blurted out. "I'm so sorry to disappoint you, but we're not engaged. You and I aren't actually going to be a part of his family, and the assassin is hunting us because Logan's in the CIA and he accidentally got me shot at so he feels guilty. That's why he's protecting me."

Abby's brows shot up. "Wow. That's a lot of info. Where do you want to start?"

"He said he loves me. I mean, he does love me. And I love him. But I can't. I can't." Skylar suddenly blurted the entire story out, including the conversation they'd just had. By the time she'd finished, she'd gone through an entire roll of toilet paper, and her mom was smiling. *Smiling.* "How is this funny?"

"Do you know that you've never cried about your marriage? In all the times we've talked about it, you've never cried."

"I've cried—"

"No, you haven't. You've been all about summoning a strong front and focusing on work." Abby gently brushed her hair back. "I was worried about you. You were making yourself hard. Your smiles didn't reach your eyes, and your bad moods were tightly controlled."

Skylar inclined her head. "I had to be hard. See what happens when I'm not?" She gestured to the pile of toilet paper on the floor.

"Yes, the tears hurt. But since I've been in Wyoming, I've seen a Skylar I haven't seen in a very long time." She paused. "Since Dad died, really, but it became so much worse after your marriage ended."

Skylar's jaw dropped open. "I said that same thing to Logan, but about you. When you got out of Keegan's truck with Falcon, you looked so alive, and I realized how long it had been since I'd seen you like that."

Abby's face became thoughtful. "I didn't realize it until you said it just now, but you're right." She smiled. "I was so worried about my baby girl, that I never thought about myself." She took a deep breath. "I grieved the loss of Dad for a long time. And at the same time, I lost you, first to your own grief, then to your work, and then to the devastation of your marriage." She took Skylar's hands. "When Falcon showed up at the police station and told me that you'd awakened some sort of assassin and we were going to go meet up with you, I was so happy."

Skylar blinked. "Happy? That's happy news?"

"Yes! It meant I was going to get to see my daughter, and that she'd gotten out and lived enough to cause mayhem." She smiled. "You used to be so much trouble as a child. You remember when you sawed up our dining room table while Dad and I were out to dinner so you could build one that was an octagon, because you felt it would fit our space better?"

Skylar smiled through her tears. "You confiscated all the power tools for a month."

"It should have been longer, but your dad won that argument." Abby grinned. "Your dad was the spirit in our household, Skylar. I didn't realize until just now how much we both depended on him to keep us light, how we'd both let ourselves slip into a weariness with life, which was the exact opposite of how he defined life."

Skylar bit her lip, emotions tight in her chest. "I thought I'd work with Dad forever, and I never got a chance."

"No, you didn't." She gripped Skylar's hands. "But when I watched you out there tonight with Logan, and his family, and Leila, I saw that sparkle in your eye again. My baby girl was back. Do you feel that when you're with Logan?"

"I do." Skylar didn't need to think about it.

Abby nodded. "I felt it the minute I met Falcon. And then Keegan. And the others. There is something about this family that's pretty remarkable." She winked. "And that Frank is a pretty interesting man. If you marry Logan and move out here, I might come stay with you for a while. You said you're sharing a house with Frank, right?"

Skylar stared at her mom. "What are you talking about? You want to move out here?"

"Baby, I've been alone for years now, and I realized today

that I don't want to do that anymore. I want my daughter back, and I want to live life as fully as I can in the time I have left. This family is pretty special, and they're opening their arms to us. If you truly love Logan, and I can tell you do, maybe it's time to jump in and see what life can give you."

"I just told you that I can't—"

"You actually can." Abby smiled. "You really can."

"But what if it doesn't work? What if it all ends?"

"It might end. It ended with Dad." Abby met her gaze. "But the time I spent with him made all the heartache that came after worth it. You can live, or you can die while you're alive." She patted Skylar's hand. "I'm done being dead while I'm alive, and you are, too. Say yes to Logan, Skylar. See how high you can fly."

Skylar's heart tightened with a longing so deep it hurt. She realized she wanted to trust him. She wanted to give this a try. She wanted it all.

Abby smiled. "I see it in your eyes, Skylar. This is the right path for you—"

The door suddenly flew open and Logan appeared, his gun in his hand. "He's found us. They tracked the breach to an internal leak, who admitted that he's on the way here. He's minutes away. Let's go."

Alarm shot though Skylar, and she jumped to her feet. "Eugene? He's here?"

"Yeah. Let's go." He grabbed Abby's elbow and started hustling them along the hall. "Chase and Ryder are taking everyone to the basement." Ahead, Skylar could hear footsteps pounding, her heart went to her throat at the thought of the children in danger. "Where's Leila?"

"She's with them." They reached the basement door and Logan gestured for them to go down the stairs.

Chase was at the bottom, a gun in his hand. "Let's go. I'll lock up once you guys are down here."

Abby hurried down the stairs as Quintin, Falcon, Brody, and Keegan approached, all of them armed and focused. Logan caught Skylar's wrist, yanked her to him, and kissed her, his eyes blazing. "I love the hell out of you, Skylar. When this is over, if you want to dump my ass, I won't stand in your way. I won't force you into anything you don't want, but know that I will love you until the day I die." He kissed her hard then set her back. "You stay the fuck alive until I get back. Do you understand?"

She nodded. "Of course—"

At that moment, she heard a shriek from the basement. They both looked down as little J.J. tried to run up the stairs. He was giggling and laughing as Chase picked him up and then handed him to Mira, who had come out after him.

Mira clutched him to her chest as she hurried out of sight, and Chase looked up at Skylar. "Come on. Now."

Skylar had run and hid when she was at Logan's. But now...she shook her head. "I can't."

"You have to," Logan said. "He'll be here any second."

"No." She stepped back. "He's after me. If I go down there, I endanger everyone." She looked at Logan. "Those are the people we love in that basement. I can't put them at risk. This is our problem. We have to fix it without endangering them."

Logan stared at her, then swore under his breath. "Chase," he said finally. "Skylar's not coming. Lock it down."

"You sure?"

"Yeah." Logan looped one arm around her shoulder and pulled her against him. He placed a kiss on her forehead, holding her for a split second, before pulling her off the landing, and shutting the door behind them.

She heard Chase run up the stairs and lock the door behind them. The moment it clicked, she knew she was stuck. She'd made her choice...and it was the right one. "What now?"

"We need to lead him away from the house," Brody said. "Away from the basement."

Logan and Quintin looked at each other, and they nodded at the same time. "Dead Man's Notch," Logan said.

"We gotta get to the barn. We're riding." Quintin broke into a run down the hall, and the others sprinted after him. The men kept her in the middle, and she had to run hard to keep even with them.

They made it to the back door, the one closest to the barn, then paused.

Logan flicked the switch, turning the driveway into darkness. "On three. Run like hell. Total silence."

Skylar's heart was thundering, but she nodded.

The little group squeezed up next to the door, as tight as they could while Logan grasped the knob. He looked at her. "Ready?"

She nodded. She had a million questions, firstly, how did they know they weren't going to be gunned down as soon as they stepped outside, but she didn't ask. This was Logan's world. She had to trust him.

"Now." He opened the door, and they tore down the stairs, their feet moving so quickly as they hit the dirt. Skylar ran as hard as she could. The men were tightly clustered, using their bodies as a shield to protect her. Men she barely knew, all of them willing to sacrifice themselves to keep her safe.

They reached the barn and ran inside. Quintin stopped to close the door behind them, as the others spread out, racing for the tack room. Logan gestured them to different stalls. It took less than three minutes for six horses to be tacked up and mounted.

Logan gestured and they rode to the far end of the barn,

the echo of the horses' hooves the only sound in the quiet barn.

They reached the double doors, and Quintin rode ahead. He leaned down and unlocked them, and then paused as Logan gave a quick rundown of the plans. Everyone nodded, but Skylar's mouth was dry with panic.

She didn't know if she could do it.

Logan looked over at her. "You got this, Skylar. I know you do."

She nodded and took a breath. "Okay."

"Okay." He reached over and squeezed her hand. "Everyone ready?"

All the riders moved into a tight cluster around her and gave their assent, so Logan nodded at Quintin. "Go."

Quintin yanked the double doors open. As a unit, the horses took off in a fast gallop, racing into the dark night. The horses' hooves pounded over the dirt as they flew across the stable grounds toward the same plains they'd ridden out on earlier with such joy.

No joy now. Just paralyzing fear driving Skylar forward.

Logan was so close on her right that her foot kept brushing against his leg. Quintin was in front. To her left was Brody. Behind them were Keegan and Falcon. Every horse was so close to her that she felt as if she could lean over and touch them.

Silently, they rode, no one speaking.

Finally, Logan signaled Falcon, who pulled away slightly. He pulled out his gun and fired several rounds into the air. None of the horses reacted to the gunshot, but she flinched, sudden panic clogging her throat as she was back in that moment at Logan's condo, when the bullets were flying and—

"Skylar." Logan's voice was low, breaking through the fear starting to paralyze her. "Stay with me. We're going to keep you safe."

Tears burned in her eyes as she looked over at him. The faint sliver of the moon gave just enough light for her to see the outline of his face. His beautiful face. The one she loved. The one who held her life in his hands. His face was calm and focused. Fierce. Determined.

He was ready, she realized. He *could* handle this. And he wasn't going to let her die. She could read it in every line of his body, in the faces of every man riding beside her. Her life was in their hands...and she trusted them.

She trusted them.

Relief rushed through her, a galvanizing relief that blew through her like a storm wiping out the tension that had been gripping her so ruthlessly for so long. She trusted them, and she knew she was right to do so. "Okay." And this time, she meant it.

He grinned. "Okay, then."

Falcon came riding up, hard and fast. "We have contact."

Skylar twisted around on her horse and scanned the darkness, but she couldn't see anything. "He's following us?"

"Yeah. He's in a truck. Lights off. But he's definitely following us."

The game was on.

CHAPTER TWENTY-EIGHT

As THEY CONTINUED TO RIDE, Logan kept looking over his shoulder.

It didn't take long until he could see the faint outline of the truck behind them.

It was closing fast.

Skylar was doing the same thing, and she clearly saw the truck when he did. "Logan?"

"He's too far away to shoot us," he said. "We have to wait."

They continued to gallop on the flat plains. To their right were hills with rocks and boulders that a truck would have trouble navigating, but they didn't ride up into them.

Because they weren't trying to escape him.

They were going to trap him and end it.

Logan had used himself as bait many times over his career. He never worried about it. He never worried about getting killed.

But with Skylar by his side, and his family around them and back at the house, the stakes were high. Too high. He cared what happened. He was worried about their safety. He was worried that the choices he'd made for the last decade were going to burn the only people he cared about.

It was too late for regret, but he knew for absolute certain that he was never going back to his job. He was never again making a choice that could bring harm to the people he cared about. Whatever he had to face tonight, he would stand and face it. Whatever came tomorrow, he was staying. No more running. Not today. Not ever.

Quintin checked behind them, and then gestured to Logan.

Logan nodded and looked up ahead. "I think we can make it." They'd had a spot in mind, but it had been a push to get to it before Eugene caught them. Not Eugene. The man hunting them went only by the name Arrow. To make Skylar feel safe, Logan had been willing to call him Eugene.

To make sure he was prepared for what he was facing, it was time for him to be called by who he was.

"We're almost in range," Falcon shouted.

"One more minute!" Logan shouted. "Come on!" He urged his horse faster, as did the other riders and Skylar. Up ahead, loomed their target. The trail they were on curved to the right between two cliffs. It was the perfect place to set an ambush.

Logan looked behind him. The vehicle was closing fast. The lights were off, and it was driving in darkness, getting closer and closer. It was going to be close. "Now!"

The pack turned right hard, galloping into the canyon. For about twenty yards, the canyon went straight, and then it made a hard right, taking them out of view of their pursuer. The moment they were out of sight, they pulled up. "Off!"

Everyone leapt off their horses, except for Keegan. They all tossed their reins to him, and then he took off with all the horses in a gallop in the direction they'd been heading.

Logan led the way up the west cliff, joined by Skylar and

Brody. Quintin led Falcon up the east cliff, while Keegan disappeared around the corner with the horses. Quintin and Falcon shot up the side of their cliff, but Logan's group was slower. Skylar was athletic, but she wasn't as fast as he and Brody were.

"Go ahead," Brody said. "I'll keep her safe."

"I'm not leaving her. You go ahead. I told you what to do."

Brody nodded and sprinted past them, while Logan stayed with Skylar as she climbed. He kept watching behind them, waiting for the truck to show up, even though he knew it wouldn't.

It was the perfect place for an ambush, and Arrow would know that.

Arrow would also know that Logan would expect Arrow not to fall for it.

Which meant that Arrow would know that Logan was expecting him to circle around and try to take him out. Which meant Arrow would do something else.

But Arrow hadn't spent hundreds of hours playing around the rocks of Dead Man's Notch with his brothers, making plans for what they would do if their father came after them.

"Here." He reached the crack in the rocks. "In here." It was narrow and pitch black. Scary as hell to someone who didn't know where it led.

But Skylar didn't hesitate. She just hurried up, sat down on her butt, and then jumped down into the darkness.

Logan followed after her, landing softly. "Skylar?"

"Here."

"Brody?"

"Here."

"Let's go." He took Skylar's hand and started leading her through the tunnels that had once been a mine. Now it was a series of tunnels through the rocks, tunnels that he and Quintin knew inside and out. It had been years and years since Logan had been in the tunnels, but old instincts knew exactly which way to go.

Brody followed behind, and Logan kept Skylar close. He knew she wanted to ask a zillion questions, but they had to stay silent.

They were close. So close to where he knew Arrow would access the mountain. There were two possibilities, one on the east cliff, and one on the west cliff. He hoped Arrow chose the west cliff, where they were.

Arrow was his problem.

He wanted to deal with it.

The tunnel became narrow, and Logan had to turn sideways to get through. It was absolute darkness, and he squeezed Skylar's hand, letting her know that she was doing a great job.

She squeezed his hand back, a little harder than necessary, and he smiled. He knew she had to be scared. They were literally sliding through a rocky passage barely wide enough for them to get through. With the darkness, they were all completely blind. It had to be terrifying for her, but she didn't even hesitate.

She was giving him her complete faith, and he wasn't going to let her down. Not fucking ever.

The path widened to a small cave that had several small openings that let in a faint bit of moonlight. With his eyes adjusted to the darkness, the faint bit of light was enough for Logan to see clearly. They had a forty-five-degree view of the plains leading up to the mountain.

Logan gestured for Brody to set up there. If Arrow tried to get up the cliff on that side, Brody would see him. *Shoot to kill*. That had been Logan's order to the team. He hoped they wouldn't have to do it.

Taking a life was a burden he didn't want on anyone. But they'd all nodded without hesitation.

Still holding Skylar's hand, he led her down another narrow crevice. They had to get down on their knees at one point, and Skylar kept her hand on his ankle as she followed him.

Within moments, they came out on a tiny ledge hidden behind a large rock. They were exposed now. If someone were above them, they would be in trouble.

But Falcon would have his gun trained on the top of the cliff from the other side, while Quintin would be down in the rocks, like they were.

Logan gestured for Skylar to crouch down, and she did. He eased around the rock and peered down at the ground.

A black truck was parked at the base of the cliff.

He was there.

Logan's adrenaline spiked, and he pulled out his gun. The night was silent. So he listened.

They'd spent hundreds of hours trying to sneak up on each other out here as kids. He knew the sound of a dislodged pebble. He knew how to track it. He knew every inch of these hills. This was where he'd first honed the skills that had saved his life professionally a dozen times.

And now he was here again. And again, it was personal—

A pebble clattered above them. Faint. Tiny. Moving maybe a couple inches. But it wasn't supposed to be there.

Logan swung around, pressing his back against the rock as he looked up, scanning the rocks above them. If Arrow was up there, Falcon would have him. There was no way to hide from the east cliff on the top.

And yet, he'd heard a pebble move.

Without taking his gaze off the cliff above them, he gestured for Skylar to freeze. They were both in the open if Arrow came down from above. It was dark, but not that dark.

He waited.

There was more silence.

Arrow was waiting, too.

But Logan could wait forever. He leaned his head back ever so slightly so he could look down at the truck again. It was still there, and no one coming up from below. Where the hell was he?

He wished he could communicate with his team, but they didn't have the technology. Even texting them would light up his screen. They were all alone out here.

Waiting.

If he didn't have Skylar, Logan would go up the side to look for Arrow, but he did have Skylar, and he wasn't going to leave her.

He risked a glance at her. She was tensed in a crouch, one hand on the rock to support her. Her hair was hanging forward over her shoulder. She was looking up at the cliff, giving the moonlight the chance to cast shadows across her face. His chest tightened as he watched her.

This woman was his future. His soul. His everything. He was never going to let her go.

As if sensing his perusal, she looked over at him. She smiled, and then a shadow fell across her. The wrong kind of shadow.

"Down!" He shouted the warning as he threw his body in front of her, twisting on his back as he fired up the cliff. Pain shot through his side, and he used his body to shove her backward into the tunnel as he kept shooting.

Suddenly, there was movement above him, and he shot again as Arrow fell past him, rolling down the side of the cliff, his gun clattering ahead of him.

Logan scrambled to his feet and ran to the edge of the ledge. He leaned over, watching as Arrow thudded to the ground. The way he landed made it obvious. "He's dead. It's over." Skylar was safe. His family was safe. His—

"Logan!" Skylar caught him as his knees buckled.

He grabbed her arm as he went down onto the ledge. Pain suddenly shot through him, a sharp, shooting pain in his abdomen. Skylar propped him up as he ripped his shirt out of his jeans and yanked it up. Blood. A hole. Son of a bitch. "I've been shot."

"Oh, my God." Horror shot through Skylar when she saw Logan's wound. There was so much blood.

"It's fine. I've been shot before." But his words were slurred, and his hand kept sliding off the wound. "Need to put pressure on it."

"I've got it." She ripped her sweatshirt over her head and balled it up as Logan slid off her to his side. "Logan's been shot," she shouted into the night. "Help! He's been shot! Help!" The words tore at her as she pressed her sweatshirt to his side. "Help! He's bleeding!"

Brody suddenly appeared beside her. "Son of a bitch. We're going to have to drag him out."

"Through the tunnel? There's no way. It's too narrow." Tears streamed down her cheeks.

Brody's phone rang, and he answered it. "Quintin! We're on some ledge on the south side. Arrow's dead. Logan's in trouble."

Skylar pressed harder on Logan's wound, and he grimaced. "Sorry." She released the pressure, but he grabbed her wrist.

"No. Keep the pressure on." His eyes were half-closed, but he was watching her. "I love you, Skylar."

"I know. I love you. Don't you dare die."

He tugged at her hair. "Skylar. Look at me."

She could hear the men shouting now, trying to find them, but there was so much blood. "What?" she said.

"I'm not going to let you go. I said I would, but it's a lie. You're my world. You need to know that. That ring is yours. Everything I have is yours. If I don't make it—"

"No!" She practically shouted the word. "Don't even say that! I need you!"

At that moment, Quintin burst out of the tunnel. "Logan!"

Skylar backed up as Quintin dropped to his knees beside his brother. He had a flashlight, and he quickly inspected the wound. She hugged herself as Quintin tied her sweatshirt around Logan's ribs. "Life Flight is on the way to the ranch. We need to get you off the cliff and back there."

"Climb down." Logan's eyes were closed. "We gotta climb down."

"Son of a bitch." Quintin looked over the edge. "We're not sixteen anymore."

"Fuck that. We're better than we were then. Where's Skylar?"

She hurried over and knelt beside Logan, taking his hand. "I'm here."

He cracked his eyes open just enough to see her. "I gotta go. Wait here. Not safe for you to climb." He smiled. "You have your life back, sweetheart. What are you going to do?"

Before she could answer, Quintin interrupted. "Tell her later, bro. We need to get you down." He draped one of Logan's arms over his shoulder, and Brody grabbed the other. Together, they dragged him to his feet.

Logan stumbled, leaning on them heavily.

Skylar couldn't believe they were going to be able to get him safely down. "How are you going to go down the cliff?"

"Carefully." Quintin dragged Logan toward the edge. "You stay alive for her, bro. You hear me? Because if you die, I'm pretty sure Falcon's going to marry her. Once he does that, then he'll be family, and no one wants him in our family."

Brody laughed. "Ain't that the truth. Let's go."

And with that, the men dragged Logan over the edge of the cliff. Skylar ran to the edge and leaned over, watching in near terror as the trio eased down what looked like a sheer rock face. Tears filled her eyes as she watched Logan's head loll to the side, and she knew he'd lost consciousness.

Below them, Falcon ran to the truck and climbed into it. She prayed he'd find the keys.

She knew it was so dangerous what they were doing, trying to carry an unconscious man down the side of a cliff. Any of them could lose their grip and fall to their death.

But it was the only way. And they were willing to do it for him.

Tears blurred her vision, and she turned away and ran for the tunnel.

CHAPTER TWENTY-NINE

SKYLAR SAT in the corner of the hospital waiting room, her knees pulled to her chest, her chin resting on them. She was so scared. She couldn't stop shaking.

By the time she'd arrived at the hospital, Logan was already in surgery. She hadn't been able to find the men who had gone in the helicopter with him. They'd already left in the truck by the time she'd gotten down the cliff, and the helicopter had met them at the house.

She wished they'd waited for her to get down and go with him, but she understood why. Logan's life was at stake, and it wasn't as if she was really his fiancée.

Keegan and Skylar had brought the horses back. Chase had helped them put the horses away, but it had still taken precious time. Now, Keegan was getting her coffee, and she was alone.

What if it was too late? What if she'd waited too long to tell Logan how much she loved him and how much she needed him? What if it had taken her too long to get brave enough to claim the man and the life she wanted? What if—

"Skylar!"

She looked up as her mom came running into the waiting room. "Mom!" The tears she'd been trying to keep at bay broke free, and she flung herself into her mom's arms. She buried her face in her mom's shoulder, clinging on for life. She remembered when she and her mom had been in the hospital, just like this, when her dad had died.

It had been so terrible, so scary. They'd both been so scared of the future, and how they would get by without him. Alone. Just the two of them. "I'm so glad you're here," she whispered.

"Me, too." Abby pulled back and framed her face with her hands. "He's going to be all right, Skylar. He's a tough bastard."

"Mom!" She laughed through her tears. "It's so awkward when you swear."

"I've been teaching her. She's a quick learner." Frank limped up, his dark face creased into a warm smile. "I'm planning to corrupt her. It's going to be fun."

Skylar covered her ears. "Oh, my God. I really don't need to hear that." But she was already laughing.

"Skylar!" Leila waved to her, drawing Skylar's attention away from her mom. "Is he okay?"

Skylar took a deep breath, wrapping her arms around Leila as the teenager fell into her embrace, just the way she'd just fallen into her mom's. "He's going to be fine. He's a Stockton. You know how tough they are."

She hugged the teenager hard, and her mom leaned in and wrapped her arms around both of them. "It's time for a Leila sandwich," her mom said.

To Skylar's surprise, the teenager didn't try to pull away. She just clung to both of them, her body trembling as she hung onto Skylar.

"He's going to be all right," Chase said. "Trust me. We're much too stubborn to die."

Skylar looked up to see Chase standing beside them, holding his foster son in his arms.

Behind Chase, she was stunned to see a flood of Stock-tons taking over the waiting room. Every brother, except the elusive Caleb. Most of the women, except the few that she presumed were home taking care of sleeping kids. The room was packed, and became even more crowded as Brody, Falcon, and Quintin walked in from wherever they had been.

Everyone was talking and hugging. The room was filled with such love and support that the tears almost started again. Abby tucked her arm around Skylar's. "This is a special family," she said quietly. "Surely you can see that?"

Leila nodded. "I know." The longing in her voice was so visceral that Skylar felt like she could almost reach out and touch the depths of her emotion with her hand.

She put her arm around Leila. "They're pretty amazing," she said. "But we are, too."

"They?" Chase turned back to them, his brows up, having clearly heard them. "What are you talking about? You all are part of this family."

Skylar managed a smile. "You know we're not really engaged. We don't have to pretend anymore."

"Not engaged?" Brody walked up. "What are you talking about?"

The whole room fell into silence at Brody's question, turning to look at Skylar. She swallowed. "We pretended to be engaged," she said. "It was a cover to keep me safe. And now that it's over..." She shrugged, her throat tight as she gave up the family she'd already started to love. "You can know the truth."

Keegan laughed. "The truth? The truth that you guys are totally in love?"

"Logan briefly regained consciousness in the helicopter, and the only thing he wanted to know was if you were all right," Quintin said. "He kept asking where you were and telling us to get you."

She looked over at him. "He did?"

"Damn straight he did," Brody said. "I thought he was going to pull his gun on us to make us go back and get you."

Tears filled her eyes. "He's going to be okay, right?"

"He is." Quintin walked up to her and pulled her into a hug. "But if he were to be a selfish bastard and die, then you need to know that you're already part of our family. He loves you, and that's all it takes. It's forever, Skylar."

"We don't need anything official to be a family," Chase said. "That's not how we are." He looked over at her mom. "You, too, Abby. You know that none of us have a mom, right? Our kids need a grandma around, and we're already counting on you."

Skylar started laughing through her tears. "You guys are crazy. What if Logan wakes up and realizes he's changed his mind?"

Chase put his arm around her and kissed the top of her head. "Doesn't matter. We love you, too. Both of you."

That did it. The tears wouldn't stop this time, especially when everyone clustered around to hug her and Abby. She felt the warmth of their hugs, the truth of their love, and she knew that this family would never abandon her or turn on her. There would be no sides taken. She could count on them. Which meant she could count on Logan, too.

He needed to wake up so she could tell him.

Please, Logan, wake up.

CHAPTER THIRTY

"LOGAN?"

He opened his eyes at the sound of the voice he'd been burning to hear for hours, and then smiled when he saw Skylar peeking around the corner of the door to his hospital room. "Skylar." His voice was rough and scratchy, but none of that mattered. Not when she was there. "You're all right?"

She nodded. "Your family thought I should be the first to come see you." She smiled nervously. "They know we're not really engaged, but they told the hospital I was your fiancée and told me to come in first. Is that okay? I could go get Chase—"

"Come to me." He lifted his hand. "I need you."

Relief rushed across her face and she hurried across the room. She grabbed his hand and sank down into the chair next to the bed, hugging his hand to her chest. "I love you," she blurted out. "You're my forever. I'm sorry I was afraid—"

"No." He shook his head.

"No?" Her face fell. "You changed your mind?"

"Hell, no." He wanted to grab her and haul her into his arms. "Come here."

"But your stitches—"

"It's fine." He got his body to move to the right and make space for her. "Here."

She smiled and climbed up next to him. He pulled her against him, and she tucked herself against his side. For a long moment, he just held her, breathing in the feel of her against him. "When I saw his shadow fall across you," he whispered. "I thought for a second that I'd screwed up terribly. That I was going to lose you. I've never been so terrified in my life."

"You were terrified?" She laughed against his neck. "You were the one bleeding all over the mountain and unconscious!"

"I'm impossible to kill. I was fine." But he knew it had been close. Closer than he'd ever come, and he knew why. He pulled back slightly so he could look at her face. Her hair was spread over his pillow, her blue eyes full of emotion. "That's it for me, Skylar. I'm not going back. Not even to pack up my stuff. I'm going to have a moving company pack it." He watched her face as he said it, trying to get a sense of where she stood.

She bit her lip, watching him.

"I want you to stay with me. You and Abby." He lifted her hand and gently removed the diamond ring. He held it between his thumb and forefinger, turning it so it sparkled. "Pretty, isn't it?"

She nodded. "It's beautiful."

"A few years ago, I was on a mission in a town in South America. I had to deal with a situation. In the process, I saved the life of a woman and her two children." He'd never forget that moment. He wasn't about to tell Skylar that he saved them by killing her abusive husband, who had locked them all up in their mansion. Her husband had been his target. The family? One of the reasons he'd done what he did. "She gave me that ring as a thank you."

Skylar looked up at him. "Really?"

He nodded. "It was her grandmother's ring. She told me that her grandmother and grandfather had been married for seventy-eight years, and they'd loved each other deeply. She asked me to take it and give it to the woman who would give me the sunshine and freedom that I'd given them by saving their lives."

"That's so beautiful," Skylar whispered.

Logan closed his fist around the ring. "She told me that it would bless me and my wife with the same beautiful lifetime of love and happiness that her grandparents had had." He smiled. "I told her I didn't have a woman. She told me to keep it until I did. That my woman was coming." He smiled at her. "And two weeks later, you moved in across the hall."

Emotions danced in her beautiful blue eyes. "And you gave it to me."

"The moment I met you, I knew the ring was yours. I didn't believe I'd ever be in a position to give it to you, but I knew it was meant for you. Then Eugene happened. A fake engagement was all I thought I'd get, but I was happy for you to have it." He took her hand and pressed a kiss to her knuckles. "But things have changed, right?"

She nodded.

"Because I love you. I always did, but now I own it."

"And I love you," she said. "I always did as well, but now it's real."

He smiled. "Hang on." Gritting his teeth against the pain, he rolled himself off the bed, landing gingerly on his feet.

"What are you doing?" Skylar quickly got up. "Get back in bed."

"I will in a sec. Come over here." He wasn't sure he could make it around the bed, manly man that he was.

Skylar hurried around the bed and took his outstretched hand. "Logan—"

"Shh. I'm busy. Don't interrupt me." He leaned heavily on the hospital bed, and then managed to get himself down on one knee, with only a few choice profanities. Once he was down, he was pretty sure he wasn't going to be able to get back up, but it didn't matter. "Left hand, please."

Skylar was grinning as she held out her hand.

"All right, then." He clasped his hands around it, looking up at her. "I love you madly, deeply, and forever. You've changed my world in a thousand ways. I swear to you that I will stand by you, protect you, and love you every second of every day for the rest of our lives, no matter what. I give you my family, my friends, my legacy, and my heart." He grinned when her eyes began to shine with unshed tears. "Skylar Jones, will you marry me, for real?"

He didn't even have time to hold his breath or get nervous, because she nodded immediately. "Yes," she whispered. "Yes, a thousand times yes. I love you, Logan. Always and forever."

Elation leapt through him, and he held up the ring. "Your finger, ma'am."

She grinned as she watched him slip the sparkling diamond onto her ring finger. "It's a perfect fit," she teased. "What a surprise."

"You're a perfect fit for me." He tugged at her hand. "Come down here and kiss me, baby cakes. I don't think I can get up."

She laughed and fell to her knees, wrapping her arms around him. He drew her carefully against him and kissed her.

His woman.

His fiancée.

His forever.

CHAPTER THIRTY-ONE

CHRISTMAS

Skylar snuggled next to Logan on the couch, grinning as the entire Stockton clan, plus their dear friends Gary and Martha Keller, gathered in Chase's living room for Christmas morning. Her mom had been flying back and forth a lot, and Skylar was so delighted she was there for Christmas.

Sitting with Zane's oldest son, who was her age, was Leila, who Skylar and Logan had been fostering. She looked so happy, but there were still times when the sadness weighed heavily in the seventeen-year-old's eyes.

She seemed to sense Skylar's gaze on her, because she looked over at them, her face lighting up as she waved to Skylar.

Skylar smiled back and blew her a kiss.

The Christmas pancakes were already eaten, bacon consumed, hot chocolate brewed by the barrel.

Logan's beautiful laugh echoed through Skylar as he talked with Zane. He was so happy. So complete. She smiled as she ran her finger over the gold band encircling his finger. Apparently feeling her touch, he looked over at her, grinning as he pulled her in for a kiss.

"I still remember that first Sunday brunch we attended together," he said. "I was so uncomfortable with all the kids and wives and chaos."

She smiled. "I remember."

"But you gave my family back to me," he said, pressing a kiss to the two rings nestled together on her ring finger. "You gave me my life. I love you so much."

She grinned. "I love you, too."

"Excuse me." A raspy, older voice rang out. "May I have the floor, please?"

Skylar and the others looked over as Frank walked over to the hearth to stand in front of the fire.

His recovery from his car accident was going so well. He was no longer using a cane, and he was getting steadier by the day. From what she'd heard from Zoey and Ryder, he'd filled out a lot from when they'd first met him, and he had agreed to continue living with them in the River House forever, even after he recovered.

He had to. He and Liam were family now.

She leaned over to her mom, who was sitting next to her. "He looks pretty handsome up there in his Christmas vest and Santa tie, doesn't he?"

Abby giggled. "He always looks handsome."

"All right." Frank grinned at the room. "Abby, I need you to come up here."

Abby squeezed Skylar's knee and hopped up, weaving around kids, unwrapped presents, and acres of crumpled wrapping paper as she navigated to Frank's side.

Frank put his arm around her and turned to the room. "I'm not gonna lie. Ryder and Zoey have been a gift to me and Liam." He nodded at them. "You guys are my kids now. You're Liam's parents."

Liam grinned, and Ryder and Zoey raised their coffee mugs to Frank. "We love you," Zoey shouted.

Frank nodded. "And I love you. All of you." His gaze settled on Lissa. "I will forever be grateful for you opening the door to the Stockton clan and all the love that comes with it. I thought I was going to die a lonely old man, and instead, I'm thriving as a happy old man getting younger every day."

There was a round of cheers and applause, and Skylar's heart filled with love. The Stocktons were so amazing how they opened their arms and hearts to anyone meant to be a part of their family, including her.

Frank's smile faded. "I'll tell you though, it ain't easy being around all this romance and lovey-dovey shit all the time, and having to go to bed all alone every night when the love of my life is off in Vermont."

There were a few catcalls, and Abby's cheeks turned pink.

Frank turned to Skylar's mom, took her hand, and then he went down on one knee. He pulled a ring out of his vest pocket and held it out to her. The place erupted into cheers, and Chase had to quiet everyone down before Frank could continue.

He gazed up at her, love etched all over his face. "My dear Abby, you brought life back to my heart when it was on the verge of closing forever. You make me feel like a teenager again. I want to spend the rest of my life taking care of you, loving you, bringing sunshine into your life. Will you marry me?"

This time, the room was utterly silent. Waiting.

Skylar held her breath. She'd seen how happy her mom was with Frank, but would she be willing to leave Vermont?

Because it went without saying that Frank could never leave Liam and the Stocktons behind.

She didn't have to wait long. Abby burst into tears, flung herself into Frank's arms and started laughing and crying. "Yes, yes, yes, yes. Of course I will. It took you long enough! We're not getting any younger, you old devil."

Frank let out a whoop and hugged her. "She said yes! We're getting married!" The room erupted into cheers, and everyone leapt up, running over to hug them.

Skylar and Logan stood up, and they made their way through the crowd. Abby saw her coming, and spoke to Frank. The two of them turned to face Skylar and Logan. "I know I should've checked with you first," Frank said to Skylar. "But I thought you might give it away. I hope you're okay with it."

Skylar said nothing. She just walked right into him and hugged him fiercely. He laughed and hugged her back. "I love you, Skylar," he whispered. "I know I'm not your dad, but I feel like you're my daughter."

"I love you, too, Frank." She pulled her mom into the hug, and then Logan wrapped his strong arms around all of them. They stood there like that for a moment, just love upon love upon love.

Then Skylar saw Leila watching them, yearning etched all over her face. She nudged Logan. "It's time," she whispered.

Logan looked over at Leila and nodded. "Time," he agreed. He reached down between the cushions of a nearby chair and pulled out a thin, flat box. "Hey, guys. It looks like we missed a present." He made a pretense of checking the tag. "It's for Leila."

Abby squeezed Skylar's hand, and everyone took their seats, anticipation on their faces. Because every adult in the room knew what was in the box.

"For me?" Leila looked thrilled. "But I already got so

much." Even as she protested, she was on her feet and heading over to them.

Skylar smiled. Christmas had been almost overwhelming for Leila. She, Logan, and Leila had spent many hours talking about how this Christmas was so different for Leila. After years of being in foster care, never belonging, rarely getting a gift for Christmas, and always worrying about what terrible thing was around the corner, it was difficult for Leila to relax.

Skylar understood. Logan understood. They'd both spent years fearing what was to come, afraid to trust the good.

She smiled at Leila as the teenager took the present from Logan. "It's just a little thing."

"All right." Leila flashed them a quick smile, then retreated to her spot on the carpet with it.

Unaware that the entire room was watching her, she bent over and carefully untied the ribbon. She rolled it up and then tucked it in her pocket, as she had done with all the other ribbons. She'd told Skylar that the ribbons were the prettiest thing she'd ever seen, and she wanted to keep them forever.

She carefully slid her fingers under the tape, unwrapping the present without tearing the paper. She then folded up the paper and put it on the pile of wrapping paper she'd accumulated from the day, which she was also planning to keep forever.

The gift box had candy canes and a Black Santa on it. Leila smiled, tracing her fingers over Santa's face. "I've never seen a Santa with my skin color before."

"The world is full of so many different colors, all of which are beautiful," Logan said. "Including Santa."

Leila smiled and lifted the lid. Inside was white tissue paper tied with a red satin ribbon. They all waited while Leila carefully untied the ribbon, tucked it in her pocket, and opened the tissue.

Inside were typed documents. Signed documents. Legal documents. Adoption documents. Adoption documents that made a seventeen-year-old girl the legal forever daughter of Logan and Skylar Stockton.

Skylar's throat tightened as she watched Leila's face as she read them.

The teenager's eyes widened, and then her hand went over her mouth. She jerked her gaze off the papers and stared at Logan and Skylar. "Is this for real?"

Skylar nodded. "You bet it is."

Logan smiled. "We love you, Leila. We want to make it official."

"But I'm seventeen. No one adopts seventeen-year-olds. I'm too old—"

"No!" Skylar ran across the room and dropped to her knees in front of Leila. "We love you, Leila. You're perfect and beautiful and you're the daughter we were meant to have."

Logan sat next to Leila and put his arm around her shoulders. "Because you're seventeen, you still have to sign them. But we already signed. If you don't want to, you'll still be our daughter in our hearts. You'll still live with us. You'll still be a part of this family forever."

Leila stared at him, then looked down at the papers again. "It says...it says that my name will change. My name will be Leila Stockton." She looked up, disbelief etched on her face. "I'll be a Stockton?"

Chase smiled. "You'll be one of us, Leila. We all love you." He gestured at the room. "Look around. Everyone is waiting desperately for you to sign that paper and officially become a part of us."

Leila did as he said and looked around. Her eyes widened as she took in the expectant expression on everyone's face. The big smiles. The love surrounding her, reaching for her.

Her gaze finally settled on Logan and Skylar. "You're too young to be mom and dad to a seventeen-year-old."

Mom. Tears filled Skylar's eyes. "I'm not that young, and even if I was, it doesn't matter. I want to be your mom, Leila."

Logan took her hand. "I know you're scared, Leila. You're scared to trust this. To believe in this. In us. But you know this family. You know we don't walk away. Take a chance on us. We won't let you down. Skylar had to teach me that I deserved love, and now it's your turn to learn that lesson." He put a pen in her hand. "I love you, Leila. Be my daughter. Be *our* daughter."

She stared at the pen with anguished longing. "I'm not always nice," she whispered.

"God," Skylar said, laughing through her tears. "None of us are always nice. That's what love is. You don't have to earn it. You're worthy of it simply because you're you. It's forever, through everything." She set her hands on Leila's cheeks, drawing the girl's gaze to hers. "I love you, Leila. You're meant to be my daughter, and I'm meant to be your mom. And Logan is meant to be your dad. You know it. Let it happen."

Leila stared at her for a long moment, then she bent over, flipped the page on the documents and signed at the little red tab. Tears were streaming down her cheeks as she looked up.

She looked at Skylar and said one word. "Mom." Her voice broke as she said it, and the room erupted into cheers.

Skylar hugged her, and Logan wrapped them up in a fierce embrace, hugging them so tightly Skylar felt like he'd never let them go. And she knew he wouldn't. He'd hold them tight in his arms forever, no matter what. And that was exactly where she wanted to be.

Her mom knelt down. "Finally, I get a granddaughter," she said. "I've been waiting forever for you!"

Leila laughed and opened her arm to pull Abby into their little hug. "Can I call you Grandma?"

"You better!"

Chase crouched next to Leila. "Hug your Uncle Chase, Leila." And then, the room descended on them, tackling the new family to the ground in a pile of hugs, love, and family.

Thank you for reading Logan and Skylar's story! **Are you new to the Stockton clan?** Read Chase and Mira's story to see how the the first Stockton brother fell hard for the woman who would heal his heart. Download *A Real Cowboy Never Says No* and start reading today!

The Harts are finally here! Fall in love with Brody as he gets a second chance with the sassy, spunky woman who he loved and lost a decade ago in *A Rogue Cowboy's Second Chance.* He broke her heart, and now she needs to trust him with her life. One-click *A Rogue Cowboy's Second Chance* to get started.

Do you love small town romance? Try *Unexpectedly Mine* the first book in my Birch Crossing series, in which a single mom rents her spare room to a distractingly handsome business exec who just might help her learn to trust again.

SNEAK PEEK: A ROGUE COWBOY'S SECOND CHANCE

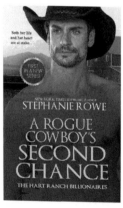

★★★★★ *"Wonderfully written, lots of heart."*
-Candy G. (Five-Star Amazon Review on A Real Cowboy for
Christmas)

Fifteen years ago, he shattered her heart. Now she needs to
trust him with her life.

★★★★★ **"Absolutely swoon worthy, lovable and
emotionally driven. Family is everything."** -Madison
(Five-star Amazon Review on *A Real Cowboy for Christmas*)

~

BRODY HART RAN his hand over the gleaming chestnut hair on Stormy's neck, pleased by how well the horse was doing. She'd been in such rough shaped when he'd rescued her, and now her coat was gleaning. Her dark brown eyes now had that sparkle he always fought to rekindle when he brought a new horse to the Hart Ranch. "Glad you found your way home," he told her.

Stormy snorted and swished her tail, impatient to get released from the cross-ties.

"I know. I'm almost done." Whenever Brody was in town, he did the shoeing for the horses who needed extra care. He'd made a study of farrier methods and honed his skills to best help the animals they rescued and brought onto the Hart Ranch.

He trusted no one else with Stormy's feet, and his care had made a difference. She'd barely been able to walk when she arrived, afraid to put weight on her broken hooves.

Now she galloped through their extensive pastures, tail held high, the purest freedom of spirit. She was why he had this ranch. She and all the others like her.

He ran his hand down her back leg and leaned his shoulder into her hip, shifting her weight off her hoof so he could lift it and work on it. He was humming quietly to himself when he heard footsteps behind him.

He didn't have to look up to know who it was. He recognized the gait of all eight of his brothers and sisters. He'd trained himself to do that back when they were homeless kids, hiding under the bridge in the dark. It had been imperative that he knew who was coming, so that he would know how to keep those under his care safe.

The habit remained today even though they were all

adults, and no one was after them, trying to drag them back into foster homes, or worse. "Hey, Keegan."

His brother spoke without preamble. "Did you sleep last night? At all? Your light was on all night."

"You stalking me?" Brody set the lightweight, high-tech shoe on Stormy's foot to test the shape. Most horseshoes were steel. A few racehorses used aluminum. He'd experimented on a lightweight, durable plastic compound. It was too expensive to ever become popular, but he didn't care about money.

He cared about his horses. And his innovations had saved Stormy's feet.

"No." Keegan leaned against the wall, his booted feet in Brody's line of vision. "Just keeping an eye on my bro." He let out his breath. "Did you find anything?"

"Nothing new." Brody lined up a high-tech nail and tapped it through the shoe and the outer rim of Stormy's hoof. "It was a false trail." Only nine of the homeless kids who'd been living under a bridge together so long ago had stuck together, taking the last name of Hart and claiming legal status as a family. But a number of others had gone through their pack during the five years Brody had held them together, not sticking around long enough to become a Hart, but always leaving behind an imprint that the rest of them never forgot.

After one of those who'd moved on had been murdered a few years ago, Brody had made it a point to track down everyone he could find and make sure they were alright. He'd located most of them, touched base, and helped out where he could. But there were a few he couldn't find, and he wasn't planning on resting until he found them all. He thought he'd located one of the women, but he'd run into a dead end last night.

Keegan sighed. "We're all adults now, Brody. It's not your job to continue to hold us all together."

"It's what I do."

"I know. But you don't need to be the guardian of everyone anymore."

Brody finished securing Stormy's shoe and set her hoof down. He stretched his back as he turned to face his brother. Keegan was wearing a dusty cowboy hat, faded jeans, and a loose flannel shirt. His short blond hair was neat, and his blue eyes blazed with the warmth that was a hallmark of every Hart.

Keegan looked like a dusty cowboy, not one of the Hart billionaires who had gotten lucky with security software when they were teenagers. The world saw his family as billionaire celebrity recluses. Brody saw his family as the only people who mattered to him, real people who were all still fighting to escape the childhoods that had sent them running for their lives to hide out under a bridge as kids.

The shadows still ran deep for all of them. But the family they had formed had given all of them the safe space they needed, no matter what demons crawled out of their pasts after them. The Harts had a rule, which Brody had made when they were all under the bridge, that no one could hold out. Emotions had to be shared. Secrets had to be revealed. No one carried their burdens alone.

It was why they'd survived, and why the Harts were thriving now.

Which was why he answered Keegan's question. "Every night I go to bed, I see Katie Crowley's face. I wonder what I could have done to save her. If I hadn't let her go to Boston—"

"Stop." Keegan held up his hand. "You have to stop that shit. You're not a god, Brody. You never had the right to tell any of us what to do or how to live. Those of us who stayed chose to stay. Those who chose to leave were following their paths. However it turns out isn't your fault."

"But she's dead—"

"Yeah, it was shitty. You don't need to tell me that. I think about her, too. But she died years after leaving us. I hate to tell you this, bro, but you aren't responsible for the entire lives of every person you've ever met."

Brody scowled at him. "She's *dead*."

"And the rest of us are alive." Keegan put his hand on Brody's shoulder. "We're all here, Brody. Eight of us, plus you. More, if you include the Stocktons, now that Hannah married into their family. Katie was Hannah's sister, but Hannah has fought to find a life again, happiness, and a family. Learn from her. Let yourself be happy, Brody. That's what you're always telling us."

"I know." Brody shoved his cowboy hat back from his head and wiped his wrist over the perspiration beading on his brow. "It's different for me. It's my job to hold everything together."

"Yeah, well, not if it wrecks you." Keegan lightly punched Brody in the shoulder. "Family meeting tonight, bro. You're the topic. I just thought I'd warn you."

Brody frowned. "Why me?"

"Because we all think you're turning into an old shit, and you need to get a life." Keegan grinned and ducked when Brody tossed a rag at him. "Seriously. You better come in your party pants or you're going to get your ass kicked. We're tired of your crap, old man."

Brody laughed, his spirit already lighter. "Who's house?"

"Bella's hosting tonight."

Bella was the older of the two Hart sisters. She was the chef for the part of the Hart Ranch that provided high-end, rustic vacation packages for big spenders who wanted to experience the cowboy life on a dude ranch. "Is she cooking?"

"She is."

"Well, damn. I wouldn't miss it if she's cooking."

"You wouldn't miss it anyway." Keegan tossed an envelope at him. "By the way, this arrived this morning by personal courier. Looks important so I opened it."

Brody took the envelope, which was, indeed, torn open. He didn't care. He had no secrets from his family. "What is it?" As he asked, he noticed the grin on Keegan's face. He stopped. "What?"

"Open it."

Brody shot Keegan a suspicious look, then slid his fingers into the envelope and pulled out a small white envelope with his name on it. That envelope was also open. He lifted the flap and saw it was a concert ticket.

Covering the name of the performer was a yellow sticky note. Someone had jotted in purple pen, "Personal invite from Tatum Crosby. She hopes you'll come."

He froze. "Tatum?"

"Tatum," Keegan confirmed.

Brody ripped the sticky note away and saw Tatum Crosby listed as the headliner for the concert. His seat was row one. Behind the ticket was a backstage pass. "The concert's tonight in Portland," he said, scanning the details.

"I saw that. You can't go, obviously. Family meeting and all."

Brody couldn't take his gaze off the ticket. Tatum Crosby. She'd swept through his little group when she was seventeen, a brilliant flash of fire, passion, and energy. She'd stayed for a summer.

A summer he'd never forgotten.

And then he fucked up, she'd left, and she'd never spoken to him again. He'd kept track of her, though. Watching her ascent to the realization of her dreams. "This can't be from her. She'd never invite me."

"Is it her writing?"

"No." She'd left Brody a note when she'd taken off. A note he'd kept for a long time as a reminder of how badly he could screw up if he wasn't careful. A reminder that had helped keep him focused on being the protector that all those in his care had needed.

He shoved the ticket back into the envelope and held it out to Keegan. "Toss it. I'll be at the family meeting tonight."

Keegan didn't take it. "I can't. I texted the Hart chat. We think you should go to the concert. See her. Family consensus."

"No." Brody tossed the envelope into a nearby trash can. "It's not from her."

"What if it is?"

He paused and looked at his brother. "She's married."

"Divorced. You know that."

Brody let out his breath. "Our fling was a long time ago."

"It wasn't a fling, and it might have been a long time ago, but she still haunts you. She's the reason why you've never met anyone else. We all know it." Keegan plucked the envelope out of the trash. "You're always telling us we deserve love. You're the one trying to marry all of us off because we all deserve the family we didn't have. But you're the one who won't even try. Because of her."

Brody walked to the end of the aisle and stared across their expansive ranch at the sun quickly rising in the sky. Tatum Crosby. Keegan was right. She had become his world fifteen years ago, and that hadn't ended when she'd left.

"You have to go, Brody. You always say that the universe hands you what you need, not necessarily what you want. Well, guess what?" He shoved the ticket back into Brody's hand. "You got handed a ticket, so you gotta go."

Brody scowled at his brother. "Why do you remember the things I tell you only when it's convenient?"

"Because I'm smart. I booked the penthouse at the Ritz in Portland for you already. They're delighted Brody Hart will be gracing them with his presence this evening." He grinned. "We're still going to eat Bella's dinner, but we're doing it without you, so you better have a good time, or you'll miss her dinner for nothing."

Brody grabbed a brush and began working on Stormy's neck. "I'm not going. It's not from Tatum."

Keegan laughed. "Of course you're going. There's no way in hell that you could possibly walk away from this invite without knowing that for sure."

Brody ground his jaw. "I fucked up. She was right to leave."

"Yeah, an eighteen-year-old, homeless, runaway trying to keep a bunch of kids alive and together made a mistake. He definitely deserves to pay for that for the rest of his life, right?"

Brody looked over at his brother. And said nothing.

"How many of her songs do you know every word to?" Keegan asked.

Brody replied without hesitation. "All of them."

"Then you need to go see her, or you'll never be free."

One-click now to get started!

SNEAK PEEK: UNEXPECTEDLY MINE

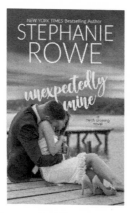

"This book wove...deep inside my heart and soul."
-Amy W (Amazon Review)

Single mom Clare is too busy for love...until a single dad rents her spare room and teaches her how to trust again.

~

CLARE WAS LIFTING the box of cupcakes off the front counter when she became aware of the utter silence of the general store. Even at the funerals of her parents, she hadn't heard this kind of silence in Birch Crossing.

Awareness prickled down her arms, and she looked at Norm, who was in his usual spot behind the front register. She could have sworn that there was amusement crinkling his gray eyes when he nodded toward something behind her.

Clare spun around, and there he was.

Griffin Friesé.

Her mystical knight in shining armor from last night.

Her heart began to race as she met his gaze. His stare was intense, penetrating all the way to her core. She was yanked back to that moment of his hands on her hips, of his strength as he'd lifted her. The power in his body as he'd emerged from his truck during the thundering rain and raging wind. Her body began to thrum, and his expression grew hooded, his eyes never leaving hers, as if he were trying to memorize every feature on her face.

He was wearing a heavy leather jacket that flanked strong thighs and broad shoulders. His eyes were dark, as dark as they'd been last night in the storm. Whiskers shadowed his jaw, giving him a rough and untamed look. His boots were still caked with mud, but his jeans were pressed and clean. His light blue dress shirt was open at the collar, revealing a hint of skin and the flash of a thin gold chain at his throat. His hair was short and perfectly gelled, not messy and untamed like it had been last night. A heavy gold watch sat captive on the strong wrist that had supported her so easily.

Today, he wasn't the dark and rugged hero of last night.

Well, okay, he still was. His power transcended mud, storms, nice watches, and dress shirts.

But he was also, quite clearly and quite ominously, an

outsider, a man who did not fit into the rural Maine town of Birch Crossing.

Then he smiled, a beautiful, tremendous smile with a dimple in his right cheek. "How's your daughter?"

A dimple? He had a dimple? Clare hadn't noticed the dimple last night. It made him look softer, more human, more approachable, almost endearing. Suddenly all her trepidation vanished, replaced by a feeling of giddiness and delight to see him. She smiled back. "She's still asleep, but she's okay. Thanks for your help last night rescuing her."

"My pleasure." His smile faded, and a speculative gleam came into his dark eyes. "And how are you?"

No longer feeling like a total wreck, that was for sure. Not with Griffin Friesé studying her as if she were the only thing he ever wanted to look at again. Dear God, the way he was looking at her made her want to drop the cupcakes and her clothes, and saunter with decadent sensuality across the floor toward him, his stare igniting every cell in her body. "I'm fine." She swallowed, horrified by how throaty her voice sounded. "Thank you," she said. "I owe you."

"No, you owe me nothing." He smiled again, a softness to his face that made her heart turn over. "Seeing you hug Katie was plenty."

"Oh, dear Lord," Eppie muttered behind her. "Now he's going to kill Katie, too."

Clare stiffened and jerked her gaze from Griffin. The entire store was watching them in rapt silence, listening to every word. Oh, God. How had she forgotten where they were? Wright & Sons was the epicenter of gossip in Birch Crossing, and everyone had just witnessed her gaping at this handsome stranger.

Assuming her decades-old role as Clare's self-appointed protector, Eppie had folded her arms and was trying to crush Griffin with her glare, for daring to tempt Clare.

Astrid and Emma were leaning against the doorjamb, huge grins on their faces, clearly supportive of any opportunity to pry Clare out of her dateless life of isolation. But Norm's eyes were narrowed, and Ophelia was letting some scrambled eggs burn while she gawked at them. Everyone was waiting to see how Clare was going to respond to him.

Oh, man. What was she doing nearly throwing herself at him? In front of everyone? She quickly took a step back and cleared her throat.

Griffin's eyebrows shot up at her retreat, then his eyes narrowed. "Kill off Katie, *too*? " He looked right at Eppie. "Who else am I going to kill?"

Eppie lifted her chin and turned her head, giving him a view of the back of her hot pink hat.

"The rumors claim that you're in town to murder your ex-wife and daughter," Astrid volunteered cheerfully. "But don't worry. Not all of us believe them."

"My daughter?" Pain flashed across Griffin's face, a stark anguish so real that Clare felt her out heart tighten. Just as quickly, the vulnerability disappeared from his face, replaced by a hard, cool expression.

But she'd seen it. She'd seen his pain, pain he clearly kept hidden, just as she suppressed her own. Suddenly, she felt terrible about the rumors. How could she have listened to rumors about him when he was clearly struggling with pain, some kind of trauma with regard to his daughter?

She realized he was watching her, as if he were waiting for something. For what? To see if she believed the rumors?

She glanced around and saw the entire store was waiting for her response. Eppie gave her a solemn nod, encouraging her to stand up and condemn this handsome stranger who'd saved Clare's daughter. Sudden anger surged inside her. "Oh, come on," she blurted out. "You can't really believe he's a murderer?"

Astrid grinned, Eppie shook her head in dismay, and the rest of the room was silent.

No one else jumped in to help her defend Griffin, and suddenly Clare felt very exposed, as if everyone in the room could see exactly how deeply she'd been affected by him last night. How she'd lain awake all night, thinking of his hands on her hips, of the way his deep voice had wrapped around her, of how he'd made her yearn for the touch of a man for the first time in a very long time.

Heat burned her cheeks, and she glanced uncomfortably at Griffin, wondering if he was aware of her reaction to him. To her surprise, his face had cooled, devoid of that warmth that they'd initially shared, clearly interpreting her silence as a capitulation to the rumors.

He narrowed his eyes, then turned away, ending their conversation.

Regret rushed through Clare as she glanced at Astrid, torn between wanting to call him back, and gratefully grasping the freedom his rejection had given her, freedom from feelings and desires that she didn't have time to deal with.

"I need a place to stay," Griffin said. "A place without rats, preferably."

Griffin's low request echoed through the room, and Clare spun around in shock. Then she saw he was directing his question to Norm, not to her. Relief rushed through her, along with a stab of disappointment.

No, it was good he wasn't asking to stay at her place. Yes, she owed him, on a level beyond words, but she couldn't afford to get involved with him, for too many reasons. Staying at her house would be putting temptation where she couldn't afford it. There was *no way* she was going to offer up her place, even though her renter had just vacated, leaving her with an unpleasant gap in her income stream.

"Griffin stayed at the Dark Pines Motel last night," Judith whispered, just loudly enough for the whole store to hear.

"Really?" Guilt washed through Clare. The Dark Pines Motel was quite possibly the most unkempt and disgusting motel in the entire state of Maine. How had he ended up there?

"Well, now, Griffin," Norm said, as he tipped his chair back and let it tap against the unfinished wall. "Most places won't open for another month when the summer folk start to arrive. And the Black Loon Inn is booked for the Smith-Pineal wedding for the next week. It's Dark Pines or nothing."

Griffin frowned. "There has to be something. A bed and breakfast?"

Norm shook his head. "Not this time of year, but I probably have some rat traps in the back I could loan you for your stay.'

"Rat traps?" Griffin echoed. "That's my best option?"

Astrid grinned at Clare, a sparkle in her eyes that made Clare's stomach leap with alarm. She grabbed Astrid's arm. "Don't you dare—"

"Clare's renter just moved out," Astrid announced, her voice ringing out in the store. "Griffin can stay in her spare room. No rats, and it comes with free Wi-Fi. Best deal in town."

Oh, dear *God*. Clare's whole body flamed hot, and she whipped around. *Please tell me he didn't hear that.*

But Griffin was staring right at her.

Of course he'd heard. And so had everyone else.

Like it? Get it now!

BOOKS BY STEPHANIE ROWE

CONTEMPORARY ROMANCE

WYOMING REBELS SERIES
(CONTEMPORARY WESTERN ROMANCE)
A Real Cowboy Never Says No
A Real Cowboy Knows How to Kiss
A Real Cowboy Rides a Motorcycle
A Real Cowboy Never Walks Away
A Real Cowboy Loves Forever
A Real Cowboy for Christmas
A Real Cowboy Always Trusts His Heart
A Real Cowboy Always Protects

THE HART RANCH BILLIONAIRES SERIES
(CONTEMPORARY WESTERN ROMANCE)
A Rogue Cowboy's Second Chance (Sept. 14, 2021)
A Rogue Cowboy Finds Love (Jan. 2022)

LINKED TO THE HART RANCH BILLIONAIRES SERIES
(CONTEMPORARY WESTERN ROMANCE)

BOOKS BY STEPHANIE ROWE

Her Rebel Cowboy

BIRCH CROSSING SERIES
(SMALL-TOWN CONTEMPORARY ROMANCE)
Unexpectedly Mine
Accidentally Mine
Unintentionally Mine
Irresistibly Mine

MYSTIC ISLAND SERIES
(SMALL-TOWN CONTEMPORARY ROMANCE)
Wrapped Up in You (A Christmas novella)

CANINE CUPIDS SERIES
(ROMANTIC COMEDY)
Paws for a Kiss
Pawfectly in Love
Paws Up for Love

SINGLE TITLE
(CHICKLIT / ROMANTIC COMEDY)
One More Kiss

PARANORMAL

ORDER OF THE BLADE SERIES
(PARANORMAL ROMANCE)
Darkness Awakened
Darkness Seduced
Darkness Surrendered
Forever in Darkness
Darkness Reborn
Darkness Arisen
Darkness Unleashed

BOOKS BY STEPHANIE ROWE

Inferno of Darkness
Darkness Possessed
Shadows of Darkness
Hunt the Darkness
Darkness Awakened: Reimagined

IMMORTALLY DATING SERIES
(FUNNY PARANORMAL ROMANCE)
To Date an Immortal
To Date a Dragon
Devil's Curse
To Date a Demon (Coming Soon!)

HEART OF THE SHIFTER SERIES
(PARANORMAL ROMANCE)
Dark Wolf Rising
Dark Wolf Unbound

SHADOW GUARDIANS SERIES
(PARANORMAL ROMANCE)
Leopard's Kiss

NIGHTHUNTER SERIES
(PARANORMAL ROMANCE)
Not Quite Dead

NOBLE AS HELL SERIES
(FUNNY URBAN FANTASY)
Guardian of Magic

THE MAGICAL ELITE SERIES
(FUNNY PARANORMAL ROMANCE)
The Demon You Trust

BOOKS BY STEPHANIE ROWE

DEVILISHLY SEXY SERIES
(FUNNY PARANORMAL ROMANCE)
Not Quite a Devil

ROMANTIC SUSPENSE

ALASKA HEAT SERIES
(ROMANTIC SUSPENSE)
Ice
Chill
Ghost
Burn
Hunt (novella)

BOXED SETS

Order of the Blade (Books 1-3)
Protectors of the Heart (A Six-Book First-in-Series Collection)
Wyoming Rebels Boxed Set (Books 1-3)

For a complete list of Stephanie's books, click here.

ABOUT THE AUTHOR

New York Times and *USA Today* bestselling author Stephanie Rowe is "contemporary romance at its best" (Bex 'N' Books). She's thrilled to be a 2021 Vivan® Award nominee, and 2018 winner and a five-time nominee for the RITA® award, the highest awards in romance fiction. As the bestselling author of more than fifty books, Stephanie delights readers with her wide range of genres, which include contemporary western, small-town contemporary romance, paranormal romance, and romantic suspense novels.

www.stephanierowe.com

For AER, my shining light.

ACKNOWLEDGMENTS

Special thanks to my beta readers. You guys are the best! Thanks to Kelli Ann Morgan at Inspire Creative for another fantastic cover. There are so many to thank by name, more than I could count, but here are those who I want to called out specially for all they did to help this book come to life: Alyssa Bird, Anita Hanson, Ashlee Murphy, Bridget Koan, Britannia Hill, Caryn Santee, Deb Julienne, Denise Fluhr, Dottie Jones, Felicia Low Mikoll, Heidi Hoffman, Helen Loyal, Jean Bowden, Jeanne Stone, Jeanie Jackson, Jodi Moore, Judi Pflughoeft, Kasey Richardson, Linda Watson, Regina Thomas, Summer Steelman, Suzanne Mayer, Shell Bryce, and Trish Douglas. Special thanks to my family, who I love with every fiber of my heart and soul. Mom, I love you so much! And to AER, who is my world. Love you so much, baby girl! And to Joe, who teaches me every day what romance and true love really is. I love you, babe!

BOOKS BY STEPHANIE ROWE

CONTEMPORARY ROMANCE

WYOMING REBELS SERIES
(CONTEMPORARY WESTERN ROMANCE)
A Real Cowboy Never Says No
A Real Cowboy Knows How to Kiss
A Real Cowboy Rides a Motorcycle
A Real Cowboy Never Walks Away
A Real Cowboy Loves Forever
A Real Cowboy for Christmas
A Real Cowboy Always Trusts His Heart
A Real Cowboy Always Protects

THE HART RANCH BILLIONAIRES SERIES
(CONTEMPORARY WESTERN ROMANCE)
A Rogue Cowboy's Second Chance (Sept. 14, 2021)
A Rogue Cowboy Finds Love (Jan. 2022)

LINKED TO THE HART RANCH BILLIONAIRES SERIES
(CONTEMPORARY WESTERN ROMANCE)

BOOKS BY STEPHANIE ROWE

Her Rebel Cowboy

BIRCH CROSSING SERIES
(SMALL-TOWN CONTEMPORARY ROMANCE)
Unexpectedly Mine
Accidentally Mine
Unintentionally Mine
Irresistibly Mine

MYSTIC ISLAND SERIES
(SMALL-TOWN CONTEMPORARY ROMANCE)
Wrapped Up in You (A Christmas novella)

CANINE CUPIDS SERIES
(ROMANTIC COMEDY)
Paws for a Kiss
Pawfectly in Love
Paws Up for Love

SINGLE TITLE
(CHICKLIT / ROMANTIC COMEDY)
One More Kiss

ROMANTIC SUSPENSE

ALASKA HEAT SERIES
(ROMANTIC SUSPENSE)
Ice
Chill
Ghost
Burn
Hunt (novella)

PARANORMAL

ORDER OF THE BLADE SERIES
(PARANORMAL ROMANCE)

Darkness Awakened

Darkness Seduced

Darkness Surrendered

Forever in Darkness

Darkness Reborn

Darkness Arisen

Darkness Unleashed

Inferno of Darkness

Darkness Possessed

Shadows of Darkness

Hunt the Darkness

Darkness Awakened: Reimagined

IMMORTALLY DATING SERIES
(FUNNY PARANORMAL ROMANCE)

To Date an Immortal

Curse of the Dragon

Devil's Curse

To Date a Demon (July 13, 2021)

HEART OF THE SHIFTER SERIES
(PARANORMAL ROMANCE)

Dark Wolf Rising

Dark Wolf Unbound

SHADOW GUARDIANS SERIES
(PARANORMAL ROMANCE)

Leopard's Kiss

NIGHTHUNTER SERIES
(PARANORMAL ROMANCE)

Not Quite Dead

Made in United States
Orlando, FL
17 April 2022

16928243R00159